Among The Shadows Of Men

Liam Mac an Ghoill

ISBN: 095690713X
ISBN-13: 978-0956907134

Among The Shadows Of Men

Had it have been on midnight's fictional shore,

Or a cloud in afternoon.

Leaves of splendour would crawl at her feet,

Smudging the grass with tranquility.

I could have bought that pain,

Had it been greater than birth.

And as I stumbled at the step of death

I could not whisper, I could not breathe

Eternal refuge,

But turned to face the trees.

Liam Mac an Ghoill

ALSO BY LIAM MAC AN GHOILL

The Moss Wall
The Chronicles of Tiny Tim
Face2Face

For the lost youth of a hidden generation

CHAPTER 1

As Oliver pushed his way through the lines of people crowding the hallway, he occasionally greeted those he recognised with a simple nod of the head or a formal handshake. The traditional aroma of whiskey and stout guided his nostrils as he hypocritically passed through the open doorway and entered the cigarette smoke filled room of the dead. As this was Oliver's first wake and he lacked the necessary skills, he guided himself through the ritual by carefully following the actions of others and presenting himself before the corpse as insincere as most of those around him. Prayerful whispers echoed off the yellow age stained wallpaper, occasionally complemented by a breath of cheap perfume, and its vain attempt at masking the results of seldom washed armpits. As he gazed around the room, Oliver noticed his old schoolmaster smiling as if the person, who had just died, had left him a large sum of money. Sitting beside the coffin on two dining chairs, his mother and Aunt Martha continued to mutter prayers under their breath. Oliver dipped his fingers into the holy water and proceeded to sprinkle some over the head of the person who no longer cared whether he was doing the right thing or not. Suddenly

1

Oliver stopped, allowing the holy water to flow freely down the palm of his hand and onto his shirt sleeve. He felt the blood begin to freeze in his veins and the sledge hammer pounding of his heart alerted Oliver to the terrifying scene before his eyes. He began to scream, he screamed from within the very depths of his innermost terror. He screamed so hard that the flames on the candles disappeared and the solitary light bulb, hovering above his head, shattered to a million small fragments. Oliver looked at the face that now stared up at him from the darkness; the face was his.

'For God's sake son get a hold of yourself', cried Oliver's mother, 'you're going to bring the bloody neighbours in on top of us'.

Oliver awoke with his brow bathed in sweat and the familiar figure of his mother hovering above him as he lay on the bed. The slow realization that he had been dreaming was a welcoming relief. The new day that had just greeted his arrival, was embraced like a long lost friend, allowing the deep pounding in his chest to subside. The nightmare's graphic and pitiless barrage of fear still clung to his memory, and Oliver knew it would take some time to subside.

'No wonder you're having nightmares', yelled Oliver's mother, 'staying up till all hours drinking and getting up to no good. Don't argue with me either; I saw you pissing in next door's flower garden'.
Oliver smiled, putting aside the frights of his earlier slumber and recalling within his mind, the teenage escapades of the night before. His two friends, John, Michael and himself had gone to the disco in Ballynease. Oliver had got so pissed that he cornered a blond with long curly hair, and asked for a dance. The realization that the person chosen was of similar

sex to himself, only came to his attention when he found himself sliding across the polished dance floor on his back, courtesy of a well aimed punch to the jaw by the deeply offended Rocker, who had failed to take on board Oliver's state of mind and body. John and Michael quickly rallied to their friend's defence, and without further ado found themselves greeting the cold dark air, at the advance of three large unfriendly bouncers. It had not been the first time the three friends had been ungracefully removed from their place of enjoyment and, as Oliver thought, it would not be the last. Oliver recalled how he came to first meet John and Michael, and how they quickly became three peas in a big screwed up pod. One evening, while approaching a bus stop in Cookstown, Oliver encountered two people with two deeply conflicting arguments and accents.

'We saved your ass during the war', boasted John,

'Hell if it hadn't have been for us Yanks, the whole fucking world would be speaking German'.

'If it hadn't have been for the English', replied Michael, 'every Yank in the good old U S of A would be lined up against a wall and shot, because they didn't have enough brains to learn Japanese'.

Oliver decided that in the interests of public safety, something must be done to defuse the situation.

'If it hadn't been for the Irish, both England and the USA would be speaking English', he interrupted. John looked at Michael; Michael looked at Oliver and burst into laughter.

'I've never heard a truer word spoken', laughed Michael, 'but fuck it, who gives a fiddlers fuck'. The three, who had been total strangers some fifteen minutes earlier, had now decided to seal their friendship by getting thrown off the bus for having a farting contest.

Michael was born in a small market town called Pickering in Yorkshire and had come to live in Castledawson with his mother two years earlier. His father had died in a motorcycle crash when he was only five and it was some time before his mother decided to move on and meet someone else. Michael's mother met and fell in love again with a policeman from Northern Ireland while he was in England on a training exercise. However, the cupids little arrows rapidly turned to poison when he came home drunk one night and tried to beat her to death. Michael tried to stand up for his mother but was rewarded with a broken nose and the exchange of his right eye for a glass one. His mother had neither the will nor the way to return to England, so both Michael and his mother were destined, for the time being, to endure the constant rains and pains of a Derry village.

On the other side of the Atlantic, in a small town in Missouri by the name of Stockton, John was born; he was raised on a small 20 acre homestead, along with his father, mother and grandmother His father depended on work at the walnut factory, whenever the season was in, and other times they made do with what they had and charity from the local church. John loved to fish at the Stockton River, hour after hour he would sit with his fishing rod and dream of faraway places, dream of places where food was plenty and the American dream was no longer just a dream. Unlike Michael's father, John's left voluntarily one spring morning and never returned. It wasn't long after that his mother decided to take up residency in the mental hospital in Springfield, leaving John with no one else but his aged maternal grandmother in Stockton and a paternal grandmother who lived in Maghera in Northern Ireland. When John's maternal grandmother took ill and had to go into a nursing home, John's grandmother Eileen in Northern Ireland sent for him, and a new way of life moulded the heartaches and unanswered questions together, to create an uneasy tolerance.

Oliver returned from his garden of thoughts by the nagging voice of his Mother.

'When are you ever going to catch yourself on', she nagged, 'when I was your age I had crossed the bloody water to England on my own, and had three jobs'.

'I bet the reason you had three jobs all in one week', mocked Oliver, 'was because you got booted out for nagging'.

'Don't be getting fresh with me lad', replied Oliver's mother, 'it's a wonder you aren't arrested for pollution, those damn socks of yours are life threatening'.

Oliver could only reply to his mother's outburst with an outward grin. He knew there was no chance of taking on his mother verbally, he had tried it many times in the past but his mother always had a superior answer. He loved his mother over and above what could have been expected of a seventeen year old and neither the changing place from child to adulthood would ever alter the course of his heart. His father however, was very much a stranger and had been so ever since he acquired the understanding of growing up. From the moment Oliver could grasp the awareness of life, his father had been a prop positioned in front of the television, behind a copy of whatever newspaper came to hand. Oliver sat before many turf fires listening to various people boast of their escapades and daring deeds while growing up as children. But never once had his father opened the door of his mind to reveal at least one episode of rascality. Not one remnant of boyish mischief had crossed his lips to allow Oliver immunity on the grounds of like father like son. Oliver often asked himself during the tiny hours when all were fast asleep, was his father real? Or did he hide some soot coloured secret that was too terrible to tell. When he was a small child, standing between the rational and who gives a shit, he had come to the puerile understanding, that his mum had dug him up from the grave. When he confronted his mother with this carefully analysed solution, the uncontrollable laughter that followed allowed him to quickly come to the conclusion, that both his parents were fucking nuts. When he was eleven years old his teacher asked,

'Ok children, for homework I would like you all to write an essay entitled, My Father, My Hero'.

Oliver wrote the title as neatly as he could on top of the page, and on his way home from school he nipped behind the hedge to plant the biggest shit on it that had ever emerged from his undersized snow white ass. When Oliver revealed what he had done in confidence to his mother, he was administered with the same display of insane laughter that he had received earlier in his life. Oliver soon learned from both these experiences that grave situations were not to be taken seriously. Oliver also quickly grasped the knowledge that as an only child, Christmas and birthdays could reap greater harvests. That a bedroom of his own was a worthily exchange for a fart free environment, and that any brothers and sisters that he might have had, would without question be either zombies, or not right in the fucking head. With all this taken into consideration, Oliver was happy to be as one with himself.

'Are you going to get up or lie there stinking all day', roared Oliver's mother. Oliver lazily removed himself from below the comfort of the warm blankets, and slowly made his way to the bathroom. The strong aroma of urine splashed the remainder from the night before into the toilet bowl as Oliver stared out the open window at the street below. Robert the registered town drunk was making his way up the footpath, carefully scanning the ground for any coins that might have been discarded unintentionally. An old red Ford Cortina spluttered along with the dark thick smoke from its exhaust declaring the inevitable, that its engine hadn't long for this world. At the bus stop he could see Annie McKenna waiting patiently for the Ulster bus that would take her to the butchers in Moneymore, to claim the bacon ends that would keep her seven children hunger free, but thirsty for the next few days. Oliver surveyed the scene before him and saw only aching people, wounded by the sword of life. If only each person could be given the opportunity to write the script of their own destiny, there is no doubt the picture before him would have changed dramatically. At seventeen he held no licence that would allow him entry into the club of time acquired knowledge, but one thing he learned fast, grasp everything with both hands because no one is going to give it to you. Take whenever the opportunity arises, because prospect never rings the door bell twice. As Oliver retreated from his thoughts, he made his way down the stairs and lay claim to the seat at the table, directly across from his father.

Oliver took no notice of the paternal mascot as he patiently awaited the deliverance of his now rumbling stomach. His mother poured the long white mug with a generous helping of tea, and produced a plate with two eggs, one sausage and a rasher of spot the meat bacon.

'Get that ate now', nagged his mother, 'I never want to see you wasting good food, and eat your crusts, there are plenty of people in those African countries who would be glad of a few crusts'.

'Ok mum', replied Oliver sarcastically. 'I will make sure that any of the crusts I don't feel up to, will be swiftly posted off to those in need'.

'Don't get smart with me you wee brat', answered his mother, 'when I was a child there wasn't a morsel left on the table; we were damn glad of every crumb. You young ones now don't know what it's like to go hungry'.

Oliver could only think back, with some amusement, at the collection his school had every Friday entitled, Friends of Lima. Every Friday morning a pupil would be designated as collector and would hold a tin can out to everyone respectively muttering the words 'Friends of Lima'. Oliver decided on one of these occasions that the fifty pence piece, that lay smouldering in his pocket, could be procured for a better use, particularly the ice cream van that sat waiting for pupils to depart from school. So, when the familiar tin was dangled before the begrudging Oliver, Oliver decided that he was no longer friends with Lima.

Oliver's thoughts were returned to reality once again by the cold sharp words of his mother.

'Two people were shot dead in Dungiven this morning', she said, 'the police claim they failed to stop at a checkpoint, so they opened fire'.

For Oliver the troubles, as it was infamously known, had been a part of his life ever since he was able to see and hear. Bombs and bullets were everyday occurrences, and even to the faint hearted, they were accepted as happenings that were here to stay; so the best thing to do was get over it and hope it didn't affect anyone you knew. Grey Land Rovers sporting dark green uniform clad police, and armoured cars with a soldier's gun protruding from the top, were part of the scenery. Oliver remembered while he was walking home from school that one of the police men called him a wee taig. It was not until he returned home and asked his mother the definition of what the policeman said, that he became aware of the sectarianism that gripped Northern Ireland.

'A taig is another name for a Catholic, son', she explained, 'there are people out there who do not like Catholics, and there are people who do not like Protestants, and if you want me to explain what a Protestant is, then they are the people who wear uniforms and carry guns. Some carry large banners with a picture of a white horse and beat large drums on the twelfth day of July. Some Catholics also carry guns, but do not wear uniforms, while others beat drums also and carry large banners sometimes portraying the virgin Mary on the seventeenth of march and fifteenth of august'.

Oliver returned once again from the past and quietly asked his mother,

'Did they release any names yet?'

'Not yet', replied his mother. 'but there is one thing we can be sure of; they are sure as hell Catholic'.

Oliver glanced at his mother and studied her thin

worn frame. He remembers back to the time when she used to take him for long summer walks down narrow country lanes, and how they would pick the wild strawberries that grew within the patches of wild grass on each side. He remembered how strong and full of life she was, always laughing and playing games and stopping occasionally to tease a cow in a field, or mock the gait of a passing local farmer. As they sat down for a rest, taking in the scenery, Oliver thought of the countless stories she told him. Tales that were steeped in fairies and goblins, of witches and leprechauns and rainbows that led to crocks overflowing with gleaming yellow gold. She would tell of the Halloween nights and of the many pranks their immature childhood minds would fashion, pranks and deeds that today her adult wits would never allow.

Oliver recalled his mother telling him of a childhood licence that granted immunity from reality,

'Hold on to your childhood son for as long as you can', she would say, 'grasp it tight with both hands because someday it will slip out of those hands, and the cruel heart rending state of adulthood will be there to take its place''.

Those days would be forever locked in the vault of Oliver's heart, allowing him the occasional glimpse as he fought his way through the thick jungle of his existence.

'They are not always Catholic', said Oliver, replying to his mother's earlier statement.

Oliver's Mother turned sharply to him and raised her voice,

'Then remind me son when a Protestant was shot by the police', she roared.

'Ok mum, don't bite my fecking head off', replied

Oliver, 'I'm just trying to play devil's advocate'.

'You're only a skip of a lad', said Oliver's mother, 'don't try to teach your granny to suck eggs, what I have forgot about this country is not worth knowing, and what I haven't forgot is how we were treated as second class citizens. When I was a young girl, coming home from a dance, the police used to stop us deliberately if they knew we were Catholic. Any men in the car would have been either beaten up or a gun shoved in their face. I suppose by being female you could say we were lucky; a slap across the face or a mouthful of spit was our portion of bigoted fury'.

Oliver looked deep into his mother's eyes, searching for any movement of hate or anger. He had often heard the stories from some of her friends when they called around to reminisce about their teenage years. But, except for her brother in law Pat, no loathing or malice could be found, no vengeful shivers would ever cross the unpolluted heart of his mother.

'Hate is a disease', his mother used to tell him. 'a disease if not treated fast could cause human beings to be reduced to nothing less than vermin'.

'Ok mum', replied Oliver. 'I'm sorry for ever trying to challenge you in an argument'. Reaching over to give his mother a short embrace, Oliver continued, 'I know I'm much superior in intellect than you, I'm off to see a friend about a dog'. Oliver swerved from his mother's playful right hook and made his way through the front door and into the cool spring air.

As he made his way down the narrow street, Oliver's thoughts returned to the night before. Ten or eleven pints of beer had crossed his lips, and he was sure the last two or three took refuge on the carpeted floor of Danny's Lounge.

'Come on', cried Michael, 'you call yourself Irish, then drink like the fucking Irish'.

And so Oliver followed his command, pint after pint until his stomach swelled with the liquid his bladder couldn't cope fast enough with. They sang songs that had no rational meaning or understanding. On their way home, in-between throwing up, they studied the stars and came to the conclusion that the world was upside down. They collectively agreed that the moon was no more than a well rounded spud and every star was a flea on a dog's back. While sitting down on a stone seat, John suggested a theory that made Oliver first laugh, then to think deeply about what John was saying.

'I think we are all dreaming this', said John in a drunken slur, 'I think we are all having a good old fucking dream in this we call our daily lives, but our true life is when we go to sleep'.

'So what you are trying to say', replied Michael in a slow alcohol manipulated voice, 'Is that instead of me going back to sleep this shit off, I'm going to wake in a life where I had only been dreaming I was getting pissed and having this fucked up conversation with two bastards who are almost as screwed up as myself'.

'Yes', replied John, 'you my friend have hit the nail on the rusty head'.

Oliver smiled when he remembered John's reply with his jeans firmly around his ankles, trying to take a piss. He remembered saying to John,

'Ok lads, let's go and kick in that person's door across the street. If anyone complains just tell them not to worry, the whole thing is a fucking dream'.

The three friends laughed until they threw up again, then laughed some more. However, Oliver's philosophical mind would not allow the theory to pass by. *How do we really know? he asked himself. What if John was right and at this very moment he was dreaming. Every word that passed between his mother and him was the remnants of a few loud snores.* It was at this moment that Oliver began to think about death. *What happens when we die?* he thought. *Where do we go when we close our eyes for the last time, and say farewell to a life, whether it be short or long?* Oliver' train of thoughts was suddenly stopped by the familiar voice of Michael calling his name.

CHAPTER 2

The entrance to Magherafelt Tech still claimed the status of meeting place and as far back as Oliver could remember it bore all the hallmarks of people in waiting. The crushed cigarette butts, flattened beer and coke cans, and the occasional sight of used condoms littered the stone and grass lined walkway. Michael's tired looking face, hung-over from the previous night's binge, called out to Oliver,

'Don't look so worried Kid, you're only dreaming'. Oliver managed a distorted smile and replied,

'I wish to fuck it was, I think I'm going to die'. The two friends managed a laugh which bordered on the edge of being genuine, while Michael lit a cigarette and slowly sent the smoke to blend with the exhaust fumes of passing cars.

'Where's John?' asked Oliver as he scraped a small fragment of suspected dog shit from his Doc Martin boot.

'Probably still in bed', replied Michael humorously, 'I bet he's scared to wake up in case he thinks he's still asleep'.

'No fear', replied Oliver, 'he always looks a dozy bastard anyway'.

The friends' affectionate criticisms of John were soon to subside as he slowly approached the meeting place, and greeted the pair with his usual gentlemanly greeting.

'I was just starting to get over this fucking hangover until I saw your two ugly heads, now I want to be sick again'. The usual feint throwing of punches were displayed, before the three friends decided that the plan, they had devised the night before, must be blatantly put into action. Oliver knew only too well how a good and noble deed, fabricated from the alcohol fused mind, could very easy be confined to history when the mind has time to recover. Many times, from above the beer glass, he swore vengeance on those he assumed had done him wrong only to call off his attack when he had time to sober up.

'So what's the score?' blurted John, 'now that you have sobered up do you still want to do the dirty deed'.

'Yes', replied Oliver, 'if I don't get this over with it will haunt me for the rest of my life'.

Oliver's last two words stalled slightly as the hidden emotion that haunted him all his life, began to leak through the strong leather skin that he had metaphorically adopted to protect him from the bitter and unmerciful elements of his existence. The humiliating and painful blows from the schoolmaster's cane could still be felt, pounding in rhythm to his heartbeat, thumping, echoing, grinding his ten year old will into submission. *For what?* Oliver thought, *for spilling the lemonade on the classroom floor? Not remembering the last line of Walter de la mare's 'The Snare?' Or perhaps not joining in with the class of robotic children complementing the schoolmaster on how a humorous and kindly bald bastard he was.* Oliver had no wish to brown nose, or stand falsely before those with illusions of authority, in order to save himself from a beating. Ever since his mind opened the window of his infancy in order to look out across the great wide open landscape of knowledge, he had accepted a spade for what it truly was, simply a spade. When he held the bright red juicy apple before him, he had no desire to paint it orange and call it an orange. For Oliver, night was what it was and day was sometimes sunny, but mostly pissing with rain. And for Oliver, the schoolmaster was no exception, he was what he was, an ugly stinking fucked up bald shit with little or no personality. His breath was so bad that if anyone ever had to administer the kiss of life, they would have to blow into his ass.

As the three friends made their way down the mud and grass covered lane, the slush that claimed responsibility for the occasional curse had been created by a heavy downpour some hours earlier.

'Can't expect anything else from the Irish weather', complained Michael, 'never stops fucking raining, at least in good old England we get the occasional sunshine'.

'Occasional sunshine my ass', answered John, 'in the States, summer is summer, winter is winter and the other two do what the hell they want. My grandma once told me, the reason the Irish were nuts has got to do with the weather'.

'What to fuck has the weather got to do with why we are nuts?' asked Oliver.

'Well', replied John, 'She said that in Ireland, people look out their window and see the sun shining, but as soon as they decide to go out lightly dressed, on comes the taps. They quickly run back in again to done the old wet suit, but when they get outside wrapped up to

16

the teeth, the sun is splitting the fucking trees. This exercise of cat and mouse is carried out over a number of weeks until the Mick is so fucking screwed up with confusion, he wants to shoot someone. My grandma says, that's why there are so many Irish in the army, because of the weather'.

'Well done John boy', answered Oliver, 'that is a first class theory on Irish personality, the recruiting sergeant asks, and why do you want to join the army boy, and the Irish boy answers, the weather Sir'.

'I'm only telling you what she said', replied John in amused defence.

'Fix the weather', said Michael, 'and the troubles in Northern Ireland will be over'.

'Ok, ok', barked Oliver, 'keep your voice down, I hear something'.

The three friends stopped beside an old rust stained gate and viewed the scene before them. A black and white collie dog walked, almost reluctantly, beside the now forty five years old schoolmaster. Oliver noticed that nothing had changed much, save for a slight limp and the greying of the few hairs he had protruding from the side of his head. His heart began to race as he donned the black balaclava that all three had brought with them, in case of recognition. He knew the time had come and there, approaching before his very eyes, was the object of his sleepless nights. Oliver also knew that as he watched the schoolmaster's expression turn from bewilderment and then to fear, there was no turning back.

The first blow that Oliver swung with his tightly clenched fist, caught the schoolmaster unprepared, allowing him to stagger against a heavily blossomed crab apple tree. As the snow like blossoms fell on

17

Oliver, the second punch caused the schoolmaster to cry out.

'No! Why are you doing this? Please you can have my money'.

'Fuck your money', yelled Oliver, 'do you think your money will compensate me for all the suffering and pain you inflicted on me you piece of shit'.

By now Oliver's anger had emerged with a ferocity Michael and John never thought possible. They knew Oliver as the laughable Irish friend whose bark was very much worse than his bite. They knew he had been cut by the schoolmaster, but how deep they never understood until now. The punches, the kicks, even the schoolmaster's own dog decided to assist Oliver by snarling and tearing at his owner's jacket sleeve. But Oliver kept on hitting, until John and Michael decided enough was certainly enough.

'Ok, enough', cried John, 'You'll kill him for fuck's sake'.

John and Michael each grabbed Oliver by an arm and dragged him away kicking and spitting blue murder.

'Calm down', cried Michael, 'you don't want to rot in jail for the rest of your life'.

Oliver took quick and laboured gasps of breath, while slowly coming to terms with the action that he had just taken. Before him the schoolmaster lay, bleeding and moaning from his vengeful onslaught. He had dreamed of this moment every night since his days interned in the schoolmaster's classroom of brutality and poisoned facts. Now his dream had been fulfilled before his very eyes. The pathetic figure of the schoolmaster, sniffing and weeping at his feet, was not what he had imagined. He expected more; he wanted the schoolmaster to fight back, to defend himself with the same ferocity that he applied to the bamboo cane, as it throttled down on his cold infant hands. He wanted the schoolmaster to stand tall and strong and fight like a man, to cry no surrender and put up one hell's blazes of a fight. But as the anger subsided and his eyes began to push aside the mist of rage, Oliver knew that it never was going to happen. He slowly but clearly began to understand that the person, lying on the wet grass before him, was a coward in plain clothes. A whimpering excuse for anything breathing; a festering scab on the flesh of humanity, who's licence to commit child abuse would soon be lost in the rear view mirror of history.

As they climbed over the old brown gate on their departure, Oliver removed his mask and allowed the cool air to dry the sweat from his face. He had insisted John and Michael, under no circumstances, were to join in on the assault. It was his justice and his only, and now he felt better. His mind began to calm, softly turning the key of his future. He allowed himself, for once in his life, freedom within his own thoughts, without the fetters of the schoolmaster's wraith to haunt him. He afforded himself a clear view of the road of life before him, and he would find a job and work hard to achieve it.

As the three friends departed, Oliver proceeded to make his way home. While dodging the potholes of the bus stop car park, he noticed soldiers approaching on foot from the entrance leading to the now dormant cinema.

'Where are you going mate?' asked a tall wiry soldier sporting a red cap.

'Home', muttered Oliver, trying not to allow his anger to show, while restraining from telling them to mind their own business.

'Where's home?' asked the soldier.

'Just around the corner and into the left', answered Oliver, allowing a thin smile to appear across his face.

'Have you any weapons on you; any guns, bombs, knives?' muttered the soldier. By this time Oliver had his arms outstretched by his side, with his legs slightly apart.

'Yes', replied Oliver, still holding the thin smile.

'Yes what?' asked the soldier, suddenly appearing more alert.

'Yes I have', replied Oliver.

'Yes you have what?' roared the soldier, which caused the other soldiers to pay more attention to Oliver who now stood in crucified style before them.

'Yes I have a weapon', replied Oliver slightly raising his voice. At this revelation, some of the soldiers began to move back, cocking their guns and pointing them with life threatening intentions.

'Ok paddy, on the fucking ground', roared the soldier who seemed to be in command. At this demand, Oliver proceeded to lie face down on the ground, arms and legs outstretched. The soldier in command, while being covered by his comrades, began to investigate Oliver's claims by roughly frisking him. As the soldier began searching for weapons, Oliver wondered how his Mother would react when she found out what had happened to him.

She always warned him to be polite to soldiers and police,

'Don't provoke anyone with a gun pointed at you son', she would tell him, 'manners is cheap so don't be a complete skinflint'.

Oliver's mind was rushing; this was completely out of

character. He had always been polite to soldiers, answering their questions and allowing them to search him without a fuss. Michael had told him that the squaddies didn't want to be here; they would rather be back home in England, but had no other choice. As a soldier you obey orders and go where you are sent. Most of the soldiers, he said, were from working class backgrounds and joined the army because they couldn't find a job. They didn't want any trouble, all they wanted was to do their whack without grief and go home. However, Oliver was unsure of what Michael told him, when heard the soldier getting pissed off standing above him.

'Where's the fucking weapon Paddy?' he yelled.

'Ok, ok', roared Oliver, 'let me stand up and I'll show you'.

At this request two soldiers helped Oliver to his feet.

'Right Paddy, where is it?' shouted the soldier. Oliver opened his legs a little wider and discharged a fart so loud that even Oliver himself was astonished. Oliver could hold back no more and exploded into a frenzy of laughter; he laughed until his sides hurt; he laughed in unison with the soldiers facing him, he laughed long enough to feel the arms of the commander drag him to the ground once again and spread-eagle him for a second time face down on the wet tarmac. Oliver still could not stop laughing, he even laughed when he saw the black boots and green trousers of two policemen approaching. However, Oliver's laughter ceased violently as the unimpressed soldier in command trampled his already crushed knuckles with the heel of his heavy mud stained army boots.

'There's something to laugh about', he spat

triumphantly. If the pain had not been greater than Oliver's portion of fun, he may have laughed some more. The two policemen, who had arrived, intervened and allowed Oliver to go on his way, leaving behind an array of chuckling soldiers with an angry one still refusing to sense any humour from Oliver's display of putrid thunder. Before the incident Oliver's knuckles had been painfully throbbing with some skin missing as a result of the blows he had introduced to the cowardly and unexpected schoolmaster. Now, with the blood quickly pouring from them, Oliver wished he had not decided to play the prank. He was no great hero when pain was concerned; ever since his childhood days being on the receiving end of the schoolmaster, pain was something he needed to avoid at all costs. But behind the thumping pain that screamed from Oliver's hands, he managed a smile, knowing that the schoolmaster had received a taste of his own foul medicine.

When Oliver entered through the back door and into the kitchen, he knew by the smell coming from the oven that dinner had been served some hours earlier. He took his place at the table and prepared for the arrival of his mother's barrage of nagging.

'What kept you till this time?' asked his mother, 'didn't you know that dinner was on the table two hours ago'.

'Yes, I knew', replied Oliver, 'but tell that to the soldiers who kept me lying on the ground for two hours'.

'My God!', yelled Oliver's Mother, suddenly noticing the blood on Oliver's hands, 'what have you done to your hands?'

Oliver never lied to his mother, but on this occasion

he decided in the interests of keeping his mother's blood pressure from going through the clouds, a white lie must be forthcoming.

'Was messing about on an old rusty go-cart that Michael had put together, and the damn front wheel came off going down the hill at Station Road', lied Oliver, trying his hardest not to give away the truth by the changing tone of his voice.

Oliver was no liar; he had been brought up to believe the truth was always the right thing. His mother told him, from an early age, that liars were the messengers of the devil. She reminded him often that the pain and heartache, most lies can cause, could only have been taught in hell itself. When Oliver was only eight years old, he remembered his Aunt Mary crying for days after days, beside the old black wood burn stove, where she used to feed him chocolate cake and tell him stories. At the time Oliver's eight year old brain could not untangle the mystery of why? All he could come to terms with was that Aunt Mary never told him stories again, and no chocolate cake could ever hold a holy candle to what she used to bake. When he was eleven, he went to Aunt Mary's funeral and his mum cried for days after it. He asked his mum at the time, why Aunt Mary died? Only to receive a tearful reply, 'Was her heart son'. One Christmas Eve night, when he was fifteen, his mother told him the story as they both decorated the Christmas tree. She disclosed to Oliver that Aunt Mary's husband, Pat, had been cheating on her with another woman. For months on end he would come home late, telling Aunt Mary he had been either working overtime, or had been out with his work pals. Aunt Mary's instinct began to ring the alarm bells but she tried to convince herself that it wasn't true. She went to church every day and prayed that she was only imagining it. She bought new clothes, treated her hair to a perm at the hairdresser in Cookstown and began to apply makeup, something she never done before. One night Aunt Mary's husband didn't return home, the next morning the postman delivered a Dear Mary letter and the wailing and pain of Mary could be heard and felt at the North Pole. Oliver's Mother told him, that Mary had sat up night, after night, day after day, believing that her husband would return, repenting, and asking for forgiveness. Gallons and gallons of midnight oil were burnt, but to no avail. Pat and Mary had been childhood sweethearts, and according to Oliver's Mother, very much in love. They had tried for years to have children but to no avail. As a result of this barren curse, arguments soon dominated the home as each blamed the other for their failure to produce children. Pat and his Hussey, as Oliver's Mother called her, moved to London and around the time they were burying Aunt Mary, as a result of a broken heart, the Hussey met someone else and Pat was left alone. Oliver's Mother told Oliver that a few weeks before his fifteenth birthday she had received a letter from an old school friend who now lives in London. Among all the fine and not so fine things she had to say about London, was the story of Aunt Mary's husband Pat. Her friend told her that Pat had now joined the ranks of the London street drinkers who, by some fate or other, now warmed themselves around a burning oil barrel and drank cheap wine or whatever alcoholic beverage that shrouded their pains and heartaches. On hearing the news about Pat, Oliver's Mother smiled as her heart sang to the sweet vengeful tune of what goes around must always come around. She hated Pat with a dark unholy rage, a fury that left her with countless sleepless nights as she wished upon him a pitiless and agonizing end. But as time passed her heart mellowed, and she told Oliver that Christmas Eve, Mary would have forgiven him, then so must she.

Oliver's reflections were swiftly brought forward to the present by his Mother slamming the black oven baked plate of dinner in front him.

'Eat that', she said, desperately trying to quell both the anger of Oliver's bloody hands and him being two hours late for his dinner. 'I'm making nothing more tonight', she uttered, 'a fellow of your age messing around on a child's go-cart; you should be ashamed of yourself'.

Oliver said nothing, except to thank his Mother for the dinner which he proceeded to eat hungrily, even the black and hard bits. A strong, steaming cup of tea accompanied Oliver's cremated dinner, for which Oliver again thanked his mother kindly.

'Ok son', said Oliver's Mother in a calmer voice, 'I'm off to bed; don't stay up too late, you have an appointment with the dole office at nine in the morning'.

'I won't', replied Oliver, while softly wishing his Mother a good night.

As soon as Oliver had finished his meal he made his way, along with the remainder of his tea, into the living room. Switching on the television, he managed to catch the tail end of the nine o'clock news.

POLICE IN LONDONDERRY HAVE ISSUED A MESSAGE TO KEY HOLDERS IN THE CITY TO RETURN TO THEIR PREMISES, AND CHECK FOR SUSPICIOUS ITEMS. THIS WARNING IS

ISSUED AFTER AN INCENDIARY DEVICE EXPLODED INSIDE THE PREMISES OF WHITE'S DRAPER SHOP ON THE STRAND ROAD, CAUSING EXTENSIVE DAMAGE. THAT IS THE END OF THE NINE O'CLOCK NEWS, GOOD NIGHT......Oliver turned the channel but nothing could lure his thoughts away from the present day. It had been an eventful day to say the least; the schoolmaster had encountered the fist of long overdue justice. He could have got himself shot, or at the least the shit beat out of him, as a result of his humorous display of bravado. Every night before Oliver decided to go to bed he thought of how or what tomorrow would bring; what glories or tragedies would the new day scribble onto his page of life? Every new day he thought, brought both life and death; somewhere a landscape would change for better or worse and, within the confines of his own feelings, he greeted every new dawn come what may. Oliver suddenly remembered his Mother's words regarding an interview at the dole office in the morning, so without further thought, decided to depart from the day gracefully and go to bed.

CHAPTER 3

'Now Oliver', muttered the policeman, 'Let's be a good boy and tell me why you killed the poor defenceless bald schoolmaster'.
Oliver looked into the policeman's eyes and replied,
'I didn't kill anyone'.
'You killed the schoolmaster', smiled the policeman, 'we found him with two hundred and seventeen stab wounds, and his throat was cut from ear to ear'. 'He told us you did it', said the policeman, still smiling.
'He's a lying bastard', roared Oliver.
'You expect us to believe the word of a seventeen year old wanker, against that of a highly respected bald bastard'.
Oliver sprang to his feet and roared,
'I'm no fucking wanker'.
'Yes you are Oliver old son, your Mother has just given a statement to that affect', said the policeman, continuing to hold a smile that resembled a laid back Cheshire cat.
'Don't try and bluff me with that one', roared Oliver, 'my Mother would never lie against her own son'.
As soon as Oliver finished the sentence, his Mother walked into the room,

'Here's a nice cup of strong tea son', she said, 'now tell the nice smiley policeman what you do in the bath and bed at night when you think your Mother hasn't the gumption to know'.

'I never ever thought you were stupid mum', cried Oliver.

'Just plead guilty to the lesser charge of murder son, then you won't have the shame of wanker hanging over you for the rest of your life', she pleaded.

'Listen to Mother', smiled the policeman, 'Mother knows best'.

Oliver turned around and ran through the open police interview room door. To his horror, the schoolmaster covered in blood and with a wide gaping hole at his throat opening and closing to the rhythm of a song, was dancing with Aunt Mary. His heart began to beat wildly, urging him to escape this terrible place, willing him to run forever. He ran into another room and there was John and Michael, both sporting large penis shaped hats on their heads.

'Tell them the truth Oliver', they echoed in unison, 'we have just signed a statement admitting we are dick heads, our consciences are now clear'.

Oliver turned and ran again, each step he took forced the pounding in his head to get louder. He was confused beyond belief; his mother and friends had turned against him and he could find no way out. The ever smiling policeman kept smiling, reaching deep within the very depths of his mind, smiling his all knowing smile, trying his utmost to get him to admit to something he hadn't done.

'Get up son', Oliver's Mother yelled, 'you have an appointment with the dole office, and if you don't turn up for it they will stop your dole'.

Oliver opened his eyes wide and stared at his Mother. The dream, he had just awoken from, was upsetting to say the least but that was the story of his life. In all his years of dreaming, Oliver never had a pleasant dream. He dreaded going to bed most nights as the spectre of nightmares were never far away. Twisted, sometimes horrific, most times upsetting nightmares had haunted him all the nights of his living existence. The one he had awoke from was no exception, he expected it before he went to bed, and he expected the same when he lay down to rest tonight.

Oliver was quick to dress, but ignored his Mother's advise to wash his teeth each Morning. While he sat at the kitchen table, to await his breakfast, his father was already perched on the chair on the other side, zombie like in his own true tradition. Oliver accepted his Mother's plate of scrambled eggs and toast, and tuned into the morning news on Radio North.

A NUMBER OF SHOTS WERE FIRED AT A POLICE STATION IN LONDONDERRY LAST NIGHT, POLICE SAID NO ONE WAS HURT BY THE INCIDENT. POLICE IN MAGHERAFELT HAVE PRAISED THE COURAGE OF A LOCAL SCHOOLMASTER FOR HIS BRAVERY. THE SCHOOLMASTER WAS ATTACKED BY THREE MASKED ROBBERS WHILE OUT WALKING HIS DOG IN FIELDS NEAR HIS HOME. THE SCHOOLMASTER MANAGED TO SCARE THE ATTACKERS OFF BY PUTTING UP WHAT POLICE HAVE DESCRIBED AS; ONE HELL OF A FIGHT. THE SCHOOLMASTER'S DOG WAS CRUELLY KILLED DURING THE ASSAULT, APPARENTLY BY THE SCHOOLMASTER'S

WALKING STICK. POLICE WANT ANYONE WHO MAY HAVE WITNESSED THE ATTACK TO CONTACT MAGHERAFELT POLICE. NOW FOR THE WEATHER…..

'What in hell is the world coming to, when you can't even go out for a walk in peace', complained Oliver's Mother. 'Now it's happening in our own back yard'.

Oliver never spoke; the news bulletin that he had just heard, had both angered and frightened him. The schoolmaster had indeed fabricated a load of bullshit for the attention of the police and, throwing in for good measure, had killed his own dog. Oliver was disturbed by the fact that not only was the schoolmaster a cold black hearted liar, he had turned around an assault from man to man, into a robbery with violence implicating two other men. Oliver's thoughts were interrupted once again by the sound of his Mother's voice.

'Be careful son on your way to the dole office, I hope the cops catch them and throw away the key; the cold hearted thugs had to kill the poor man's dog'.

Oliver wanted to jump from the table, stand before his Mother and empty the truth out before her. But he knew he had to be calm, to control his anger and fear, and stand firm. Even to reveal the truth would break his Mother's heart, if not kill her. His Mother was an honest woman, a loather of violence, and a firm believer in the upholding of the law. Oliver rose from his seat, thanked his Mother for the breakfast, and proceeded to make his way to the dreaded dole office.

A cold breeze accompanied Oliver as he made his way along the footpath which would lead him to the dole office; where he would be humiliated, degraded and looked upon like something that had just been scrapped off the bottom of a shoe. He was seventeen years old, had four O'levels and most things he would be asked to do, whether technical or educational, he knew he could accomplish. Oliver knew he needed a job; he wanted to do more with his life. He desired the things all young people wished for, a car, nice clothes and a girlfriend. He needed to be able to hold his head up and say, 'I am an essential member of society'. He didn't want the thirty two pounds and eighty pence dole money he received every fortnight, but he had to accept it humbly. After giving his mother half, the rest he could easily blow on one night out with his friends. The half he give to his mother would then be taken back in drips and drabs over the following two weeks while he awaited his next payment. His life went from one social security cheque to the next, and Oliver knew it had to end. *Perhaps the meeting today would shine some hope into the darkness of his present situation*, Oliver thought, *maybe today would be the day of days, the moment when his life would turn the corner and step on to the street of fortune.*

Oliver made his way through the two swinging reinforced glass doors, and across the short corridor that would lead him to the information desk.

'Yes', muttered the receptionist, 'can I help you?'

'I have an appointment', replied Oliver.

'Name?' asked the receptionist.

'Oliver McKenna' answered Oliver.

'Ok, you can take a seat in the waiting room around the corner and first on the left', said the receptionist, at the same time spluttering out a short sharp cough.

As he sat down on one of the chairs in the waiting room, the receptionist coughed again. Oliver recalled the receptionist as she sat in Tom's bar in Magherafelt every Friday night, chain smoking unfiltered cigarettes and drinking whiskey raw from a half pint glass. Her husband used to be a part time policeman, that is until one morning he climbed into the driver's seat and it exploded, killing him instantly. Now she smoked and drank with a ferocity that would soon allow her to accompany her husband. When Oliver heard the door open from the room across from his chair, and a small grey haired man call his name, he arose and walked into the interview room. The grey haired man beckoned him to sit down on the small plastic chair at one side of the table, while he sat across on a higher chair on the other side. Oliver smiled inwardly, as Michael's words came flooding back.

'Listen Oliver', he said, 'the person interviewing you will choose a higher chair than you for the simple reason; he can look down on you. It's psychological; they can intimidate and frighten you into falsely believing that their shit smells like fucking roses, and because they have a bigger chair, they're the king or queen of the fucking castle'.

Oliver looked up at the small man across the table and just as he was about to speak, said,

'Excuse me Sir, this chair is very painful on my back, do you mind if I stand?'

The man looked at Oliver somewhat shocked at what he had just heard, and spoke,

'please be seated, this will only take a minute'.

Oliver stood up, lifted the chair and placed it on the other stack of chairs at the corner of the room. He then stood before the table and looked down on the little man, who now resembled a schoolchild sitting at the desk.

'I, ah, would prefer if you would sit, I'm straining my

neck', muttered the man.

'I am sorry Sir', said Oliver defiantly, 'my back is killing me, you could stand up too Sir if you wish'.

The man said nothing, until he shuffled through a number of cards he had in his hand, then he spoke,

'Take this card, the address of the employer is wrote on the back, you must find your way to his place of employment today. Under the government rules and regulations, we are obliged to assist those on unemployment benefit to find suitable employment. These same rules also state that, if a suitable situation is found and the claimant refuses to engage, then his benefit will be discontinued for a period of no less than six weeks. Is this understood?'

Oliver could barely speak, he wanted to grab the little man and kiss him, to cry out loud and thank him with all his soul. Month after month for the last year, he had been called to these meetings, but still no job. Now today, the bells of dignity were ringing out loud for all those dreams inside his mind to hear. He gulped once, then again, fighting to keep his emotions from bursting forth and tumbling the walls of his teenage defences, and exposing the inner weakness that life had forced him to hide. He was happy beyond belief for, from this day forward, he could call himself a man.

'Did you hear what I just told you?' asked the man.

'Ya ye yes', replied Oliver trying to keep the emotion from his voice, 'I will take the job, thank you very much'.

Oliver left the dole office and quickly made his way in the opposite direction from that in which he came. Each step he took was long and deliberate, his breath laboured and he could feel the blood flow around his body like a river that had just burst a dam. He thought of how his mum would react when he arrived home later and told her the good news. He imagined the envy of John and Michael when he flashed the contents of his pay packet before their poverty smitten eyes. He could hear the musical horns singing from beneath the bonnet of his new black Ford Capri, and the girls gathering around when he pulled in at the diamond to display his wheels of glory to the jealous eyes. *He deserved this job*, he thought to himself. He recalled the long nights studying for his O' levels, while his bedside lamp burned long into the night. He only took on four in order that he could concentrate fully on the subjects he had chosen. He remembered the almost uncontrollable shaking as he took his place in the examination room, and opened his mind like never before. And he recollected that Saturday morning, after a long night of tossing and turning, when he opened the letter and stared at the four A's smiling up at him from the paper. His mum had put her coat and hat on to rush out and spread the news, forgetting she still had her bedroom slippers on. And last but definitely not the least, the spending of the twenty pound his dad's sister Martha presented him with, inside a congratulations card.

Oliver stopped and stood facing the building that destiny had afforded him. The building was grey; the window frames were yellow and in addition to the boring architecture, there was the foulest smell that had ever crossed the path of his nostrils. Oliver approached the building slowly and knocked on the worn yellow door.

A voice from within roared,

'Come in, the door's open'.

Oliver turned the handle to be greeted by a tall fat man sporting a brown peak cap with a pipe protruding from his mouth like a long chimney that had just been constructed sideways.

'I have been sent from the dole office', said Oliver, simultaneously handing over the card that only an hour earlier had held so many of his dreams.

The man removed the pipe from his mouth and turned around to call someone in from the back,

'Mervin, come here a minute'.

At this request, another smaller but still oversized man, wearing the same brown peak cap, arrived on the scene.

'Take a luk at tis Mervin', he muttered.

Mervin looked at the card and raised his eyes to view the figure of Oliver now standing at his right hand side and spoke,

'Have ya ever cleaned out pig houses before?'

'No', replied Oliver.

'Have ya ever worked on a farm before?'

Once again Oliver could only answer

'No'.

'Well', said Mervin, 'there's always a first time for anything, can ye start now?'

'I have no work clothes or lunch', answered Oliver.

'We ca soon fin ye some wellies, and there's plenty a food in the pigs trough'.

At the closing of these words, both the man and Mervin began to laugh, both displaying rows of black and brown stained teeth.

Suddenly Mervin stopped and stared at Oliver, almost as if he offended him in some way and spoke,

'What foot ya kick way?'

Oliver raised his eyebrows and replied,

35

'what do you mean what foot I kick with, I can kick with both feet if the situation calls for it'.

'What he means', said the tall fat man, 'Are ye a left footer, Catholic, or a right footer, Protestant?'

Oliver could only stare at the two figures before him and curse from within the confines of his deepest thoughts. His dreams had already been swiftly put to the sword, as soon as he walked through the door. Now he was facing the cruel, ugly face of sectarianism, and the humiliating forge of dogmatic intolerance within Northern Ireland society. Michael was a Protestant and his best friend, yet never did religion raise its dirty head to paint each other with opposing brushes. Oliver had adopted an attitude of judging people by their actions and words; by the way they helped or opposed him, and never would the rod of creed conduct how he felt. Oliver decided there was one way and one way only to deal with the situation before him. Perhaps if he had been older and wiser, educated to academic level, or had just acquired more knowledge from wiser people than him, he may have dealt with the incident in an orderly fashion. But as he was not either of the aforementioned, the only words he could think of were

'Stick your job up your swine skinned asses you fat fucks'.

Oliver left the room with a speed far greater than he had entered it, and made his way along the pothole smeared road. He occasionally looked over his shoulder while he gathered pace, to see if the two pig farmers had decided to pursue him with violent and unhealthy intentions. To his relief, they had chosen to remain within their shit soaked environment, allowing Oliver to slow his steps and take in his present predicament. He recalled the little man's words in the dole office, and knew he was broke for the next six weeks at least. The Ford Capri, the healthy wage packet and string of beautiful girls had now taken a tumble of the cliff edge of his gullibility. He would have to tell his Mother the truth about what happened, if not, how would he explain the absence of a dole cheque every fortnight? As the peril of the state of affairs that he had found himself in began to subside, Oliver's heart began to ache. He knew the little man in the dole office had sent him to the pig farm on purpose, a lesson for Oliver's refusal to be looked down upon. He began to curse himself for his arrogance, for his Jack the lad attitude towards those who held his future according to their mood. He prayed that he could turn the clock back or that he would soon wake up to the sound of his Mother's voice once more allowing him the chance to try again. But Oliver knew he had prayed before, and still the shit always flew in his direction. Perhaps it was karma for what he had done to the schoolmaster the day before? Maybe it was his absence from Sunday mass? Or some distant ancestor had been cursed for stealing the witch's gold? Whatever it was, Oliver had to embrace the self assurance that it wasn't his fault. He had to try and hold his head up, to keep his courage intact and endure the many thorns that would be laid out before him. At seventeen he accepted the common conception that he stood between the great pillars of maturity, and the wetting of eyes was strictly forbidden.

As Oliver sat down on the summer seat facing the diamond, he surveyed the scenes before him. Ford Cortinas, Hillmans, Austins and Vauxhalls moved lazily back and forth, each on their journey to achieve their goals. Robert, the town drunk, was yet again scanning the ground with his thirsty eyes in the hope that some form of currency would jump up at him from the footpath. Oliver remembered his Mother telling him the story of Robert, and how he had not always been a drunk. Robert, she told him was once a fine young man, well mannered and respected by many. When he turned eighteen he left home and went to England to join The Irish Guards. Like many young men, both past and present, he was attracted to the glamour of uniforms and guns, and the chance to see the world. Before leaving, Robert asked his fiancée Winifred to marry him and she said yes. They planned he would sign up for three years and she would work in the local shirt factory. During that time they would save everything they possibly could and at the end of the three years, would purchase a small farm outside Draperstown and get married. The farm was owned by a man who owned two pubs and had agreed a price to sell it to them in three years time. Low and behold the three years ended and Robert came home to Winifred with a heart full of love and a pocket full of money. But what happened next was disputed by the pub landlord, and clarified by those who lent an ear to the conversation between Robert and the pub landlord, and afterwards with the landlord's wife. Apparently, his Mother told him that the landlord took Robert into a back room and filled him with whiskey till it was running out of his ears. He then persuaded Robert in his drunken state to cut cards for doubles or quits, that is if Robert wins he gets to keep both the money and the farm, but if he lost he gets nothing. Low and behold, Robert lost and the landlord threw him out onto the street like a dog. As Oliver recalled, his Mother told him that she had spoken to someone, who was in the bar that night and who saw the pub landlord's wife slip her husband a pack of cards. Whether the cards were marked or not was not in question his mother told him; what was in question was the pub landlord's intentions in getting Robert so drunk that he was unaware of what he was doing. That, on its own, was proof enough that a crime had been committed. On hearing of what happened, Winifred had thrown her engagement ring into the Curdian River, and left Magherafelt and Robert forever.

'Good afternoon young fella, you couldn't spare a shilling for a bag of chips?' begged Robert.

Oliver reached into his pocket and felt the fifty pence he had been holding onto for a hamburger, he removed it and handed it to Robert,

'There you are'.

Robert took it from Oliver and thanked him adding,

'This has got to be the poorest town in the world; I have never ever found as much as an old penny, God bless you son'.

As Robert left to make his way to the off-licence, Oliver hoped that if there was a God, he would bless him real soon.

CHAPTER 4

The houses and barns got smaller as Oliver made his way up the steep mountain path. Heather and sheep blotted the landscape on each side of the path, and as he ascended step by step, the grey rocks began to reveal themselves from behind the thin mist. Oliver had tramped this path many times, many times he had inhaled the sweet aroma of heather through the seasons of his childhood. Whenever his heart was low, or his mind unable to digest the sadness of his life, he would visit the cairn alone and free his thoughts from all obstacles. As Oliver neared the top he observed the pile of stones heaped one by one by the countless visitors who came from around the world to pay their respects to their ancestors. Emigrants Glen as it was named was where many people over the centuries caught the coach for Derry or Belfast. From there they would leave their land and travel to distant places in search of a better life. Some found their fortunes, while others died in foreign wars or as paupers in the country where the grass was thought to be greener. Now the survivors' ancestors climb the mountain to place a stone in memory of someone who departed from there, long before their time. Now thousands of stones rise above the heather, going up above the highest peak and climbing above the clouds as if to create a symbolic stairway to heaven to allow the spirits to make their way home.

As Oliver sat down on a rock beside his favourite place, he tried to view the scenes below, but the now thick watery clouds were blocking his view. He had arrived to examine his conscience, to look through the tunnel of his soul, and search for light. His visit to the dole office and pig farm the day before, had punished his self esteem and challenged the very reason of his being. He thought of those who had left this place in years gone by, and related to how they must have felt. How they put their backs and hearts to the yoke that lay before them, only to be defeated by hunger and burning thatch roofs. Oliver knew, the yoke that had been laid before him was overwhelming to the point that his mind and soul were crumbling. 'What chance had he to live a normal happy life, when the dark path of sectarianism had been laid before him every step he took?' he thought. The blood and tears, the pain and fear, the hate and suspicion had all wormed their way into Northern Ireland society like a thriving cancer. He wondered how many more young people like him were sitting somewhere, trying to make sense from the curse that they had inherited. Trying to find a yellow brick road that would lead them away from the bleeding streets, and to a place where there was life before death.

Oliver's thoughts were suddenly disturbed by a tall figure standing before him.

'Good afternoon', he said.

'Hello', replied Oliver somewhat startled.

'That damn mountain is tough, wouldn't want to be

doing that every day', he said in an out of breath tone of voice. Oliver began observing the figure before him, who stood about five feet seven inches tall and wore blue jeans and a black wax like jacket. His black boots looked as if they had only been worn once, and as he caught the stranger's eyes, he noticed the dark brown hair and a face that bore all the hallmarks of a well slapped backside.

'My name is Oliver', said the stranger reaching out to politely shake Oliver's hand. Oliver stood up, took the stranger's hand and smiled,

'Please to meet you Sir, my name is Oliver too'. When the two persons of the same first name finished laughing, Oliver spoke,

'What takes you all the way up here?'

'I guess I'm taking a walk up memory lane, used to come here when I was a boy, a great place for thinking and clearing the head', replied the stranger.

'You don't live around here anymore, I guessed that from your accent', said Oliver.

'No, moved to the states many years ago, couldn't find a job so like millions more of unemployed Irish, I went off to seek my fortune', replied the stranger.

'And did you find it', asked Oliver jokingly.
The stranger smiled and said,

'well I didn't get rich, made a good living working for a company who supplied private security firms', he replied. 'One thing I wasn't sorry about and that was leaving this God forsaken country behind'. While the stranger turned to try and get a glimpse of the valley below, Oliver thought about what he said and God forsaken was indeed what it was. His mother used to say that God had nothing to do with the bombings and shootings, so why does everyone have to blame him. Oliver's thoughts were interrupted again by the stranger speaking,

'Do they still burn turf on the fires?'

'Yes', replied Oliver, 'but it's hard to get it cut with a spade, they brought in new machines and it squeezes all the good oils out '.

'I promised my wife I would get her some to bring back with us, she loves the smell of it burning', muttered the stranger while still trying to see through the clouds.

Oliver remembered that they still had some good stuff lying at the back of the coal shed and spoke,

'I will get you some'.

The stranger gives up on the idea of getting a panoramic view and turned back to Oliver and replied,

'Thank you very much'.

'Did you see that old car you passed before you decided to climb the mountain?' Said Oliver.

'Yes', replied the stranger.

'I will leave it in the boot of that tomorrow', said Oliver.

'You mean the trunk?' Smiled the stranger.

'Ok, the trunk it shall be', replied Oliver grinning at the thought of how the stranger had become Americanised.

The stranger thanked Oliver once again and departed as suddenly and quietly as he had arrived. Oliver envied the man for taking the brave step away from a place where hope was now confined to fairytales and books written by wise men and women. It was getting late in the evening and the mist had still not cleared, so Oliver decided that hunger had taken precedence over his unscrambling of thoughts, and began to make his way back down the mountain.

When Oliver entered through the back door of his home and into the kitchen, all was quiet. He shouted out for his mum and walked into the living room to find it empty. Oliver returned to the kitchen and found the note that his mum had left, perching upright like a sore thumb on top of the table. The note read, GONE TO BRIAN MCKENNA'S WAKE, I HAVEN'T DONE ANY SHOPPING YET SO YOU WILL HAVE TO MAKE DO WITH BREAD AND CHEESE…..MOTHER. Oliver rummaged through the cupboard and fond enough bread and cheese to make himself a healthy sandwich. With a strong cup of tea which would have made his mothers look like muddy water, he began to feast hungrily and thought about the evening he had planned with John and Michael. It was Michael's birthday and they had decided to meet at Danny's Lounge at six o'clock. The absence of Oliver's mother had somewhat put a foot in the door of his enjoyment, as he had only four pound to his name and he wanted to borrow a fiver off his mother. He would just have to throw what he had in the kitty and drink of the boys until next time.

It didn't take Oliver long to get a quick wash and dress up in his best wrangler jeans and jacket. The traffic had accumulated owing to the added presence of those coming home from work. Robert's heart sank as he breathed in the smell of diesel fumes from passing lorries and the occasional tired tractor. He would have given his right arm for a chance to be one of the waged, to be able to come home in the evening tired, hungry and fulfilled. He knew when he left the pub tonight with John and Michael he would be penniless, and his four pound would be flowing down some urine stained alleyway. But for now he would hide those thoughts away, tuck them neatly behind the falsehood of his momentary existence until tomorrow, when those same thoughts would taunt him again and again with their soul scorching truth.

Oliver was unaware that the grey land rover had pulled up behind him, until four policemen jumped out shouting,

'Get your fucking hands in the air'.

As Oliver quickly did as he was told, one of the policemen began roughly frisking him and then turned to the others and said,

'he's clean'.

The policemen grabbed Oliver under both arms and violently flung him into the back of the land rover.

'What to fuck is going on', roared Oliver as his head connected violently with the hard metal floor.

'Shut your fucking mouth you little dip stick', growled a policeman.

Oliver felt the heavy boots of the policemen deliberately press intentionally as he lay face down.

'For fuck's sake you're hurting me', roared Oliver.

'No', laughed one of the policemen, 'this is hurting you'.

The policeman drew his baton and applied it to Oliver's head with enough force to knock him unconscious. As Oliver began to drift off to the place where pain and worry are put on hold, he could hear the laughter of the policemen drifting further and further away.

When Oliver slowly awoke he found himself inside a cold lonely police cell, with walls sporting all the hallmarks of people who had arrived and left before him. Etched onto the grey painted wall facing him, he could make out the words *thee who enter here abandon all pope*. Oliver noticed that the word pope used to spell hope, that is until someone thought it would be amusing to replace the letter h with p. On his left Oliver read *Robert was here*. Oliver began to think of Robert the town drunk and wondered how many cold winter nights he had deliberately got himself arrested to get a bed for the night. He began to come to terms with what had happened, and could think of no other reason why he was there, other than the schoolmaster. He moved his hand over the top of his head and stroked the painful lump that had swollen as a result of the baton, compliments of a sadistic cop. There was dry blood on his forehead and upper lip, prompting Oliver to begin to realise he had been here for some time. His arrest had been sudden and violent and bore all the remnants of a snatch squad sent to hunt down suspicious looking characters, or characters described by the schoolmaster. Oliver knew that he must apply all his strength and will, if he has any chance of walking the streets a free man again. He had been arrested before for kicking a door on Main Street, but had been let out after the owner refused to press charges. But now this was different, this was a whole new game of football and he needed to play the game well.

Oliver heard the footsteps getting closer to his cell door and suddenly stop. The door flung open and there before him stood a man in a dark suit and wearing a white shirt and blue tie.

'Ok young man', he said, 'get up and come with me'. Oliver arose from the hard black plastic coated bed and followed the man up the long corridor and into a room which was clearly marked Interview Room. As the man sat down on a chair on the other side of a table, he looked at Oliver and said

'Sit down son'.

As Oliver proceeded to sit down he answered the policeman with the words,

'I'm not your son'.

'Thank God for that', replied the man sarcastically, 'I wouldn't want my son to be spending the next ten years in prison'.

Oliver said nothing as he looked at the man across from him and tried to weigh him up. He looked like a decent man, his grey side burns and bald head afforded him an age far in advance of Oliver's seventeen. The lines running across his forehead added support to Oliver's belief, that the man was a plain clothes cop and had many years to know what he was doing. The man spoke again,

'Now Oliver, I am going to come clean with you, I am here to help you and at this moment in time I am the only friend you have got'.

The man shuffled through some papers while rubbing his head a few times with the palm of his hand.

'Let me introduce myself', said the man, 'I am detective sergeant Martin and you Robert are going to tell me why you are here'.

'I thought you might be able to tell me', replied Oliver sarcastically, 'If none of us know, then I may go now'.

'Well I'm sorry Oliver, but we both know full well why you are here, and you young sir will be going nowhere', replied the detective, at the same time staring at Oliver hoping to find a flicker of guilt from his eyes. Oliver said nothing as he held the detective's stare.

'Ok then', said the detective, 'where were you the

day before yesterday?'

'None of your business', replied Oliver defiantly.

'But it is my business', said the detective, 'you and your two friends John and Michael were trying to rob and beat a defenceless man, and only for the fact that you were cowards, he probably would have been as dead as his dog that you killed'.

Oliver tried to keep the fear that was building up inside him from showing, he was worried that the schoolmaster's lies could overflow onto him, and now here they were staring him right in the face.

'I don't have a clue what you're talking about', said Oliver still holding his stare.

'Don't sit there and tell me lies Oliver', said the detective now slightly raising his voice, 'the man has identified all three of you, Michael and John were arrested hours ago and have confessed, now let's start again'.

'If Michael and John have confessed', replied Oliver, 'then why in hell's fuck am I here?'

'Because', replied the detective, 'they have cleared their conscience and named you as the third man, both have got bail and are now sitting at home, and if you don't come clean you are going to Belfast Prison'.

'Then why do you need me to make a statement', asked Oliver, 'if Michael and John have implicated me in something I didn't do, why don't you fucking charge me and send me to prison'. The detective pushed his chair back and stood up,

'Because I'm trying to make it easy on you', he said, now raising his voice, 'I have a son your age and I don't want to see you rotting in jail, if you come clean then I can get you bailed and out of here, I will even speak in court on your behalf'.

For one small moment Oliver thought he might be telling the truth, but he began to quickly analyse what the detective had said, and came to the conclusion that John and Michael would never have admitted trying to rob the schoolmaster or kill his dog. The detective was only going on the lies the schoolmaster told him, and as much as Oliver wanted to expose the schoolmaster for the cowardly liar he was, he was not going to sacrifice his freedom.

'Listen', replied Oliver, 'I have an alibi for the day this alleged attack happened'.

'Then we need to check it out', said the detective, sitting down on the chair again.

'I can't', replied Oliver.

'Why not?' asked the detective raising his thick grey eyebrows.

'Because', replied Oliver, 'I was shagging someone else's wife, and she would not be happy if her husband found out'.

At the closing of this revelation, a knock suddenly came to the door.

'Come in', said the detective.

At the detective's request, another man entered the room. He too wore a black suit, white shirt and blue tie and outweighed the first detective by at least five stone. On his head he sported a thick mop of greasy black hair, and on closer inspection, Oliver recognised him as walking around the town most Saturdays with his wife shopping. In comparison to the ugly overweight figure before him, the man's wife was beautiful and slim with long blond hair. Oliver remembered a rumour Michael heard that she would shag anything that moved, and the husband was a jealous bastard.

'This is my colleague detective constable Black', said detective Martin, 'If you don't want to tell me the truth and save yourself, then I'm sure my partner here would like to spend some time with you on his own'. Oliver looked at detective Black and spoke

'I take it he's gay too?'

At this statement from Oliver, detective Black without warning threw himself across the table and grabbed Oliver by the hair,

'You fucking piece of shit I'll kill you', he roared. At this display of anger detective Martin grabbed his colleague and commenced to restrain him.

'Now, now Robert, calm down, remember the last kid we had in here, you beat him half to death, you need to control your temper', he said calming detective Black down. 'Now go outside Robert and calm down, I'll call you back if I need you', said detective Martin. At this request the second detective proceeded to make his way to the door, while simultaneously delivering a cold menacing stare in Oliver's direction. At the wake of Robert leaving the room, detective Martin looked at Oliver shaking his head from side to side,

'You shouldn't have said that, now you have really pissed him off', he said.

'Well', replied Oliver, 'when you said he was your partner, what else was I to think'.

'Ok smart ass', said detective Martin, 'let's get back to what we were discussing, you have an alibi and I want to know who it is'.

'I can't', replied Oliver, 'she said if her husband ever found out he would kill her first then come for me'.

'I assure you we will keep it strictly confidential', said detective Martin, his voice now portraying an air of impatience.

'How in hells fuck are you going to keep it confidential', replied Oliver with a slight urgency in his voice, 'her husband is a cop'.

Detective Martin rose from his chair once again and stared at Oliver,

'You lying little shit', he yelled.

'I'm not lying', said Oliver, 'she has blond hair and a body to die for and said her husband makes her sick'.

As soon as Oliver uttered the last word, the door flung open and detective Black came storming into the room. Oliver felt the punches rain down upon him like the hoofs of a wild boar. He tried to defend himself by crawling under the chair, but to no avail. Detective Black kept punching, kicking, and using his baton to beat him without mercy. The blood was beginning to sting his eyes and all he could now see was a red curtain and a screaming madman, inflicting a terrible rage on every part of his body. He cursed himself from within as he wished with every ounce of life still left within him, that he could retract every word he said. But it was too late, the few moments of sarcasm and fun had been paid with a severe chastisement.

The two glowing red eyes that Oliver now looked up at, could only belong to someone sent to escort him to hell. As the sky above him began to make sense, the stars, speckled sparks on a black sheet of endlessness and a perfect sphere of light bore responsibility for the understanding that he was not yet dead. He sat up on the damp field and dismissed the cow that found his presence fascinating, and began to painfully gather his thoughts. Every part of his body ached; his head felt that it had just been put through a mincing machine, and his throbbing ribs reminded him that breathing was not going to be easy. He remembered clearly what had happened at the police barracks, knowing precisely that he was not waking up from another nightmare. What he didn't know was how he ended up in the field, and what time it was?

Oliver commenced to get on his feet, but it took several attempts to do so. He wanted to die, but most of all, he wanted to get back home and look in a mirror to see how much of his face he had left. The beatings he had received both before and inside the barracks, were against any laws that he had heard of, but he knew it would be futile to protest. The cops would deny ever laying eyes on him, never mind arresting and assaulting him. What did cross his mind was, what would he tell his mother? If he told her the truth, she would go to the barracks in such a rage and get herself arrested. Even worse, take a heart attack on the way there. Oliver knew he had to think of something, and as he slowly and painfully made his way towards the lights of Magherafelt, the cogs in his mind began to turn slowly but surely.

As Oliver turned the handle on the back door of his home, he did so as quietly as possible. When he entered the kitchen, to his relief no one was up so he made his way to the small bathroom at the bottom of the stairs. Gently he closed the door, turned on the light and with his heart beating wildly he faced the mirror before him. As he viewed the damage inflicted on his face by the pissed off cop, Oliver could see something that had just finished twenty rounds with a heavy weight boxer. He began to wash his face with the slow flowing warm water, and to his relief most of the damage was dried up blood and dirt. He was no medical expert, but Oliver could breathe through his nose relatively well, so as far as he knew his nose was not broken. On finishing up, Oliver softly made his way up the stairs, into his room and under the crisp clean sheets of his bed.

CHAPTER 5

When the new day arrived it appeared both as a ray of sunshine taunting the pupil of Oliver's swollen right eye, and the proverbial figure of his mother standing before him. Before he went to sleep, Oliver had gathered together enough of his senses to create an excuse that would be in keeping with his battered appearance. He knew his mother would demand an explanation, and an explanation in keeping with her nervous disposition was what she would get.

'My God Oliver', roared his mother, 'What in the name of Jesus happened to you?'
Oliver gathered himself together and sat upright on the bed, trying desperately to hide the pain that was now squealing through his body,

'Don't panic', he replied, 'I fell down that hole the council dug in Queen Street'.

'Did they not cover it, or put some sort of warning on it?' cried Oliver's mother.

'They probably did', replied Oliver, still trying to keep the results of the day before from showing on his face, 'but someone must have removed it and I didn't see it in the dark'.

'Look at the state of your eye', she roared, 'you need

54

to go to the hospital with that'.

'No', replied Oliver, 'hospitals are for wimps'.

'Wimps my arse', replied Oliver's mother, at the same time bending over to take a closer look at Oliver's puffed-up eye, 'that eye needs looking at or you could lose your sight'. Oliver knew in his own mind that hospital was not a good idea. First they would want to know how it happened, where it happened and if he had any other injuries. Oliver knew he could hoodwink his mother, but not the trained eye of a doctor. An examination, followed by a phone call to the council would soon reveal that the hole that he had allegedly fallen into was only about a foot deep. Then the stress and worry of his mother would cause him to be interrogated for the truth, and that he could not tell. The beaten he had received the day before from a policeman who had probably arrived at the end of his tether, was as far as it went. Oliver was prepared to forget, knowing the schoolmaster incident however blown up, would now be swept under the carpet. The police would deny that they ever had arrested him, owing to the controversy that might evolve from his treatment, and Oliver had no qualms about trading a couple of years behind bars for a few bruises. Oliver turned to his mother, forced a smile and said,

'It will be ok, you worry too much, sure I don't even feel any pain'.

'Listen son', replied Oliver's mother, 'if you notice flashing or blurring of that eye you need to go to hospital, please son promise me'.

'I promise mother', replied Oliver, still trying to force a smile, 'so don't you be worrying and get the teapot on'.

As his mother departed the bedroom, Oliver slowly struggled out of bed and onto his feet. He ruffled slowly to his wardrobe and reached his hand to the top, pulling a small plastic bag from the corner. As he opened the bag, Oliver found a number of morphine pills that Michael had given him a few weeks earlier. From the bedroom he made his way into the bathroom and commenced to swallow two of the pills, helping them on their way down by a swig of water from the cold tap of the wash hand basin. As Oliver looked in the mirror his eye had indeed rose through the night and had began to blacken. He sprinkled some water over his face and sat down on the toilet to allow the morphine some time to free him from the violent pain that was still laying claim over his movements. He remembered when Michael had told him of a friend of his who regularly got beatings by gangs of thugs, and had kept morphine pills as an alternative to going to the hospital. He laughed at Michael when he offered him them, but as he felt the pain beginning to slowly subside, he was glad he had taken him seriously. As he rose from the toilet feeling slightly dizzy from the affects of the morphine, he descended the stairs and followed the smell of bacon and sausages coming from the kitchen. As he sat down at his place at the table, he suddenly remembered the promise he had made to the other Oliver the day before.

'Are there any turf left in the shed?' he asked his mother.

'A few in a bag, but hardly enough for a night's burning', replied Oliver's mother as she placed his breakfast on the table before him.

'A Yank I met yesterday asked me for some', said

Oliver, 'he wants to bring them back to the States I believe'.

As Oliver finished the last word, he noticed the morphine was causing him to slur and quickly corrected himself as he spoke again.

'I suppose the smell of burning turf will remind him of the only good thing he left behind'.

'Well if it makes him happy, give him whatever there is in the shed', replied his mother, 'he might get more use out of it than I did, I can't get the blooming spade stuff to burn and those new machines they use to cut turf now are squeezing the oils out of it and leaving nothing but mush'. Oliver quickly finished his breakfast and before leaving he thanked his mother.

'Remember what you promised me son', she yelled as Oliver made his way out through the back door, 'If that eye gets worse go to the hospital'.

'Will do', replied Oliver at the same time reaching into the coal shed and taking hold of the remaining turf.

As Oliver waited for the bus which would take him to the bottom of the Mountain, he wondered how John and Michael had fared. He did not believe the detective when he told him they were charged. He was disappointed he did not make it to the birthday party; he knew his mother would be good for a few pounds when he got back, and he would catch up later. As the bus pulled up he paid his twenty five pence fare and commenced the short journey. As Oliver stared out the window, he surveyed the passing houses, fields and trees with his good eye. Everywhere he looked he saw beauty, but beneath that beauty was ugliness thriving from the fodder of hate and religious indifference. He wondered if some day, like the Oliver he was bringing the turf to, he too would leave it behind and go seek a place where the waters were not turning red with the blood of innocence. He remembered the old people telling him stories from World war two, and how religion and suspicions were buried and everyone united against a great evil sweeping across the world. Oliver wondered if another greater iniquity came again, would the people of today face it with the same determination and courage as their forefathers did, or would they continue on their path of darkness, blinded by greed and selfishness.

As the bus moved away, Oliver made his way to the place where he agreed to leave the turf for the other Oliver. He stopped beside an old rusted Morris Minor car and proceeded to open the boot. To Oliver's surprise, another bag had been left and when he looked at the outside he noticed a note taped to the side that read, FOR OLIVER, A GIFT WHICH I HOPE YOU WILL NEVER NEED. As Oliver opened the bag and took a peek inside, he smiled inwardly and closed it up again. He removed the gift that the other Oliver left for him and replaced it with the turf, wishing that he had more to leave him. As he proceeded to depart, Oliver took a quick glance at the mountain above him, but knew he was in no fit state to be facing the steep grassy path today. He shook his head at the idea and carried on his way to catch the next bus back to Magherafelt.

When Oliver returned, no one was at home so he made his way upstairs to his room. Opening the wardrobe door he slipped the plastic bag that the other Oliver had left him inside. As Oliver noticed the pain creeping up on him again, he took two more morphine pills from the top of the wardrobe and put them in his pocket. Looking around his room he noticed how neat it was, compliments of his fussy and caring mother. Unlike John and Michael's rooms which resembled something that had just been the victim of a hand grenade tossed through the window, Oliver could always depend on his mother to clean up his wreckage. As he made his way back down the stairs and into the kitchen, he noticed one of his mother's notes accompanied with a fresh crispy five pound note attached. HI SON, HOPE YOUR EYE'S NOT BOTHERING YOU, REMEMBER YOUR PROMISE. I WONT BE BACK TILL LATE SO HERE'S A FIVER TO GET YOURSELF SOMETHING….MOTHER. Oliver deposited the money deep into his jeans pocket and smiled to himself, *that will get a few beers* he thought.

As Oliver locked the back door behind him, he slipped the key under the yellow gas tank and proceeded to make his way up the town. The town was quiet save for one or two cars passing by, and the occasional tap of shoes as people calmly went about their business. As Oliver approached the roundabout across from the diamond, a police land rover passed him and fortunately for Oliver, moved off out of sight. Oliver hurriedly made his way around the corner, and took the first door on the left into Danny's Lounge.

As Oliver sat down on the table beside his two friends John and Michael, John looked at him coldly and failing to notice his injuries said,

'Where to fuck have you been, are we not good enough to play with anymore?'

'Well kids', replied Oliver, 'it's a long fucking story'.

'Tell us about it', replied John, still holding the cold stare, 'we have all night'.

'Ok kids', replied Oliver, 'but I'll make it short'. Pulling his chair closer to his two friends, Oliver proceeded to fill them in on the events leading up to last night. When Oliver finished, John arose from the table and shortly returned with a cold pint for Oliver.

'Here kid, I'm sorry for the dirty look, but we were just pissed off you didn't turn up last night', said John. Michael reached over and placed his hand on Oliver's arm and spoke,

'I knew there was something wrong, I felt it in my bones and when I saw you walk in just now with that black eye, my suspicions were found to be right'. Oliver took a long swig from his pint and spoke

'Well kids, thanks to the beating the cops gave me, we are now free from any accusations being made about the schoolmaster'.

'Holy fuck', said John slightly raising his voice, 'a terrible fucking price to pay, they could have whacked you and no one would have known it was them'.

'There are some bad evil bastards among those cops', said Michael, 'and from now on we are going to have to watch our backs'. Almost at the same time as Michael finished his sentence, someone threw ten pence into the old worn jukebox in the corner, and the three friends listened quietly to the song *Heaven Can Wait* by Meatloaf. As the words flowed over to their table, Oliver's mind began to wander back to the day before and how Heaven or Hell as the case may be, waited for him. He began to reflect on all the deaths he had heard about, and all the young men like himself who's lives violently ended. He wondered what had came into their mind when they realised that death had arrived, and a chill began to crawl up his spine as he thought about his own death. He began to ask himself the questions, how would he face death? Would he stand up tall and fearless, or would he grovel on the ground whining with the piss running down his leg? His thoughts were quickly returned to reality with the sound of John's voice,

'Ok Ollie old son, time to go up and get us another round, Michael is broke'. Oliver arose from the seat and made his way to the bar counter. As the bar lady approached with her usual yellow-stained toothy smile, he politely ordered three pints and waited for them to be poured. As he waited Oliver ran his good eye around the bar, scanning the few customers who had taken up temporary residence. At a lone table in the corner next to the jukebox, sat an old farmer sipping his bottle of stout and glass of whiskey. At the table straight across from him, a man and woman sat almost zombie like, occasionally bending their elbows in unison to sip from their wine glasses. Perched on a high stool at the bar to Oliver's right sat a middle age man, dressed in a grey pinstriped suit and sipping at a glass of beer while reading a copy of the local newspaper. As Oliver returned to his table with the pints, he put his head close to his friends and whispered,

'Do you see that ass hole sitting at the bar with the fancy suit, he's a fucking cop'. Michael and John slowly and inexplicitly began to raise their eyes towards the man at the bar.

'Doesn't look like a cop to me', whispered Michael at the same time reaching down to empty some of the contents of his glass down his throat.

'Nor me either', said John in a slightly higher voice than Michael. Oliver looked at his two friends and put his hand up to his brow in a feint resemblance of being disappointed, and whispered,

'Are you two fucking stupid, or did the few drops of beer that you have just consumed kill off the remaining four brain cells that you have between you?'

'Ok smart ass', whispered John, ' let's see professor Oliver explain to us how in damn fuck, he has come to the swift conclusion, that there is a cop sitting at the bar'. Oliver looked at John and winked with his good eye,

'You can smell them', he replied.

'And tell us dear Oliver', whispered John sarcastically, 'what in fuck's name does a cop smell like?'

'It's simple', whispered Oliver, taking another swig from his glass, 'they smell of shit'. At the closing of this statement John looked at Oliver somewhat amazed, then at Michael and suddenly all three burst out laughing. The three friends laughed so hard that Oliver had to hold his ribs, as the pain began to disagree with his sense of humour. When the three friends calmed down, Michael looked at Oliver and said,

'You are so full of shit you think you can smell it of everyone else'.

'You think so, well I'm not fucking joking', replied Oliver, 'I knew an old woman once who told me to beware of anything that smells of shit, and that bastard up there is fucking leaping'.

'Ok lads', replied John, 'let's say for arguments sake that all cops smell of shit, but we could also add that farmers stink to high heaven too'. Oliver looked at John as if he was dumbfounded by what he had just heard,

'So are you trying to tell me that the man sitting at

the counter with a fancy set of duds on is a farmer?'
asked Oliver.

'Well farmers do wear suits too', replied John.
Oliver gathered closer to his two friends, threw a
glance towards the man at the bar and spoke,

'listen lads, there are two types of shit, one kind is
the type that removes itself from the ass of various
animals, humans and birds to name but a few, but
cops smell of a different kind of shit. You could wash
them, scrub them with a wire brush and steep them in
bleach, but all in fucking vain, because it's not in their
bodies, but in their spiritual presence'. As soon as
Oliver had finished, he reached for his glass and took
pleasure from the cold beer passing through his mouth
and down into his stomach. He expected his two
friends to laugh, but to his surprise they stared at him
in silence. As he positioned his pint glass back on the
table he spoke,

'What to fuck is wrong? You are looking at me as if
I'm a lunatic who just escaped from the fucking nut
house'. John smiled at Oliver and reached over
putting his hand gently on his arm,

'Don't worry Oliver old son, we won't tell', he said
amusingly.

'Fuck off', replied Oliver as he pushed his hand
away.

'Listen Oliver', said John, 'Every single person in this
bar is fucked up in the head, including us; the people
they have locked up in the mental shops are the sane
ones'. John looked over at Michael and began
laughing, suddenly all three were joining in on the
amusement, until John suddenly stopped and spoke in
a serious tone of voice,

'I have a grandmother in Missouri who can see and

speak to the dead'. Oliver and Michael now threw John a strange look, while Michael expressed a sincere concern for both John and his grandmother's sanity,

'I always knew Yanks were fucking loopy, now I have the evidence here before me'.

'Ok lads', answered John, 'Let it go'. Oliver looked deep into John's eyes, seeking out some glimmer of falsehood, but he could find none. He knew John was no lunatic, and as far as he had seen from the time they had first met, John was one clever kid. Now he knew from within his own experiences of people, that John had something worth listening to.

'Don't listen to him John', said Oliver, 'he's almost pissed and he has only drunk two pints'. Michael turned to face Oliver, ready to inflict him with a barrage of obscenities, but Oliver placed his finger over Michael's lips and said,

'Let's hear what he has to say'. John took a drink from his glass before getting close to his two friends and began to tell them in a subtle voice.

'When I was a kid, I looked on my grandmother as one weird cookie. Every night before she went to bed, she would go outside and sit under an old oak tree facing the chicken shed. She would mumble things, sometimes even smile and laugh to herself, and other times calling people's names. I used to get shit at school from the other kids, it was all over the county that my mum was in the nut house, and the way my grandmother was behaving, they would say she was next. I got into a lot of fights and always got the blame for starting them, so the head teacher told me not to come back. For the first few weeks I didn't tell my grandmother, I used to sit beside the Stockton River, sometimes I would curse my family, but most times I would just cry. Then one day my grandmother appeared behind me as I sat at the river, and sat down beside me. She told me she knew I was expelled from school the first day it happened, that her mother who had died some thirty years earlier told her. When I asked her why she didn't confront me before, she replied that I needed time in peace to reach within myself and untangle all the threads of anger that had been spun by the spinning wheels of life'. Oliver and Michael were now engrossed in John's story, so absorbed that they hadn't realised that their glasses were empty.

'Hold everything', said John suddenly realising it was his turn to buy the beer, 'I'll be back in a jiffy'. Oliver sat in silence, not only was he patiently awaiting a new glass of cold beer, but the continuation of John's story. The revelation that John had madness in the family did not halt his inquisitive mind. He knew that John's mother had taken a mental breakdown, owing to her husband deserting her and the hardships of life that he left behind. And from what John had told him of life in rural Missouri, his grandmother was as tough as old work boots. It wasn't long before John returned and presented the three full glasses to the table before them.

'Ok Johnny old boy, lets here more', said Michael as he positioned himself comfortably on the chair.

'Right lads', said John, 'When we left the river that day, I went back home, but my grandmother told me she had business to attend to, so she left for town. I attended to my chores, feeding the chickens, making sure the brown mare grazing in the field had water, and sawing some wood for the fire. When my grandmother returned a few hours later, she smiled at me and said, you can go back to school on Monday, all is well. When Monday morning arrived, I gathered my school bag, along with the knots in my stomach, and made my way to school. When I entered through the school gate almost ready to throw up, all I could hear were the other pupils calling out, 'hi John, welcome back John'. I was gob smacked to say the least, but even more so when I was met with the schoolmaster grinning and calling me his friend'. Michael interrupted by asking,

'What to fuck happened, did your grandma threaten them with brutal death, or cast a fucking spell?'

'No', replied John displaying a smile, 'she reminded the schoolmaster how his first wife really died, and not by suicide as he led everyone to believe'.

'Holy shit', said Michael, 'I fucking love it, tell me more Johnny old son'.

'There's not much more to tell', replied John, 'from then on I respected my grandma and believed in her great gift. One thing she did tell me though, that I would inherit her gift'.

'And have you?' asked Michael.

'Yeah sure I have', replied John, 'I was talking to your grandfather the night before last'.

'Fuck off', said Michael, his voice echoing a tone of belief.

'No I'll not fuck off', replied John, 'He told me to give you a message'.

'You are taking the piss', said Michael, in a manner of excitement from his voice.

'I'm not taking the piss', replied John.

'Well what did he want you to tell me?' asked Michael.

'He wanted me to tell you', replied John trying to

keep the quiver from his voice, 'to stop wanking so much or you'll end up as blind as a fucking bat'. All at once Oliver and John began to burst into laughter, and were soon joined by Michael who quickly discovered the humorous side of the story. The three friends laughed so loud that they began to draw attention from the few patrons in the bar, who themselves began to laugh without ever discovering what they were laughing at. As the three friends finished their drinks, they made their way outside and into the cold air of the night.

'We'll have do this more often', said Michael as he buttoned up his wrangler jacket in anticipation of the cold walk home.

'Yeah', replied John, 'If only we had the money to do it with'. Oliver looked at his two friends, and saw two reflections of himself. They too were broke and fed up with the way life was dealing them the wrong cards. Thoughts began to creep into his mind, but Oliver quickly put them aside, as he knew his mother would cringe if she knew what he was thinking.

'I have to hit the road guys', said John, 'have an early morning appointment at the dole office'.

'Well', said Oliver, 'Give one of the pig farmers a punch for me'. John turned to Oliver and shouted back as he made his way home,

'I will do'.

As Michael said good night, Oliver commenced on the familiar journey home, and the comfort of his soft warm bed, he began to wonder what nightmare awaited him tonight.

CHAPTER 6

'Hi Oliver, can you hear me I'm talking to you?'. Oliver jumped up from his bed, but was quickly stopped from leaping onto the bedroom floor by the pain that had not gone away. He had slept well throughout the night, save for the passing army helicopter that had woke him up around three o'clock, as it flew low over his house. The voice that he heard in his sleep bore all the hallmarks of the story John had told them of his grandmother the night before. The voice speaking to him had an American accent and sounded old, and Oliver could only shiver as the voice still echoed in his head. He had heard many stories throughout his seventeen years of life, stories of ghosts, of fairies and things that could not be explained. The story John had told them the night before had shook him most of all because of two things, first the person was living and speaking to the dead on a regular basis, and the second being that John had convinced him it was true. He had no inclination to delve into the unexplained world of reaching to those beyond the grave, but time after time that world would allow itself access to his thoughts. However real the world looked from the simple window of his mind, Oliver would perhaps by chance, see a reality that others wouldn't. He had thought many times about his present situation, and asked the question often, what did his future hold for him? A couple of pints in the local pub, and a burger or two were all the excitement his meagre funds would allow him. Oliver wanted more, he wanted to experience the age of youth behind the wheel of a fancy car, and a beautiful girl to show off to. He craved for a healthy wardrobe bursting with the latest fashion, and afford as much beer as the bar could hold. He envied some of the kids in his town who had rich parents, parents who could supply their kids with all the trimmings of stimulation. He was sick with embarrassment, and every day for the past year, he was aching with the throbbing of deprivation. He had a conscience, and that conscience hung around his neck with the weight of a thousand buses. But every day that weight got lighter and lighter, every time humiliation arrived to slap him across his face, that heavy load he carried began to crumple and fall by the wayside. He had made up his mind to pay a visit to the local parish priest Father Ned, and seek out the answers to the questions he had been asking himself every morning he opened his eyes to a life of nothing. Father Ned was renowned for his level thinking and theological skills; he also had the reputation for using his fists whenever the opportunity arose. As Oliver climbed out of bed and proceeded to get dressed, he knew all the punches that Father Ned could throw at him couldn't make him feel any worse.

As Oliver made his way out through the back door and onto the street, he bumped into the postman and asked

'Any mail for me today?'

'Nothing today', replied the postman as he continued on his way.

Oliver thought by some stroke of luck, the dole office would have overlooked the incident of the pig farm and sent him his payment as normal. But once again luck had played little part in his expectations, and with a sigh of disappointment he continued on his journey to the parochial house.

The parochial house looked grey from a distance, and as Oliver got closer the grey began to stand out like a giant grave stone. One tall hung over the entrance as he made his way through the black wrought iron gates, while another stood like a giant green sentry beside the dark chocolate coloured door. Oliver was not confident of a hospitable greeting as he reached to knock the door and send warning of his presence. It had been years since Oliver paid host to St John's Church, and stood among the self confessed saints of the town. He could not blame his mother for not trying, as Oliver remembered the yells and threats of eternal damnation she would fling on him every Sunday morning, until she came to the long drawn out conclusion that Oliver was going straight to hell. As the door slowly opened, a pale faced little old lady, dressed in a blue and white flower pattern dress, greeted Oliver,

'Good Morning, can I help you?'

'I have come to see Father Ned', replied Oliver.

'Is he expecting you?' replied the little old lady at the same time opening the door wider.

'No', answered Oliver, 'but it is important that I see him.

'Please come in and wait in the hall, I will see if

Father Ned is free', said the little old lady.

Oliver walked through the front door and accepted the chair that the little old lady beckoned him to sit down on. Above his head and facing him on the wall was a picture of a Gaelic football team, and at the bottom it read, *Derry under 21's 1967*. Left of the photo was a large Sacred Heart picture, and on the wall over the door to his right, hung a crucifix. Oliver felt uncomfortable and inferior, as his school days leading up to Holy Communion began to return to his memory. The priest always dominated the classroom as soon as he walked through the door, a God like figure who he was always taught to first fear, and respect second. He remembered a story his mother told him about a priest called Father Tom, and how he could employ magic to counter any violence instigated towards him. One day Father Tom was travelling on his bicycle to a place called Drennen, to attend a parish member who was on his death bed. As part of his journey he had to pass through a Protestant village, and like many priests before him, the occasional ration of abuse and sometimes physical violence was administered by those gathered at the corner. On this particular occasion a few men were standing at the corner chatting, and when they saw the priest, identified by his collar, they took their penises out and began to simulate masturbating while laughing. As the story was told, Father Tom pointed his finger at the men and said 'Stay like that until I come back'. It took most of the day for the priest to attend the dying man and other clerical duties, and as he returned late in the evening, the men were still standing there and nevertheless performing the by now, all knowing and self humiliating act of masturbating. Whether it was true or not, for a long time Oliver didn't take any challenging rude chances with priests.

'Father Ned will see you now', said the little old lady. Oliver arose from the chair and followed the little old lady down the hall and into the room on the left. As she departed the room, closing the door gently behind her, Father Ned rose from his armchair beside the window and shook Oliver's hand,

'Good morning young fella, please sit down', he said. Oliver thanked father Ned and sat down on the chair opposite the priest beside the window.

'What is so important, that would take a young man like yourself to visit me without first making an appointment?' asked Father Ned, at the same time offering Oliver a view of his pearl white teeth. Oliver looked up at the priest and began to stare straight into his face, In addition to the two rows of perfect white teeth that he had just witnessed; Father Ned had a healthy tan and a fine crop of black hair. Oliver looked into his eyes hoping to discover a blink of insincerity, perhaps to uncover some dark secret or recognise a weakness in his faith. Oliver had always prided himself on character detection, and weeding out quickly those who had guilt written all over their conscience. But Oliver could see neither good nor bad in Father Ned, and realised that whatever questions he choose to ask, would be at his own peril.

'I've been doing a lot of thinking these last few months father', said Oliver, 'and a question keeps coming up time after time, and I cannot find the right answer'.

Father Ned leaned back in his chair and turned to look out the window,

'Thinking is a healthy thing young man, it helps

stimulate the brain cells and helps us to challenge the decisions we take on our journey through this existence'.

'Unfortunately', replied Oliver, 'the brain cells that are being stimulated are all for the wrong reasons'. Father Ned turned from staring out the window and began to look Oliver in the eyes. Oliver returned his stare, holding his gaze firmly, not daring to allow any frailty in his senses that would allow the priest to dominate the proceedings.

'Then let me tell you son', said father Ned, returning his gaze towards the window, 'Murder is a mortal sin, if you are trying to find some lame excuse or crack in the system of the laws of both God and man, then let me remind you, there is none'.

'My qualm is not about the taking of life father', replied Oliver, 'but about living it'.

Father Ned calmly rose from his chair and walked across the room towards a large portrait of a priest hanging solitary on the wall facing the window. He stared at the picture for some time, as if he was silently asking the painting for some guidance or answer to the question that Oliver was about to ask. Oliver turned to look at the priest and with some hesitation began to speak,

'Is it a sin to steal father?'

Father Ned suddenly turned to Oliver and sharply said

'Yes, it is a sin to steal, did your parents teach you anything?'

Oliver was taken aback by the priest's sudden onslaught; he knew he must keep calm at all costs if he was ever to acquire the knowledge that he so much needed.

'I mean father, is there ever a time when it is right to

steal?' asked Oliver.

Father Ned walked over to Oliver and spoke,

'If you know the bastards who broke into St John's primary school, tell me now'.

'I know nothing of any break in father, and I have never stolen anything in my life', replied Oliver, the blood now rushing to his face, 'I only came here for a simple philosophical answer to something that has been eating me alive for months'.

Father Ned walked back to the chair beside the window and commenced his searching for what it was he was looking for on the other side of the glass.

'Forgive me son', said father Ned, I had no intention of accusing you of anything, been under a lot of pressure lately'.

'It's ok father', replied Oliver, thankful of the priest's apology.

'Ok son', said Father Ned, 'the question asked by you this day, is an arrow that has been aimed at me by many people over the years. When is it right to steal? To take from others what is not yours is a sin that few can deny. If I am starving, is it right to steal food? All stealing is a sin, however dire my situation, but a question to be asked, if I am starving are the pains of hunger stronger than my ability to reason, and to such an extent that it is no longer me who steals the food, but the intensity of my starvation. Father Ned and Starvation, could be argued are two separate entities, therefore if that argument is found to be sound, then it is not me who has committed a sin, but Mr Starvation. Oliver began to assimilate what Father Ned had just told him, he began to ask himself if the hunger for change, the scarcity of the means to make those changes, could be placed in the same category as Mr

Starvation. Oliver commenced to seek more answers from Father Ned,

'Now that we have settled the argument in relation to the stealing of food', asked Oliver, 'but how does the same argument fare in relation to other necessities such as a roof over our head, the clothes on our back, or the means to travel without needing to walk or catch a bus'.

'What you are saying', replied Father Ned, 'is it ok to steal things that we do not need to live, or put it another way, not an essential ingredient of survival?'

'Yes and no', replied Oliver, 'We need the clothes on our back, or we would freeze to death in winter, and likewise the roof over our heads. We may not need the means to purchase alternative transport, such as a car, but if I had no money for a bus fare, or there was no bus route to where I needed to go, I would have to walk, perhaps in the snow or rain for a hundred miles, thus causing pain and severe discomfort to my being'. Father Ned looked at Oliver and smiled,

'young man', he said, how old are you?'

'Seventeen', replied Oliver.

'Well, for a seventeen year old you sure know how to draw water from a stone', replied Father Ned. Oliver smiled back at Father Ned, something inside him began to reflect a liking for the priest, and he loved his answers because they allowed him an opening in which to dwell deeper on the subject,

'Just a kid with a lot of questions', replied Oliver.

'Well that is a pretty good argument', said Father Ned, 'the same principle could be applied, if the cold and wet, or perhaps the shame of being naked had overcome my mental state, then once again it is not me who committed the sin. However the argument in relation to the car is another matter. Is it right to say that walking, even in snow or rain can cause us to take leave of our senses? I believe that laziness could pack a strong punch towards that argument'.

'But what if, say we tried hard to get a job in order we can exercise our basic human rights, a right to fairness, a right of equality, a right to escape a depressed existence', replied Oliver.

'Inter arma enim silent leges, in times of war the law falls silent', said Father Ned, 'It would be fair to lay claim to the validity of that statement son, there are few in Ulster who would argue that a state of war does not exist. In times of war, accepted forms of behaviour are adopted, which in normal peaceful circumstances would be unlawful. When I say accepted, I do not mean the killing of unarmed civilians, I am merely stating that the stealing of food and water, trespassing, or if you must, pinch a vehicle in order for you or your family to escape death or persecution'. Oliver began to unravel all the information that Father Ned had told him, and to his excitement all the questions he had been struggling to find answers to, were now laid bare before his very mind. He had been fighting a war all his life, against those who had ten times more than they needed. The town and country he lived in was as much his as those who drove about in fancy cars, smoking cigars and coming home to large houses. He had tried hard to reach for his slice of the financial cake, and each time it had been snapped away from him by greed and sectarianism. Oliver now knew his way forward, no longer would the smog of confused values cause him to lose his way, nor conflicting morals bar his path to equality. Oliver arose from his chair and turned to

Father Ned,

'Thank you Father for answering my questions, but its time I made my way home in time for lunch, you know how mother's are', said Oliver.

Father Ned arose and shook Oliver's hand and replied,

'Yes indeed son, I have a house keeper here and if you're one minute late, you get the Gestapo interrogation as to why'.

Father Ned followed Oliver to the front door and opened it allowing Oliver to taste the cool air,

'God bless and I hope you reach the end of your rainbow', he said.

'Thank you again Father', replied Oliver, 'I believe I'm almost there'.

As Oliver made his way along the grey footpath and past the local bank, he smiled both evidently and within his heart. He began to view all those passing by, whether on foot, bicycle or car as potential adversaries in his declaration of war. A police car passed by as he continued down Broad Street, and as he turned slowly to look, he noticed the cops were staring in his direction with leers of suspicion. Oliver turned right into Murphy's street and spied Michael sitting lazily on top of a summer seat that leaned against the wall outside Jane's Hair Dressers. As he approached Michael, he shouted jokingly,

'You waiting to get your rollers in?'.

'Fuck off', replied Michael, while feinting a punch at Oliver as he took a seat beside him, 'my mum's in getting her hair done, been in there a fucking hour now smoking and yakking'.

'Why don't you fuck off home?' said Oliver.

'Can't', replied Michael letting out a sigh, 'she promised me a fiver if I wait, she's scared shitless of

Robert the drunk'.

'For fuck's sake, Robert is harmless', replied Oliver.

'Tell her that', said Michael, 'one evening he grabbed her ass and she's terrified ever since'.

'He grabs everyone's ass', replied Oliver laughing, 'he even grabbed mine'.

Both Michael and Oliver laughed together until Michael spoke again,

'Done anything exciting today?' asked Michael.

'Nothing much', replied Oliver, 'Just been to the parochial house to see Father Ned'.

'What fucking took you there?' asked Michael as he turned to Oliver in disbelief.

'Don't worry old son', replied Oliver smiling, 'I haven't turned religious, just wanted a few answers from a theologian who knows what he is talking about'.

'For fuck's sake kid', said Michael, 'If you needed to talk to a theologian, Robert the drunk would have given you all the answers you needed'.

'But this one was free', replied Oliver, 'Robert would have wanted a feel of my ass'. Michael laughed out loud only to stop momentarily to speak,

'How do you know Father Ned wasn't looking at your ass?' laughed Michael.

'Because I have heard from a reliable source that he has a couple of female friends he visits more often than others', replied Oliver.

As the two friends' laughter faded, Oliver turned to Michael and spoke,

'Did you see John?'

'Will see him later on, why anything planned?' replied Michael.

'I want to discuss something with both of you,

something I believe affects all of us' said Oliver.

'You mean being unable to rustle up a shag between us', replied Michael jokingly.

'Speak for yourselves, but seriously, I want to meet later on', said Oliver.

'What about Danny's Lounge? I could murder a pint', replied Michael.

'No, too many ears', said Oliver, 'there is a picnic table under the trees just across the road from the Grammar School, how about meeting there around five'.

'For fuck's sake', replied Michael, 'you must be planning a fucking mass murder, if you want us to sit out there in the fucking cold freezing our balls off'.
Oliver arose from the seat and smiled at Michael,

'Be there at five, and you will find out', he said.

'Ok captain', replied Michael mockingly.
Oliver departed from Michael and hurriedly made his way towards home. He realised he was five minutes late, and his mother would perform her usual nagging ritual. But Oliver knew that this wasn't the reason why he was quickening his pace, the excitement flowing through his veins like a child the day before Christmas, had allowed other priorities to take precedence over the expectation of his mother's wrath. Oliver's world had become clear, his destiny was now within reach and he knew that today, was his first day of freedom and the beginning of a life worth living.

CHAPTER 7

'A fucking bird just shit on my head', complained John as he greeted Oliver, 'Michael told me you needed to talk, but over a nice pint would have been more civilized', as he tried to wipe the bird droppings from his wrangler jacket with spit and a black wool hat.

'Birds shit is good luck', joked Oliver as he sat down on the summer seat beside his two friends.

'Any type of shit supposed to be good luck', said Michael.

'How to hells fuck can shit be good luck', complained John, 'I only bought this jacket two weeks ago and what the fucking birds eat around here, it will probably burn a hole in it'.

'Never worry', replied Oliver, 'If what Michael said about shit being lucky, and what I have planned goes right, you can have yourself a thousand wrangler jackets'.

John looked at Oliver and raised his eyebrows,

'You're not surely planning to rob Dawson's clothes shop, knowing our luck we won't find a thing to fit us', he said.

'Fuck Dawson's clothes shop', replied Oliver, 'we

need to go for the hard stuff'.

'Yeah right', replied John grinning widely, 'like the shoe shop next door, now that is the real hard stuff'.

'I was thinking more in line with the shop five doors down', said Oliver.

Both John and Michael suddenly became silent, each turning to the other in disbelief at what they had just heard. Oliver decided to break the silence by helping them to make their mind up as to what shop he was talking about,

'Yes kids', he said, 'the fifth shop down is the bank'.

'You really are taking the fucking piss, you brought us down here to come out with that crock of shit', replied Michael angrily.

'No shit intended', said Oliver, 'I'm serious, I have decided to give up the fruitless task of looking for a job and catch myself on'.

'And how to fuck do you intend to rob this bank', replied John, 'walk in with your dick hanging out and wait until everyone dies laughing'.

'No worry Johnny old son, I won't ask you to go in first', joked Oliver, 'I will be the first in the door and I will be armed'.

Michael stood up from the seat, walked a few small paces forward and turned towards Oliver,

'You have truly lost it kid, what in the name of fuck brought that idea into your tiny brain', he said.

'I've been thinking about it for a long time', replied Oliver, 'every night before I went to sleep I thought about it, the interview with the pig farmer was the last straw'.

'Did you also think about the risks', said John, 'or was there no room left in your head, you know if you're caught it's ten years behind bars, and worse, you could get blown away by the cops'.

'Yeah, yeah, yeah, I have let that cross my mind a few times', replied Oliver, 'but what also crossed my mind was the state of affairs I am in now. All I am doing is existing, living a life that is meaningless and empty, moving from one day to another with blue moulded hope and the fading glimmer that things might change. But they never do, there are no jobs for me in this screwed up society where whatever church door you walk through, determines what your future is going to look like. I am fucking pissed off with pen pushing assholes dictating my life according to whatever mood they are in. We are living in a war zone, and the enemy is everywhere, if I walk into a bank and rob the living shit out of it, metaphorically I am on a bombing raid, retaliating against an adversary that has blasted the crap out of my soul since the day I arrived on this stinking earth. I have been left with no alternative but to fight my enemy with fire and if need be, burn them to the fucking ground'.

John and Michael again remained silent, a lorry passed by causing a vibration to release the few trapped raindrops from the tree above their heads. A horn sounded from somewhere up at the diamond, and in the distance a dog barked, possibly signalling the shadow of a passing stranger. The three friends remained silent, each within their own thoughts, each wrestling with the spectres of their own fears. Oliver turned to view the long row of terraced buildings that made up Broad Street, and recalled the countless days that he had walked up each side, glaring through the shop windows with nothing in his pockets but exhaust polluted air. He remembered the May Fair each year that echoed with the feet of people laughing and spending money, and the alcohol soaked breath of farmers staggering from the pubs. All his life he wanted to have the freedom to put his hand in his pocket, and buy whatever he fancied, to walk through the wide open door of the Corner Bar and drink lemonade from a tall slender glass until it flowed freely from his ears. To eat sweets and ice cream until he was sick, and fire slugs at the rifle range until he had won every prize. To some he might have been regarded as greedy, but in truth, all Oliver ever wanted was to be free. '

'Ok lads', said John interrupting each of their thoughts, 'I need a fucking pint'.

John returned from the bar counter with three frothing pints of beer, and sat them neatly on the table. He lifted one quickly to his mouth and to Oliver and Michael's amazement, swallowed half with one gulp.

'For Fuck's sake kid take it easy', said Oliver, lifting his own glass up and taking a few small sips, 'you're not on a beer drinking contest'.

John turned to Oliver and replied,

'If what you say is the truth, then I need to start practicing for all the pints I will be able to afford'.

'Thinking about this is scaring the living shit out of me', said Michael, trying not to spill his beer as a result of his shaking hand.

'Calm down kid', replied Oliver, 'a couple of pints and you'll soon lose the nerves'.

'Just slam it down your throat in one heavy gulp', said John, 'that will sure as hell kill anything trying to push the shit out'. Oliver laughed while Michael forced a smile and John sent the remaining half of his glass in hot pursuit of the first half.

'You're talking of fear and being scared', said Oliver

as he stared at Michael, 'but what scares me more than anything, is the fear of allowing things to remain as they are'.

'I could live with the Status Quo ok', replied Michael.

'Well then', said Oliver, 'let things be as they are, I'm not forcing you to do anything against your will'.

'I think Oliver has got the right idea', said John, staring into his empty glass, 'why live life with nothing when you can have plenty, all it takes is the speedy growth of a pair of iron balls and a brain with enough wit to plan a healthy escape'.

'We have known each other for awhile now', said Oliver, 'I would trust no one else, or to rephrase it, I have no one else to trust. We all have borne the bruises of life's punches, we were born for the hang man's noose and there are few arguments which have stated otherwise. Each of us have fought against the system, pushed our way through the storm only to walk into another one. I for one am sick and tired of my life's lot, and with or without your help. I'm going to change it'. Michael was next to finish his pint after John, so he made his way to the bar to retrieve three more of the same. While Michael was away John spoke to Oliver in a low voice,

'I want to make enough money to go back to the States', he said.

'If we plan and execute things right, you will have enough money to return to the moon', replied Oliver before he emptied the remainder of his glass.

'I want to go back to the farm, take my grandma out of the old folk's home and enjoy her company for the few years she has left', said John.

'Have you heard from her recently?' asked Oliver.

'Got a letter last Tuesday, she said she wasn't feeling well and hoped I could come and visit her', replied John.

Oliver noticed John's voice change when he mentioned his grandma's sickness, and hoped within himself that John would indeed get enough money to return. He thought a lot about America these last few weeks himself, and the thought of going there to live had slowly begun to grow in his mind. In America it wouldn't matter if he was a Catholic, no one would slight him for trying to better himself and he truly believed that anyone with a few thousand dollars to invest, could make a dream come true.

'Is there room at the old farm for another one?' asked Oliver.

John looked at Oliver somewhat in disbelief and said,

'You're joking me kid'.

'No', replied Oliver holding John's stare, 'I've been thinking about it for a long time, I really want to go back with you, get out of this God forsaken hole and start a new life'.

'Shit man, you are fucking serious', replied John in excitement, 'of course there is room, my grandma would be happy to meet you, and holy fuck, we could drain the Stockton river dry together and shovel the fish into our brand new truck, shit, forget about draining it, we'll dynamite the son of a bitch'.

Oliver smiled as he heard the excitement in John's voice, a joy that was quickly beginning to mirror the growing exhilaration from his own heart. As Michael returned with the three pints, John hurriedly told him the news.

'You won't be fucking lieve it kid, Ollie and my good self are planning to return to the good old U S of A', said John.

'Return', replied Michael, 'I didn't know Oliver had been to the states before'.

'What I mean', replied John, 'is, I am returning, and Ollie is coming along for the ride'.

As Michael lifted his pint to his lips to take sip, Oliver noticed the shake had gone. He also detected an air of jealously from Michael's tone of voice and quickly moved to calm any of Michael's fears of being ostracised.

'Do you know what I think', said Oliver, 'I believe that nothing could ever work out unless the three of us were together, so Michael will have to come with us, even if we have to kidnap him and hide him aboard a ship'.

John also detected Michael's change of tone and replied,

'Too fucking true'. John lifted his glass and said, 'here's to us, may our friendship be like my last girlfriend's legs, they never parted'.

Oliver joined John in the toast and then Michael rose his glass faking a reluctance, but happy to be included in operation USA.

'What you mean? You never had a girlfriend in your life, never mind a last one', said Michael humorously.

'Don't kid yourself kiddo', replied John, 'I have more women's fingerprints on my ass than the whole FBI have on record'.

'I didn't know you were into that kind of thing', said Michael fighting back his laughter.

'Well what do you expect', replied John triumphantly, 'I'm a hot blooded male fully loaded with hormones and wagging for a shagging'.

'You mean wanking for a spanking', said Michael,

still bursting to hold back his laughter, 'that's why there's so many finger prints on your ass'.

The three friends burst into laughter, causing Oliver to send a spray of wasted beer across the table and onto John's snow white tee shirt. John still laughed as he wiped the remnants of beer from his tee shirt and through his enjoyment, Oliver's heart glowed with warmth towards his two friends. The days that he walked and talked, laughed and quarrelled with John and Michael would stay within his memory for the rest of his life. He loved his new found friends, and had no doubt if the day ever arose in which that friendship would encounter the ultimate test, he knew taking a bullet would be a lesser pain than betrayal. Oliver recalled the people who had come and went in his life, the boys and girls throughout his school days, people he had met in the potato fields, while attending the local disco and the people who could have been his friend, but decided to turn their heads for one reason or another. Friendship beyond his family was as hard to find as a job and virtually nonexistent if you hadn't got a job. Oliver believed that destiny had put them together for a reason yet to be unfolded, and some day in this world or the next, that providence would be as clear as spring water. Oliver's thoughts were interrupted by John lowering his voice to speak,

'Ok kid, what are our plans?' Oliver took a sip of his beer and said,

'First of all we need a few codes in case we are overheard'.

'What do you have in mind?' asked Michael.

'First, I believe when we are referring to doing the business with the banks, we should say, we are going to gather potatoes. The first potato field should be named Taylor, and I believe we should go gather potatoes at Taylor's very soon'.

'Good show', replied Michael grinning, 'What to fuck is it with you Irish and potatoes?'

'Well', replied Oliver, 'I thought it might be better than going to gather Yorkshire Puddings'.

'You don't gather Yorkshire Puddings you dumb ass', said Michael, 'you have to bake the fucking things'.

'Potatoes are fine with me', replied John as he finished a sip of his beer, 'carry on Ollie kiddo, the thought of gathering potatoes at Taylor's is giving me a stiff'.

'If the fucking cops catch us you'll be getting a stiff all right, a stiff in a wooden box', said Michael.

'No one will be ending up in a box', replied Oliver, 'keep our heads and leave the planning to me'.

'Ok', said John, 'but we also need a code word or words for the cops, hit us with that one kid'.

'The cops are farmers', replied Oliver, 'so whenever we are intending to go gather potatoes, we need to watch out for the farmers'. John first looked at Michael waiting for him to say something, when he realised Michael had nothing to say he turned to Oliver and spoke,

'I thought the farmers wanted us to gather the fucking potatoes, if that is so, then why do we have to fear them?'

'Well it's like this', replied Oliver allowing a cheeky grin to appear across his face, 'the farmers don't know we're going to gather their spuds, in normal circumstances the farmers pay us for gathering the potatoes, and whatever we gather they take home and store in a shed. But in our case we are gathering the spuds unbeknown to the farmer and taking them home to our shed instead'.

'So what you're saying in real terms is, we are going to steal the fucking spuds', said John.

'Very good Johnny old boy', replied Oliver sarcastically, 'you have hit the rusty nail once again firmly on the head and you deserve a pint'.

Oliver arose from his chair and made his way to the bar, the barman greeted him with one nod of the head and Oliver ordered and paid for three more pints of beer. Without waiting the few minutes they would take to pour, he made his way towards the stench of the men's toilets. As he entered the room of stale urine and a hint of historical vomit, he made his way to the enclosure of the toilet bowl and locked the door firmly behind him. Outside and leaning against the urine wall were two men, and the objects of Oliver's secret embarrassment. All his life had had a problem urinating in front of others, a phobia that stayed with him and would not go away. Instead he would always retreat behind a locked door in the pretence that he needed a dump. He quickly finished removing the remains of John and Michael's pints and made his way back to the bar to collect his order. As he returned to the table to Oliver's horror, John decided to open his mouth a little wider than was expected,

'You hiding your dick again behind the shitter door?'

'What you mean?' replied Oliver beginning to glow bright red across his face.

'I mean Ollie old kid, that all the time I've known you and whenever we go to the toilet together, you need a shit', said John, 'that could mean one or all of several things. Either you scare the shit out of yourself on a regular basis, your dick is so small you need enough time away from the view of others to find it, or you are really a woman dressed up as a man. So what's it to be kiddo?'

Oliver tried to turn the situation in his favour, or at the least get them to laugh it off,

'Ok you have got me, I admit it, I'm a woman', replied Oliver.

'Shut to fuck up John and let's get down to the serious stuff', muttered Michael in a low voice.

'Yeah', replied John mockingly putting a finger to his lips, 'we need to plan our getaway after we grab those spuds'.

'I hate to break up your moment of amusement', said Oliver in a more serious tone of voice, 'but it's going to happen tomorrow'.

John and Michael suddenly went quiet, the beer that had claimed responsibility for the giddiness and air of humour, had now retreated leaving behind the remnants of sobriety.

'I know you may have had other plans kids' said Oliver, you may have believed the idea, after a few days might drift off into the sunset. But in all truthfulness, I have faith in the saying, why leave until tomorrow what can be done today. Today is Wednesday that leaves only tomorrow to hit it and the rest of the weekend to spend some of it. My Mum and Dad will be out all day tomorrow, so just call at the house as early as you can. If any of you don't want to go through with this, I won't hold it against you. You don't have to tell me or make your minds up now; just don't turn up at the house tomorrow'.

Oliver drained the last of his pint and stood up to leave,

'I'm off now kids, need to keep a clear head from

here on'.

Michael and John still sitting quietly at the table wished him goodnight, not wishing to say whether they would see him the next day or not.

Oliver entered through the back door like he had done so many nights before. And like so many nights before, the house was silent save for the sound of snoring coming from his Mother and Father's room. The usual note of DINNER IN THE OVEN was perched on top of the kitchen table, but Oliver ignored it and quietly made his way up the stairs and into his bedroom. Before turning on the small bedside light, Oliver pulled the curtains and removed his heavy Doctor Martin boots from his sweat soaked feet. Normally he would have laughed into himself when he thought of his mother's reaction when she walked into his room in the morning and sniffed them. But tonight he allowed no space for humour, no place would be kept within his head for anything other than what lay in the very near future. Oliver knew he was now standing before the edge, and the bank in Magherafelt was his only lifeline from the dark cold waters below. He could have easily backed off and turned to face his tormentors with humble acceptance. He could crawl among the remains of his existence, searching for the scraps of institutionalized fairness and perhaps one day he may find it. But Oliver knew that equality was a long way off, too long for him to wait. He hoped that Father Ned was right, and exceptions could be made to the rules of war. He hoped that when Friday night arrived, he would be climbing into his own bed knowing that all the potatoes were neatly packed in his own shed. And he wished that tomorrow morning; John and Michael would knock on his door, because in all honesty he did not want to face the dragon on his own. As he removed his jeans, socks and Wrangler Jacket, he slipped under the cool sheets of his bed. He would leave his clothes lying bunched up on the floor as he had always done, and with no doubt in his mind he would toss and turn through the night like a ship on a storm drenched sea. And as he reached to turn the light off beside his bed, he knew there was one thing he would do different before he went to sleep, he would pray.

CHAPTER 8

'Everyone on the fucking floor now', roared Oliver as he stood inside the age old building. He watched old ladies and men, students and staff look at him as if he had just arrived from a spacecraft. He wasn't frightened; he had pictured this moment in his mind a thousand times and diluted his anxieties and ghosts by his detailed planning. 'Get on the fucking floor I said', roared Oliver once again.

As Oliver turned around to see what position Michael and John had taken up, he was surprised to see no sight of them and quickly realised he was alone. He knew he had to be strong and show no fear; he had to express his violent intentions towards those who did not respond to his threats. Oliver walked towards an old man standing beside the desk and put his gun to his head,

'If you are not on the floor in three seconds, I'm going to blow his fucking head off'.

Still nothing happened; everyone just stared at him as if they didn't care, as if Oliver had no intentions of carrying out his threat. As Oliver squeezed the trigger he let out a roar

'I fucking warned you, this is what happens when no

one listens'.

Oliver waited for the bang to echo from every wall in the building, he waited for the man to fall bleeding and lifeless before the feet of the terrified customers, but nothing happened. He was even more surprised to see a man dressed in a white coat emerge from a door which led into a room and calling out

'Who's next?'

The old men and women, the staff and students pointed at Oliver and with one simultaneous voice replied,

'He is'.

Oliver looked into the face of the man who he had just pointed the gun at, he smiled and said,

'It's ok son, you can go first'.

He now looked at the gun in his hand and to Oliver's horror, there was nothing there but a bright yellow banana. The man walked towards Oliver and helped him into the small room within the building. As he beckoned him to sit down he spoke,

'Now young man, tell us your name'.

Oliver suddenly felt naked and he soon discovered all he had on was a pair of his mother's pink and white flowered knickers. His heart began to beat widely, the blood rushed to his face and small droplets of sweat began to form across his brow. He could not understand how things had got this way, he had planned it so well with every detail analysed and reanalysed until it was fool proof. He decided to reluctantly answer the doctor's question with a question of his own,

'Can you tell me your name first?'

'Certainly', replied the man, 'my name is Doctor Nutt, but my patients call me nut'.

'But I thought this was a bank', replied Oliver in astonishment.

'Hummm', answered Doctor Nutt, 'you're not the first person who thought that and you certainly will not be the last, as a matter of fact we have two patients here in the other room with the same idea, they are just waiting to be transferred'.

'Transferred to where? asked Oliver.

'To my home', replied Doctor Nutt.

Doctor Nutt stood up and beckoned Oliver to follow him into the next room, he opened the door and ushered Oliver inside. To Oliver's amazement John and Michael sat at a table eating cream buns and drinking tall glasses of milk. John was dressed in a navy blue stripped dress and Michael was wearing nothing but a purple bra.

'These two had the same idea', said Doctor Nutt, 'they said something about a bank too so I guess you can be my patient also and accompany them to the nut house'.

John and Michael stopped eating and looked at Oliver, John said,

'Don't worry kid; anyone can get it wrong the first time, first time, first time, first time'.

Oliver jumped from his bed and found himself landing on the bedroom floor with a loud thud. He could hear John's words still echoing in his head as he slowly gripped reality and realised that he had escaped from yet another nightmare. He turned his eyes towards the alarm clock on his bedside cabinet, the time read eight forty four. He picked himself off the floor and sat down on the side of the bed, rubbing his head with both hands to try and relieve the pounding headache that had now arrived like a downpour of rain. He knew what day it was, and he also knew that the night's sleep had softened the plan and attempted to add doubt to the logic of the whole idea. In the past Oliver had put together acts of bravado which he swore to carry out, but after a good night's sleep, the ideas soon became discarded among the refuse of madness. But today, insanity would stay with him like two peas on a dinner plate, awaiting to be devoured together and digested in the pits of hell. Oliver got dressed quickly and made his way down stairs, he was surprised to see another mother note left on the table which he simply translated as she won't be back till late. If it had have been any other time, Oliver would have questioned or indeed wondered about his mother's frequent absence from home, which was contrary to her character. His mother never left home much, save to do the shopping or go to mass on a Sunday morning. She would be busy every day cleaning and cooking, or reading a book. On Saturday nights she would sit up to watch the late film, and Oliver more times than not had returned home to find her snoring noisily on the armchair with only a small white dot visible on the television screen. For the most part whenever she went out, his father was left behind sitting at the fire and content to be so. But now they were together often, something Oliver had not seen since he was a young child. As he shrugged it off, he proceeded to make himself a strong cup of black coffee. Coffee was all he would put in his stomach today, for he needed his wits to be running on all fours. As he waited on the kettle boiling, he sat down at the table and began thinking about John and Michael. Perhaps he had asked too much of them, and began to question his own motives for asking them along. Yes he knew they were not happy the way their lives were going, and like him they had no hope of ever changing them for the better. John wanted to return to the States, and there was little doubt that both Michael and he would join him. The noise of the kettle boiling returned Oliver back to his task of coffee making, but was soon followed by a familiar knock on his back door.

As John and Michael sipped the strong black coffee that Oliver managed from the jar of instant, an eerie air now floated over Oliver's kitchen. The three friends sat in silence like condemned men awaiting the drop at the end of a rope, or a barrage of bullets from a firing squad. All that could be heard was the precise tick of the grandfather clock coming from the hall and the occasional sniff from Michael's recently acquired runny nose. Oliver decided to shake the silence by asking,

'How did you both sleep last night?'

'Like shit', replied Michael.

'Like a baby', answered John sarcastically, 'that is, one who was up all night from teething'.

'I slept ok myself', said Oliver, 'save for a thumper of a nightmare'. Sweeping the question of sleep to the side', continued Oliver, 'I want to give both of you the opportunity to back out now if you want, I promise you I will not think any less of you'.

'Well', replied John, 'I done a lot of thinking about it myself, and I know there is no way I'm ever going to get back to Missouri to see grandma, not on a fortnightly dole check'. Michael turned and smiled at John before speaking,

'To be honest kids, the thought of it has given me the runs', he said, 'I'm fucking terrified and like both

of you I'm flat broke and in my present situation, I'm going nowhere as fast as a bullet'.
John took a sip from his coffee and looked at Michael saying,

'Did you have to mention bullets, now you're going to give me the fucking runs'.

'We are all scared', said Oliver, rising to leave his empty coffee cup in the sink, 'but there is one thing no one can deny if we carry out this thing today, we're no fucking cowards'.
Walking back to the table Oliver said,

'Right kidos, follow me upstairs and I'll show you the armour'.

John and Michael followed Oliver upstairs and into his bedroom, the last one gently closing the door behind him. As John and Michael sat down on the bed, Oliver made his way to the corner of the room and lifted the carpet. With his penknife he wedged a piece of floor board up and from the hole and removed a black plastic bag. Walking over to John and Michael on the bed, he sat down beside them and removed the contents wrapped in an old grey tea shirt.

'Holy shit man', said John in an air of amazement, 'For fuck's sake what are you going to do with that, that's not a gun, it's a fucking cannon'.
Oliver held the Webley .455 up so that John and Michael could see how well he had kept it over the years. It had belonged to his grandfather who was a soldier in the First World War, and had been in the house long before he was born. At the beginning of the troubles when the police and army began to search Catholic homes for weapons, his mum had taken him for a walk one fine spring morning, and threw it into the nearest river. Unbeknown to his mum, and still

only seven years old, Oliver returned on his way home from school, and recovered it almost drowning in the process. In addition, Oliver had removed some of the bullets from its hiding place some months before, so now he had all the protection he needed if the police or army attacked his house again. As he grew older and acquired more knowledge of the politics of Northern Ireland, he knew it was not the army or police he might need to use it against, it was loyalist murder squads who were killing Catholics in their homes. And as Oliver frequently removed it from its hiding place to oil and polish, he had faith in his ability to use it, and the courage to keep that faith company. Michael interrupted Oliver's reflections by saying,

'I'm off to the toilet again, that thing has just give me a bowel movement'.

As Michael quickly made his way to the toilet, John asked Oliver,

'Can I hold it?'

Oliver handed the gun to John, who held it out in front of him like a child with a new toy,

'Fuck it man it sure is one baby', he said in excitement.

After he played with the gun for a few minutes John handed it back to Oliver and asked,

'What's the plan kido?'

'We'll wait until Michael gets back from the bog', he replied, putting the gun on top of the bed. As soon as Michael returned pale faced and sweating, Oliver began to fill his friend in on the plot.

'I have three black masks, they are balaclavas that can be worn as hats, and as soon as we go through the door, we can pull them over our heads. What I propose is to highjack a car shortly before we make our move, this will allow less time for the disgruntled car owner to run crying to the cops. Michael can do the driving, he's the one who claims he can drive, and we need someone on the outside with their foot hovering above the accelerator'.

'What do I do if the cops land on the scene while you both are inside?' he asked.

'If you see them coming blow the horn three times and wait as long as you can', replied Oliver, 'but if they get too close and we are not out in time, get away as fast as you can'.

'Then what to fuck man do we do?' asked John.

'We find our own way out', replied Oliver, 'there's a back door which leads to a lane that goes all the way to Shaw's Quarry, we will just have to take our chance that the cops don't think about it too soon'.

'Any plans on where we drive to if we do manage to pull off this madness', asked Michael.

'There is an old derelict farm about fourteen or fifteen miles on the other side of Desertmartin', replied Oliver, 'we can drive the car into the barn, close the doors and hang around until the smoke clears'.

'Fuck sake man you have it all figured out', said John managing a smile at Oliver, 'if we get through this I'm going to plant one sucker of a kiss right on those bloodless looking lips of yours'.

'If that's what I'm to expect, then I hope we get caught', replied Oliver jokingly.

'Don't joke about it', said Michael still pale and sweating, 'it might fucking backfire'.

'It won't backfire', replied Oliver trying to sound confident, 'I have every faith in the whole plan, and I trust both of you with my life'.

Oliver commenced to hand out the balaclavas and said the words that they all had been dreading,

'Ok gang, let's do it'.

As Oliver and his two friends entered the cold air, all three were silent in their own thoughts. All three had gathered the pits of their stomachs together and began walking the walk of walks. Oliver's heart was thumping loudly, sending vibrations to his eardrums as he fought with his knees to try and stay on his feet. He knew he had to be brave, to stay focused and try to hold the others together. He was shaking wildly but tightened his muscles and took deep breaths. From the side of his eye he saw a blue ford Cortina pull up on the other side of the road, and one middle age man began to disperse from the vehicle. Oliver followed by his two friends approached the car and Oliver produced the gun,

'Hand over the keys we want your car', he said nervously.

The man looked at Oliver holding the gun and his eyes opened wide with fear,

'I na na need the car', he replied in a quivering voice.

'Now! Now!' roared Oliver.

The man quickly dropped the keys into Oliver's hand and began walking in a fast pace away from the car. Oliver handed the keys to Michael and said,

'Ok kiddo, let's drive'.

Michael jumped in to the car and took his place behind the steering wheel as Oliver got in beside him, and John into the back seat. Michael turned the key and fired the car into life, not caring to look if anything was coming and proceeded to drive towards the centre of the town. Oliver knew this was the easy part, and as his legs still vibrated in rhythm to the roar of the engine, he prayed into himself for strength to carry on. A few minutes later Michael pulled outside the bank and turned to Oliver and said,

'Good luck lads'.

Oliver opened the front passenger door and along with John stepped out onto the footpath. He noticed that only a few cars lined the street and one lady with a shopping basket entered Diamond's fruit and vegetable shop. As he made his way up the steps that led to the bank's front door, he knew this was it, his world was about to change. The two large oak doors lay wide open like the jaws of some wild beast beckoning its victims to enter and be devoured. Oliver and John walked through the doors, pulled the balaclavas over their heads and shouted

'Robbery, everyone on the floor'.

Behind the counter of the bank a woman teller looked at Oliver and John, first with surprise and then terror. Two men and a woman stood at the customer side of the counter, and acted in the same way as the teller. Oliver shouted to the customers,

'On the fucking floor now, or I'll blow your fucking head off'.

The two men and woman soon realised from the tone coming from Oliver's voice, that the wise thing to do would be to comply. Oliver's heart was beating loudly with fear, and as he approached the counter he could not show that fright as he pointed the gun at the teller and roared,

'Money on the counter NOW!'.

John quickly jumped over the counter and along with the teller began to fill a large cloth bank bag with bank notes. Oliver looked at his watch, he had allowed no more than seven minutes inside the bank, and now five of those were almost gone. He caught John's eye and nodded for him to check the door behind the counter. John had just finished filling the bag with money along with help from the female member of staff, and he turned and entered the door. Oliver reached over and grabbed the bag, while carefully watching both the customers on the ground and the female teller. He glanced at his watch again, six and a half minutes had gone and John had still not emerged from the door. Suddenly to Oliver's surprise, two more male members of staff materialized from the door,

'Hold your hands up where I can see them', shouted Oliver.

All three members of staff stood side by side with their hands high in the air, and as Oliver looked at his watch, almost eight minutes had past. He now shouted at Oliver,

'Ok Peter time to go'.

John returned through the door with a cloth bag in each hand, and jumped back over the counter.

'No one move for half an hour or I will be paying you a visit some night, I know where you all live', shouted Oliver.

Oliver and John ran from the bank and hurriedly climbed in beside Michael in the car,

'Get to fuck out of here', shouted Oliver. Michael put the car into gear and stepped heavily on the accelerator and sped off towards the bottom of the town.

'Keep going on this road until you see a crossroads, and then take the left turn', said Oliver, his voice now beginning to relinquish the shiver.

Oliver watched as Michael drove the car expertly, he

knew all was not yet well as around any corner or side road, a checkpoint could be waiting to stop them using fair means or foul. He was not sure how he would react to a policeman standing in the middle of the road signalling them to stop, while others pointed their guns in their direction. He would like to be able to tell Michael to attempt to drive through, while he discharged a few rounds. But Oliver knew that would be suicide, and being responsible for the death of his two friends, was something he was not prepared to take on board. Michael turned left at the crossroads as Oliver had instructed,

'Ok kid keep on this road for about three miles, you will see a bright red barn on your right, a few yards past it there is a road on the same side, turn down it', said Oliver.

'For fuck's sake man', shouted John, 'I caught the man in the bank trying to hide these two bags and guess what? They are stuffed with fifty and hundred pound notes'.

Excitement began to fill Oliver's mind, and he hoped with all his heart and soul that they would make good their escape. Oliver knew that all three of them deserved it, they had been terrified, yet they carried on and an ill deserving wind had no God given right to blow in their direction. Oliver turned around to John who was sitting in the back seat with a large smile glowing across his face,

'Sorry to burst your bubble kid, even if we get to our destination safely, we can't go around spending money like it grows on trees, we need to be careful and plead poverty for a few weeks'.

John's smile still remained as he replied to Michael,

'I can wait for as long as it takes kido, as long as I

know I'm fucking rich'.

Oliver could only laugh at his friend's reply, for he knew John was right, it didn't really matter how long they would have to wait, as long as they all knew what they were waiting for. On passing the red barn, Michael slowed and turned right onto a rough narrow road lined with potholes.

'Ok Michael old son', said Oliver, 'you're doing fine with your driving test, now follow this road for about four or five mile. As soon as you cross over a narrow hump backed bridge there are two white pillars on your left, stop there and I will open the gate'.

'I take it this is the Irish M1 motorway', replied Michael as he fought with the steering wheel in an attempt to avoid the potholes.

'What do you expect', answered Oliver, 'we would have plenty of money for roads if it wasn't for limeys and Yanks coming over and stealing it'.

'Better in our pockets', said John still holding tight to his smile, 'the Mick's would only piss it against the wall'.

Michael slowed down on arriving at the two pillars, and Oliver stepped out of the car before approaching the gate. Before opening the gate, Oliver carefully viewed his surroundings in search of prying eyes; on finding none he opened the gate and closed it behind him as Michael drove the car through. Oliver walked up the grassy lane that led to a yard that looked like it had not been visited by anyone for quite some time. Michael slowly followed him until he reached a brown rust stained barn, and allowed Oliver to open the doors wide before he drove inside. Oliver quickly closed the doors, and walked over to an old bale of hay and sat down. The barn although slightly dark, allowed enough light from a few cracked roof lights and a side window. As Michael brought the engine to a stop, John emerged with the three bags of money and emptied the contents on the dirt floor before Oliver. Michael and John each pulled up a bale of stale hay, and sat down facing Oliver. For several minutes no one spoke, each had his own thoughts to deal with, each requiring the moment of silence to smooth out the creases in their nerves, allowing them to return to their former selves. A mild wind began to arrive, slightly moving the loose sheets of corrugated iron. From somewhere across the valley a cow could be heard, and just outside the barn doors, a crow called out a greeting as it flew overhead. Oliver raised his head from its resting place on his hands and smiled,

'Do you want to know something kids? We did it'.

CHAPTER 9

Almost three weeks had passed since Oliver and his two friends had robbed the bank. On counting the money, the three friends discovered that they had boldly removed the grand sum of eighty five thousand pounds, give or take a few hundred. From Oliver's share he purchased the old barn where they hid the car after the robbery, and the ruined house next to it for what he thought was a bargain price of fourteen thousand. Oliver was now content with the knowledge that they would have a base to escape to after further robberies, safe from pursuing cops both on the ground and in the air. Against all the plans he had preached about pleading poverty for a substantial time after the bank job, he had purchased a black Ford Capri and filled his wardrobe with the latest fashion. Both Michael and John had also lavishly splashed out with their dangerously earned wages; Michael had bought his mother some expensive pieces of furniture, claiming he had won a fortune betting on the horses. John decided also to extend his wardrobe and in addition, sent a considerable sum to his grandmother in Missouri. All three had broken the number one rule on avoiding suspicion, but Oliver knew that being poor for so long, the temptation was overwhelming. He too had given his mother a few hundred, and like Michael an unexpected day at the races had blessed him with good fortune.

'Are you sure it didn't come from that bank robbery?' his mother asked him half heartily.

'Ok mum', Oliver replied, 'I did it, I walked in with my pin stripe suit and Thompson machine gun and shouted out, hit the dirt, its Machine Gun Kelly'.

'They think the IRA did it', said Oliver's mother, 'Annie from the bottom of the road said that there must have been about twenty men armed with rifles, and dynamite if they didn't open the safe'.

'You know how Annie exaggerates', replied Oliver as he tried to keep the amusement from his voice, 'I bet there were only ten men and no dynamite'.

'No matter how many there was', said Oliver's mother, 'I can't but help praising them for their courage and tenacity, especially in broad daylight and in full view of the police camera pointing down from the police station'.

Oliver froze, he knew about the police camera, everyone knew about it, he walked past it many times, and mooned it when he was drunk. He excused himself from his mother and made his way upstairs to his room, closing the door tightly behind him. Oliver sat on the bed dumbfounded by his mother's revelation, he began to feel fear churning from the pit of his stomach and he wanted to scream loudly into the face of his stupidity. He had planed everything precisely, combing the strands of every scenario and congratulating himself on a job carried out to perfection. Now the police camera had appeared, and he knew both John and himself had their faces uncovered for a few seconds before entering and exiting the bank. What comfort he could take from his mother's unexpected slap on the mouth was the fact that three weeks had passed and neither had his front door been kicked in, nor had he been snatched by any police land rover while walking up the street. Someone had told him once that the camera never works, and it was only there as a deterrent to those with dirty deeds on their minds.

As Oliver began dressing to go out for the night, he tried to shrug the worry from his mind and replace it with thoughts of disco lights and females. John and Michael had asked him to drive them to Cookstown, and all three for the first time in their lives, would pay the Bally Ballroom a welcome visit. They never had the money or dress to enter the classy nightclub before. Michael said it was a place where professional people hang out, and suggested we might fit right in with our new duds, and a pocket full of money. Oliver wasn't worried if his driving wasn't up to the standards required of an accident free society, or that he would get turned away at the nightclub door owing to him not yet reaching the age of eighteen. In a country where bombs were almost an everyday occurrence and armed men walked the streets, the simple laws were cast aside to allow space for the complicated ones.

Oliver turned the key and the engine of his black Ford Capri roared into life, a few seconds later he was travelling at speed towards the centre of the town and his arranged meeting place with John and Michael. Oliver had Michael to thank for teaching him to keep the car between the hedges, and not raising the pedestrians into the air. Oliver laughed to himself as he recalled his driving instructor Michael pleading for him to stop the car, and reciting language that could never be repeated to the faint hearted. As he pulled up at the diamond to allow John and Michael to climb into the car, he noticed a police car parked outside The May Day clothes shop.

'Hi kids', said Oliver greeting his two friends, 'did you notice the pigs parked over there?'

'Yeah', replied John as he fastened his seatbelt, 'been watching them, I guess they have fuck all else to do, they should be out chasing them damn robbers'.

Oliver moved off, driving around the roundabout and down the Cookstown road. The sight of the police car had left him feeling uncomfortable, and when he looked in the rear view mirror, his heart missed a beat as he noticed the police car follow them close behind.

'The fucking cops are on our tail', said John nervously.

'I know', replied Oliver, 'caught them in my mirror'.

'Do you think they'll pull us in?' asked Michael who in addition to a fastened seatbelt, was clutching a strap hanging from the roof with both hands.

'I don't know', replied Oliver slightly pressing on the accelerator.

'Ok kid', said John, his voice beginning to shake, 'when you get out on the straight, step hard on the gas'.

'No', answered Oliver, 'that's exactly what they want us to do, we'll keep to the speed limit and if they try to pull us in, then we hit the gas'.

Oliver continued on to his destination, occasionally watching the mirror for any sign of the police car turning off. He was frightened; the thought of going to prison had been keeping him awake at night. He wanted to enjoy his life, now that he had the funds to do so and all the things he dreamed of were now at his fingertips. He still wanted to go to the States with John and Michael, but all had agreed that another couple of banks needed to cough up, in order for them to have any chance of a secure future there. As the three friends finally arrived in Cookstown, Oliver turned the car towards John Street, following Michael's directions, and on doing so, the police car followed suit.

'Still behind us kids', said Oliver as he carefully kept within the thirty mile speed limit.

'Right', said Michael, 'just past the fish and chip shop on your left, turn in there and the Nightclub is straight in front of you'.

Oliver turned left as Michael directed and to his relief the police car drove on.

'Need not panic anymore kids', said Oliver excitingly, 'the pigs have decided to leave us alone'.

'Thank fuck for that', replied John uttering a sigh of relief, 'they just happened to be on the same road as us, probably on their way to the police station at the top of the town'.

'True children', said Michael as he unclipped his seatbelt, 'we're not the only ones who use the main fucking road to Cookstown'.

'Yeah he's right', added John, 'we're getting paranoid over nothing'.

As Oliver turned the ignition off he turned to John and said,

'I have reason to be paranoid; I left out something that might fuck up our chances of getting enough time to spend our loot'.

John looked at Oliver and said,

'What is it kid, for fuck's sake, you didn't drop our

birth certificates on the bank floor?'

'Not just, but I forgot the fucking camera pointing down from the police station', replied Oliver, with a worried look written across his face.

John sat silently for a few minutes, then turned to Michael in the back seat and said,

'No fucking wonder they make jokes about the Irish, how in hell could anyone be so stupid that they would forget the cop's ever watching eye'.

'Did you think about it?' replied Oliver.

'I sure did kiddo, and this may surprise you, but even the Limey in the back there brought it up too', said John now displaying a large grin across his face.

'What to fuck is there to grin about?' replied Oliver, 'the fuckers could have seen our faces'.

'No Siree kido, could never have happened', said John, reaching out to pat Oliver gently on the back, 'while you were figuring out the finer details of the plan, Michael and my good self sat on top of Roger's roof and with one shot from my air rifle, I put the fucker's lights out'.

A great rush of relief began to flow through Oliver's body; the thought of the camera staring down the street had given him no rest. Now he knew that demon was gone, and the cops had nothing left to point the finger at. He wanted to reach over and plant a kiss on John's face, to embrace him with a tremendous hug and thank him from the bottom of his soul. But Oliver could not show any cracks in his manhood, and instead discharged a bulging fart that had been brewing up inside him all the way to Cookstown.

'Bastard', roared John and Michael together as they swiftly departed from the car.

At the door of the nightclub the two neatly dressed doormen did not give the three friends a second glance. As they walked through the door and into an array of flashing lights and dancing bodies, Oliver surveyed the scene before him and liked what he saw. The club had two bars, one on the left as they walked through the door, and the other straight ahead. Numerous tables were scattered around, and couples danced closely on the dance floor to Status Quo's 'Living on an Island'. John noticed an empty table and beckoned his two friends to follow him. As John and Michael sat down, Oliver proceeded to the bar to order the drinks. A fresh faced clean cut lady wearing a low top green dress quickly arrived to take his order; Oliver was so impressed by her efficient manner that on receiving his three pints he tipped her a five pound note.

'Thank you Sir', the lady said as Oliver left and returned to the company of his two friends.

'This is one classy joint', said John as he took a sip from his pint.

'I've seen better', replied Michael as he too drank thirstily from the cold pint of beer.

'For fuck sake here we go again', said John as he looked at Michael, 'I bet you never set foot in a nightclub in your life before this one'.

'Have been to more nightclubs than you have had wanks, and that's a lot of clubs', replied Michael in defence.

Oliver interrupted the argument by commenting on the three girls sitting at the table next to them,

'How about those three, they look ok'.

'They look fine to me', replied John, 'but you and the experienced night clubber here have no chance'.

113

Oliver laughed at John's remark, but deep within his own self conscious mind he knew John was right. The place they were in was a hangout for high fliers who were educated and had greater expectations than a no hoper like himself. At seventeen he was quickly becoming aware of the boundaries in social circles, and knew he would have a better chance of pulling a girl in a potato field, than a place like this. To Oliver's amazement, Michael had finished the last dregs of his pint and made his way towards the bar in search of another round.

'That kid is going to drink the bar dry tonight', said John humorously as he finished his own pint. Michael quickly returned with the drinks and commented on the service,

'Now that was one quick barmaid, she had those pints pulled faster than I could get the money out of my pocket'.

'I wonder if she is as quick at pulling other things', said John while at the same time stealing a glance towards the bar.

'I guess I will be able to let you know before the night's out', replied Michael boastfully, 'I tipped her a five and she smiled at me, where I come from that means yes with a capital Y'.

'You tight fisted bastard', said Oliver, 'I tipped her ten and she called me darling'.

'Well sorry to disappoint you kids', replied John, 'where I come from that means screw the customers for what you can get, take a look towards the bar she's smiling at that ugly bastard with a face like a boiled spud'.

Oliver and Michael looked in the direction of the bar, just in time to see their sweetheart coming on to what looked like something that had just crawled out of the grave.

'Listen kids, I will give you a bit of free advice about women', said John, 'they come on to you like you are the greatest thing since sliced pepperoni, while all the time they are looking over their shoulder for something better. My grandma used to tell me, go out with all the intentions of looking for a rock, then maybe someday you will find a diamond'.

Michael replied to John's statement by pointing to a table,

'Like those rocks over there'.

'Those rocks over there will do', said John, 'whenever the next slow dance comes on we'll make our move'.

At these words Oliver felt the bees buzzing around inside his stomach. He knew if he was going to make a move with his two friends, he was going to need something stronger than beer.

'I'm off for another round fellow wasters', he said, 'does anyone want something stronger?' John rose from the table and said,

'Sit down kiddo, it's my round'.

'Get me a double whiskey', said Oliver.

'I'll go for the same and another pint', said Michael as he finished off the pint he had ordered a short time earlier.

John left the table and quickly returned with three pints, two glasses of whiskey and a glass of vodka. Michael lifted the whiskey to his lips and before downing it he said,

'To us, tonight and to our conquests'.

The three friends lifted their glasses and with one swig, emptied all three. Almost as soon as they finished their toast, Reo Speed Wagon was announced to the tune of 'Keep on loving you', and the three friends armed with false courage, made their way towards the table where the three girls were sitting eagerly awaiting their knights in shining armour.

'May I have the pleasure of this dance?' asked Michael in his best groomed English accent.
The lady with the black curly hair and wearing a navy blue glittering dress, smiled and arose to join Michael on the dance floor.

'Hi babe, care to join me for a twirl?' invited John.
The tall lady with short blond hair and dressed in a black open top blouse and cream coloured mini skirt, revealed two rows of tobacco stained teeth and made her way to the dance floor in the company of John.

'Would you like to dance?' asked Oliver politely.
The remaining lady with long red hair flowing down her back and wearing a tight black dress looked at Oliver, smiled and said,

'Piss off small fry I only dance with real men, come back when you have grown a few pubic hairs'.
Oliver was stunned, never in his life did he feel so humiliated, never since the day he had opened his eyes, did he experience such an assault on his character. He thought hard for something to say, for a few retaliatory words that would allow him to walk away with his dignity still intact.

'No hard feelings lady', replied Oliver, 'just give me a shout at the end of the night and I'll give you a lift back to the old people's home'.

At the closing of this statement, Oliver made his way back towards the entrance and straight into the men's toilets. As he entered the toilets he quickly walked into the toilet booth and locked the door. Oliver felt like screaming, he was filled with both anger and distress and fought back the tears that wanted to escape from his deep blue eyes. For the first time in his life, he had both the money and confidence to find a girlfriend, now all that he had left was a thick wad of money and a decimated self-esteem. His Mother had always warned him to know his station in life and never go wandering in search of a higher place. The taller you try to climb she would say, the further you have to fall. Oliver heard the Other men enter the toilets, some boasting of their conquests, while others vomited their hard earned cash upon the urine stained floor. As Oliver was about to finish urinating, he briefly heard someone call out,

'Does anyone own a black Capri with a HJI registration?'

He hurriedly pulled up his zip, flushed the toilet and walked to the person calling out.

'Excuse me,' said Oliver, 'you mentioned a Ford Capri?'

'Yes', replied the tall heavily built doorman, 'someone has just run into it'.

Oliver was now angry, the episode in the dance floor had lit the fuse, now he was ready to explode. He made his way towards the car park, taking long furious steps and swearing to commit murder most foul when he confronted the criminal, who dared to damage his newly washed and polished pride and joy. As Oliver reached his car, there was no one there. He frantically began to check for damage and to his relief, all he could find were a few small scratches on the rear bumper. Out of the blue, Oliver heard a soft female voice speak from behind him,

'Excuse me Sir; are you the owner of this car?'

Oliver turned around and to his surprise, a lady with long blond hair and sparsely dressed in a thin black mini dress, stood shivering before him.

'I am', replied Oliver, not daring to meet her stare for fear of giving away his innermost desires.

'I'm so so sorry', she said shaking, 'I caught your bumper with my car while reversing, if there's any damage, I will pay for it'.

Oliver quickly assured her that the damage was light and she need not worry.

'Are you sure?' She asked.

'Yes', replied Oliver, 'everything is fine, get yourself out of the cold you look freezing'.

The lady smiled and said,

'I am freezing, thank you'.

Oliver began to walk back in the direction of the nightclub, and without invitation the lady began walking beside him.

'At least let me buy you a drink', she said politely.

'Its fine', replied Oliver shyly, 'you don't need to buy me a thing'.

As Oliver walked through the door and back into the nightclub, the lady still stood beside him.

'If you won't let me buy you a drink', she said displaying her best smile, 'then how about a dance?'

Oliver was taken back, not long ago he had just received the biggest humiliating punch he had ever received in his life, now someone had come along out of the blue looking to dance with him. Oliver looked across the dance floor and spied John and Michael now sitting at the table with the two girls they had asked to dance. Both his friends had watched with humour as the lady he asked to dance had turned him down, and he knew they would taunt him for days to come. He turned to the lady who had arrived from God knows where and said,

'How about letting me buy you a drink first'.

'Fine by me', she replied.

Oliver beckoned her to an empty table out of his friends' view and asked the lady,

'What would you like to drink?'

'A glass of brandy if you please Sir, I need warming up', replied the lady graciously.

Oliver made his way to the bar and ordered a pint of beer and a double brandy. The smiling barmaid was eager to serve, but her smile soon disappeared when Oliver paid for the drinks without throwing another five pound note in her smiling direction. As Oliver sat down at the table, the lady thanked him for the drink and added,

'This is a nice place, is this a regular haunt for you?'

'Been here a few times', lied Oliver, 'I guess when you look at the same faces a time or two, it gets boring'.

'I know the feeling', said the lady as she sipped on her brandy, 'by the way my name is Mary and yours?'

'My mum christened me Oliver but I have been known by a few others I care not to name', replied Oliver.

Mary laughed and reached over to put her hand on Oliver's arm,

'Don't worry', she whispered, 'I won't tell a soul'.

Suddenly Mary leapt up as Art Garfunkel's 'Bright Eyes' began to play and pleaded,

'Please, please dance with me, I love this song'.

Oliver reluctantly picked himself up from his chair and followed Mary onto the dance floor. With the lights turned down, Mary put her arms around Oliver's neck and slowly they began to move to the rhythm of the music. For the first time Oliver began to notice the lady who had shuffled her way into his life, like a paper bag being tossed into a garden on a windy day. She had long blond hair with green eyes and a light brush of green eye shadow complemented her wide open stare. Oliver began to sense the aroma of her perfume and as she pressed her body close to his, his heart began to yearn for the moment to last for eternity. He caught a glance of John and Michael staring in his direction with expressions of disbelief, and he smiled to himself as he imagined what John would be saying now,

'What to fuck, she must be blind'.

Oliver and Mary danced in silence, each within their own thoughts and both not daring to disturb the moment. But as the song came to an end, Oliver knew that endings such as this unfortunately were part of his life and both Mary and himself returned to the table.

'Thank you for the dance', said Mary as she reached to take another drink of her brandy.

'You're very much welcome', replied Oliver as he too reached to lighten his glass.

Oliver was not quite sure how to deal with the situation, and as he looked at Mary sitting next to him at the table, his heart began to flutter in several different directions as he began to realise that the lady sitting next to him was beautiful.

'What took you here?' asked Oliver.

Mary smiled as if thankful Oliver had broken the silence and replied,

'I heard about it from a friend so I decided to give it a try, unfortunately I was late back from work so I guess I have arrived just as the ball is ending'.

Oliver looked at his watch and the time read 01.55. He was stunned by how quick the time had passed, and wished he could turn the clock back and have at least another hour with Mary.

'Will you have another drink before the bar closes?' asked Oliver.

Mary finished the brandy and set the glass on the table,

'No more for me thank you, I'm driving, but you could walk me back to the car if you don't mind', she said.

Oliver was grateful for the invitation and was only too happy to escort the beautiful Mary back to her car. As they made their way out and into the cold air, Oliver decided that if there was only one thing he ever done in his life, it would be to try and see Mary again.

'Will you be back here next week?' asked Oliver as he stopped beside Mary's car and watched her as she put the key into the lock. As Mary stopped, Oliver awaited the inevitable, the words that would be flung at him like a glove from a heavy weight boxer. The voice of the lady he had earlier asked to dance was still ringing alarm bells in his head, and round two of the same treatment could only be expected.

'Are you asking me on a date?' asked Mary as she turned to look Oliver in the face.

Oliver braced himself for the slaughter of his self esteem, but was taken back when Mary said,

'If you are, you surely don't expect me to wait a whole week'.

'How about tomorrow?', asked Oliver trying hard to keep the excitement from his voice, 'I'll drive us to Portrush and we can see how the seagulls are getting along'.

'Hummm', replied Mary, 'I'm working until two tomorrow so how about you pick me up at the Diamond in Magherafelt around three'.

Still trying to prevent his happiness from escaping Oliver replied,

'That suits me fine'.

Mary opened the door to her car, but to Oliver's surprise, she turned and kissed him gently on the lips and said,

'Until tomorrow'.

Oliver stood astonished as he watched the tail lights of Mary's car leave the car park, turn left and disappear. Crowds of people began to swarm the car park, as the night at the club came to an end, but Oliver still stared in the direction of Mary's car. The sound of John's voice brought him back to life,

'Hi kiddo, how much did she cost you for the night?'

Oliver smiled at John and replied,

'Not one penny'.

'Whatever kiddo, Michael and my wonderful self are going back with our new found babes, so hit the road without us and we will see you sometime tomorrow', said John.

'Ok', replied Oliver, 'you stink the fucking car out anyway'.

At the sound of a woman's voice calling John's name he staggered off and left Oliver standing on his own. If it had have been any other night Oliver would have cared, perhaps jealous and broken hearted that he could not find someone to love. But tonight as he started up the car and proceeded to find his way home, there was only room for one thing in his mind, tomorrow at three o'clock.

CHAPTER 10

As Oliver sat up on the bed he stole a glance at the clock on the bedside locker and breathed a sigh of relief. Oliver's memories of Saturday mornings had mostly been related to the night before, and how many pints he could gather the money up for. Pumping headaches, nausea and words of never again always greeted Oliver after a Friday night at the pub, but nothing had ever prepared him for a Saturday morning like this. He began to recall the night before and began asking the question, how someone as beautiful as Mary wanted to go on a date with him.

'Take it from me kiddo', John would remind him, 'beauty is skin deep but ugliness is bone deep, so there is no chance for you unless you strip all your flesh off to the bone and start again'.

'You're no fucking oil painting yourself', he would say in defence.

'But kiddo', John would say displaying two rows of perfect teeth, 'I have the touch, or what you say in Ireland, a gift of the gab'.

'Well that so called gab is a pretty big one', Oliver would reply, trying to get one over on John.

Oliver knew he was not much of a catch, whether in

looks or wealth. He had very little social skills and far less when it came to chatting women up. John was right, he wasn't much of a catch and if he was a fish caught in a net, the fishermen would quickly throw him back. But Mary must have noticed something he thought, some sparkle or flicker must have aroused an attraction. Oliver brushed aside any John influenced ideas and decided he needed to get himself out from under the covers and throw his ass into gear.

As Oliver walked into the kitchen his mother was at the table reading her usual morning paper.

'Good morning dearest mother', said Oliver.

'Good morning my ass', replied his mother, 'I never saw you rise before twelve on a Saturday, so I guess today is no exception'.

Oliver rubbed his hands over his mother's hair playfully and said,

'I have decided that Saturday mornings will have a whole new meaning for me, that is I will be up, dressed and bright eyed and bushy tailed'.

'And pigs will fly', his mother replied sarcastically and pointing to the clock on the kitchen wall, 'do you call that a whole new meaning?'

Oliver looked at the clock and to his horror the time read twenty five minutes past twelve.

'That clock is wrong', he said in a panic.

'No I checked it with the news this morning', replied his mother.

Oliver was angry, not just at the kitchen clock for being so truthful, but at himself for not winding the clock in his room and setting the alarm. He had approximately two and a half hours to change the ignition points in his car, get bathed and ready and meet Mary at the diamond. Oliver headed for the back door and entered the fresh air as his mother yelled,

'What about your breakfast?'

On reaching the car Oliver opened first the boot to retrieve his tool bag and then the bonnet. Changing points was a quick and easy job for those with ample experience of mechanics, but Oliver had not benefited from experience so like all DIY mechanics he had to study the job out and hope he makes no mistakes. As he took to the task, Oliver heard familiar footsteps walk towards him and say,

'Leave the fucking thing alone or it will never start again'.

Oliver turned his head around while still under the bonnet and replied,

'Go fuck yourself'.

John laughed out loud and decided to poke his head in and block the sunlight.

'Move your big head'; said Oliver, 'I need to be quick with this'.

'What's the hurry then', asked John as he continued to block out the sunlight.

'I have a date at three and I slept in again', replied Oliver as he turned the screwdriver to remove the offending part.

John remained quiet for what seemed like a long time, as he removed his head from Oliver's view he said,

'Listen kiddo, don't tell me you're off with that blond you met last night?'

Oliver continued with his task and replied,

'You have hit it on the nail Johnny old son, blond and beautiful'.

John suddenly and without any prior warning to Oliver raised his voice

'For fuck sake Oliver', he roared causing Oliver to

bang his head on the bonnet, 'she's no fucking good, and there's me all this time thinking you had something between those big fucking ears'.

Oliver removed himself from his task and stood facing John, he was not only angry at the bump he just got on the head, but also by how John attempted to dictate who he should be going out with.

'Why don't you fuck off and mind your own business', he replied in anger, 'you never met her before in your life so what to fuck do you know?'

'I might not have met her', answered John, 'but I have met her kind, listen Oliver, something is not right here I sense it'.

'What's not right?' roared Oliver, 'is it not right that you and Michael can go out every fucking weekend and shag your brains out, and whenever I get a chance all hell breaks loose'.

'Listen Oliver', said John as he tried to calm Oliver down, 'that babe you danced with last night was too good for you, she wants something'.

'What do you mean too good for me?' asked Oliver, 'am I some low life who just crawled up out of the fucking bog?'

'No', replied John, 'you got to trust me on this one kiddo, ask yourself the question, what does a tall pretty and most likely educated woman want with a seventeen years old ugly kid on the dole?'

Oliver began to think about John's question, he had already asked himself the same question on his way home from the nightclub, and concluded with the idea that people are attracted to each other in different ways. At the time Oliver knew his two friends would be jealous, but he could not have comprehended the extent of that envy until now. For once in his entire life he had a chance of love and perhaps more, friend or no friend, John was not going to put a wedge between Mary and himself.

'What I would like you to do for me John', said Oliver trying to introduce composure to his voice, 'is fuck off and leave me to stand or fall on my own two feet'.

Oliver continued with his task and as he heard his friend's footsteps drift off into the distance, he felt sad that John had forced him to take sides.

The tall picturesque figure of Mary smiling in his direction, sent shivers of excitement through Oliver as he pulled up to allow her to climb in beside him.

'I was beginning to think you wouldn't turn up', said Mary as she gently slammed the passenger's door of Oliver's car.

'Had a little trouble with a flat wheel', replied Oliver, leaving out the truth of the mechanical trouble for fear of Mary categorizing his car as only fit for the junk yard.

'The flat wheel', said Mary as she threw a sideward glance at Oliver, 'Is the world's oldest excuse for being late for an appointment'.

Oliver said nothing as he made his way down the main street and onto the open road. The road to Portrush was mostly minor roads through mountains high and low, with the occasional fresh water river joining the assortment of cows and sheep. It was not until a slow moving tractor emerged from a side lane, forcing Oliver to apply the brakes, that Mary broke the silence.

'I don't like farmers, they think they own the roads', she said as she pulled the window down to allow the fresh air to cool her face.

'Well', replied Oliver, thankful that the silence had

been broken, 'they do keep us all from starving'.

'I will agree with that, but what they are feeding us is another thing', answered Mary.

'What do you mean by that?' asked Oliver as he indicated to turn left onto another road.

'Have you ever heard of growth hormone?' asked Mary.

Oliver thought hard for an intelligent answer to Mary's question, he had heard his mother mention it to a friend and picked up on the assumption that growth hormone was given to Cattle.

'I believe it's used in some cases to increase milk production and allow them to but on more beef', replied Oliver.

'That is correct Oliver', said Mary at the same time turning to give Oliver a look of being impressed, 'but those hormones can cause a lot of problems to humans. The farmers know we give their milk to our most precious possessions, our babies, yet they still carry on using it'.

'But what are we supposed to do about it', asked Oliver, as he pressed hard on the throttle to overtake a slow moving lorry.

'Very simple', replied Mary, 'don't eat meat or drink cow's milk'.

Oliver turned and smiled at Mary before he said,

'How are we supposed to live without beef or Milk, we would fail away to nothing'.

Mary smiled back and lunged the next revelation at Oliver like four aces being tossed on the poker table,

'I don't eat meat or drink cow's milk and I am perfectly healthy', she said.

While Oliver thought about what Mary had just told him, he had to agree she was a picture of health and purity. He also knew that if he wanted to remain in Mary's beautiful presence, he would have to toe the lovers line.

'Ok', said Oliver, after some recollection of his thoughts, 'you have convinced me that in order that I might live to the ripe old age of forty, I must cast aside the evils of cow's flesh'.

At the closing of these words, the beaches and cliffs of Portrush now stood before them, and to Oliver's surprise, Mary began to jump with excitement as she saw the amusement arcade getting bigger before her eyes.

'Oh!' cried Mary in excitement, 'I love this place'.

As Oliver pulled up in the car park beside the candy floss stand, Mary reached across and kissed him on the cheek. Oliver could smell her perfume and the warmth of that one small kiss sent quivers of excitement through his heart. He remembered John's words, 'She's no good', and reminded himself of how wrong John had been. How wrong John had been was further confirmed as Mary took Oliver's hand in his, and together they walked in heavenly motion towards the amusement arcade.

The jingling of coins falling into slot machines and the laughter of children added little to Oliver's present mood. The swing boats and big dipper were something Oliver choose to ride for no purpose other than to be with Mary. Oliver had visited the arcade many times in the past with his mother. Every summer if weather permitted, along with his mother he would take the bus early in the morning and spend the whole day jumping over the waves, or rolling down the sand dunes. The happiness he felt at the time had no relation to how he felt now, for Oliver's world was changing from the first moment he met Mary.

'I hate the weather in this country', said Mary, as Oliver and her sat on the deck chair looking out across the Atlantic Ocean.

'I don't blame you', replied Oliver, 'here we are in the summer and we still have to wear coats'.

'I want to move out of this God forsaken place', said Mary as she tried to peel the last remaining flake of paint of the chair, 'somewhere hot like Florida'.

'Or like Missouri', replied Oliver, 'I have a friend who told me that every season of the year goes by the book'.

Mary abandoned the idea of trying to remove the paint off the chair and with a half smile asked Oliver,

'What does he mean by the book?'

'I asked him the same question', answered Oliver, 'and he explained it like this. In the winter it snows and rains and freezes the balls off those who have them. Spring brings in the awakening of life and thawing of bones. Summer brings heat and dust mixed in with a few allergies and the fall shakes it all off to prepare for the winter. Now what we have here he told me, was hailstones in the summer, then autumn gets so screwed up it doesn't know what to do. Winter is waiting for spring to let it know when to piss off and spring is so far up winter's ass that the mad march hare is running around singing Christmas carols'.

Mary stood up and began walking towards the town, Oliver was taken by surprise and watched her for a few seconds. Mary stopped and turned to Oliver,

'I need a drink, are you coming?'

Oliver arose and followed Mary through the car park and down the side street that led to a place called The

Sea view Bar.

As they entered the bar the inside was already buzzing with the sound of intoxicated laughter and the thick smell of cigarette smoke. A few tables still remained unclaimed, so Mary asserted her right to the one nearest the door and sat down.

'What are you having?' Asked Oliver as he removed his denim jacket and threw it over the back of the chair.

'Something very strong', replied Mary.

Oliver made his way to the bar and on catching the barman's attention; he ordered a double brandy for Mary and a pint of beer for himself. As he awaited his order he began to think about how Mary's mood suddenly changed. First they were talking about the weather, and out of the blue she sprang from the chair like a bluebottle fly escaping from a rolled up Sunday newspaper. He wondered what would have caused this sudden change and remembered the words of his father,

'Never try to understand women', he said, 'most of the time they can't understand themselves'.

As he collected his order and made his way back to the table, Oliver was relieved that Mary had a smile for him as he returned.

'I'm sorry Oliver', said Mary as she took the glass of brandy from Oliver's hand, 'It's that time of the month when every woman has the God given right to act a little crazy'.

Oliver lifted his glass touched it to Mary's now almost empty brandy glass and said,

'Here's to God given rights'.

Mary poured the last of the remaining brandy down her throat and as quickly as she sat her glass on the table, Oliver moved to the bar counter to refill it. While waiting for Mary's second glass of brandy, Oliver decided that a call of nature must be answered and responded by making his way to the gents. The smell of urine and disinfection greeted Oliver's nose as he hurriedly made his way into a cubicle to hide his embarrassment of passing water in front of others. Oliver began to wonder how the day would end, and if Mary would feel the same way about him as he did for her. Time had travelled faster than he hoped and as he washed his hands on the small white sink, he could see the sun was beginning to disappear below the horizon. He made his way to the bar and collected Mary's brandy, allowing a smile in her direction as he made his way back to the table.

'There you are baby', joked Oliver, 'another glass of hard stuff to soak your sorrows in'.

'Thank you', replied Mary, as she lifted her glass once again to toast, 'may all our sorrows be forever submerged'.

Oliver joined her in the toast allowing the cool beer to flow abundantly down his throat and into his empty stomach. As he relaxed beside Mary Oliver wanted to ask her a thousand questions. He wanted to look inside her soul, to know what she liked and didn't like. He yearned to follow the footsteps of her dreams, to walk hand in hand in the fields of gold and fall asleep in her arms, closely guarded by cupid and his arrows of love. Mary suddenly interrupted Oliver's thoughts,

'Is everything ok Oliver?' she asked as she pulled her chair closer to him.

Oliver looked into Mary's eyes, he looked at her long flowing blond hair, the smoothness of her soft white skin and the small emerald green earrings hanging from her ears. He heard Mary's voice echo from rose petal lips,

'Is everything ok Oliver, you don't look too well?'
Oliver noticed Mary's face begin to swerve from side to side. He perceived her voice floating off into the distance and within the grumbling crash of table and chair; Oliver took leave of those around him and introduced his falling body to the cold hard slate floor.

CHAPTER 11

A light aroma of mould greeted Oliver as he slowly arrived at the unfamiliar surroundings. The sun had allowed a faint presence through the gap in the faded brown curtains and as Oliver afforded himself a glimpse around the room, he noticed from a copper coloured clock perched on top of a dressing table that it was 8.14 am. As he frantically searched his mind for some vague picture of remembrance, the hammers of what felt like a vicious hangover pounded the caverns of his skull. Oliver began to recall the moments he had in the bar and the sudden departure of Mary. At the thought of Mary, Oliver sprang from the mattress and managed to regain enough strength to sit at the side of the bed. As he followed his eyes around the room again, he could see no sign of Mary and by the looks of the bedcovers, he had been alone on his place of rest. He could not remember drinking enough to allow himself a disability, nor could he recall the events that led him to the room he found himself in. On reaching over to a small table beside the bed, Oliver lifted a note and began to read. DEAR OLIVER, HOPE YOU HAD A PLEASANT NIGHT'S SLEEP, I'M SORRY YOU COULDN'T HOLD

YOUR DRINK, BUT YOU KNOW WHAT THEY SAY, PRACTICE MAKES PERFECT. I TOOK THE LIBERTY OF MAKING MY OWN WAY HOME AND HAVE LEFT YOU MY PHONE NUMBER TO CALL SOMETIME IF YOU LIKE. MARY

Oliver folded the piece of paper and placed it inside the breast pocket of his denim jacket that hung loosely over a chocolate coloured chair. He had mixed feelings of shame, bewilderment and sadness. The first true date he had ever gone on had ended in a pounding headache surrounded by a haze of unanswered questions. He had wanted to make a lasting impression on Mary and prove to her he was more mature for his years. That impression was now wrinkled by the moments that have now passed, and the days ahead have yet to prove if those wrinkles can be smoothed out.

As Oliver gathered himself together and departed from the room, he was greeted by the aroma of bacon and sausages cooking from some kitchen in the building. At the bottom of the stairs he was greeted by a small pot bellied man smoking a strong cigar.

'Good morning sir', said the man, 'did you enjoy your room?'

'The room was fine', replied Oliver, 'how much do I owe you'?

The man removed the cigar from two rows of tobacco stained teeth and replied,

'Fifteen pound should do the trick'. Oliver removed a twenty pound note from his jeans pocket and handed it to the man saying,

'Keep the change'.

Without waiting for a reply, he made his way across

the sand, through the crisp morning air and onto the car park where his Ford Capri sat solitary and dew stained. As he opened the door and positioned himself behind the steering wheel, Oliver hoped that the car would start without any trouble. As much as he enjoyed driving into the car park, that was now equalled to how fast he wanted to leave it. To Oliver's relief the car was on friendly terms and without further ado, he allowed the throttle no mercy as he made his way home to Magherafelt.

By the time Oliver had pulled up beside his house, the headache had almost subsided. What Oliver longed for most of all was a large mug of tea, followed by another and if he was still craving his morning caffeine, then he might have one more for the road. The simple pleasures of the homeward bound had put a smile on his face, and the realization that his mother's reaction to him staying out all night was going to be ear shattering. As he turned the key on the door and made his way through the short hall and into the kitchen, Oliver could never have expected the greeting that was waiting for him. His mother arose from the chair and flung her arms around him, holding him tightly and muttering

'Thank God you are safe son, oh thank God you are safe'.

Oliver could only hold his Mother's embrace for as long as it took him to recover from the surprise and when he did he said,

'Ok Mum I only stayed away one night, it's not as if I've been away for years'.

While his Mother retreated from her embrace, Oliver noticed her eyes were red from crying and as she proceeded to pour him a cup of tea, he could not fail to notice her hand was shaking.

'For heaven's sake Mum get a grip of yourself', said Oliver, I visited a friend till late and fell asleep on the sofa'.

As soon as Oliver's Mother finished pouring the tea she sat down opposite Oliver at the table and once again to Oliver's surprise began crying. Oliver was taken aback by his Mother's behaviour and began to sense something was wrong. He knew his Mother more than anyone else, and he was sure that one night away from home would have allowed him a different greeting than he got.

'Pull yourself together Mum for fuck's sake and tell me what's wrong?' asked Oliver slightly raising his voice.

Almost simultaneously his father walked into the kitchen and spoke,

'John and Michael are dead', he said.

Oliver sat quietly on the chair and reflected with deep shock on the words that had been spoken by his Father. The clock that had always asserted its right to produce moderate ticking noises around the kitchen, had now been paused to give way to the silence of death. As far back as Oliver could remember, the word dead on its own was as terrifying as the act itself. He knew that death was a dark empty place in reality where no one ever returned, and he understood the pain and despair from those who were left. 'John and Michael dead?' he began to ask himself, 'that is not possible'. But behind the mask of mirrored questions Oliver knew it was true, he knew he would see his friends no more, and from this moment on, he would curse the very words that his father uttered. He would remember this moment with contempt for those who did not deserve to live, and he would spit at the very thought of this terrible memory. Oliver slowly returned to the ticking clock and the sound of his Mother's weeping and spoke,

'How did it happen?'

'According to the news', answered his Father, 'they drove through a police checkpoint at high speed, so the cops opened fire. They didn't release the names until an hour ago, and when we heard we have been worried sick not knowing where you were at'.

'I know one thing for sure', said Oliver trying to keep the shaking from his voice, 'the cops are lying bastards, there is no way either John or Michael would be crazy enough to drive through an armed checkpoint'.

The words Oliver echoed in his friends' defence were not just designed as a cloak to disguise the dull ache that had now gripped his heart, for in all honesty he knew they would not even dream of attempting such a suicidal mission. The times they had spent together allowed Oliver the opportunity to acknowledge not only their strengths, but also their weaknesses. John and Michael were nobody's fools, and Oliver had learned from previous incidents involving the cops, that no matter how many questions you asked, none of the answers were to be believed. Oliver arose from the chair and looked at his Mother and said,

'You can stop crying now Mum, I'm alive and I'm off to bed for a lie down'.

As he made his way up the stairs he could feel his legs getting weaker as the blow from the news he had just received began to take its toll. As he staggered into the room, Oliver managed to close the bedroom door behind him before he collapsed on the bed, and allowed the dryness of the bed quilt to absorb the flood of cruel tears.

'Can I get you something', asked the barman as Oliver made his way to the bar counter.

'A pint of beer would be great', replied Oliver as he scanned the room in search of customers.

'That will be £500', said the barman as he positioned the beer before Oliver.

'£500', gasped Oliver, 'surely you have got to be joking'?

'No joking tonight sonny', answered the barman, 'with my customers deciding to go elsewhere, a man has got to make a living from someone'.

'And you think that someone should be me'? asked Oliver.

'And why not', answered the barman, 'you are the only one here'.

'I haven't got £500', pleaded Oliver in his defence.

'Stop telling lies', answered the barman, 'the parish priest had one too many in here last night and told us all about it'.

'Told you all about what'? asked Oliver somewhat bewildered.

'Well a couple of things, and one being that you and those two other wet behind the ears rascals robbed the bank down the street', answered the barman.

'He's a liar', replied Oliver trying to keep the guilt from his voice.

'Priests don't lie', replied the barman, 'and besides he even managed to let slip that you give him two grand to keep his mouth shut'.

'The squealing bastard', said Oliver in anger, 'I'll kick his bony ass, but not before I get my two grand back'.

'As a Protestant I would welcome the ass kicking, but forget the cash sonny, he spent it here last night along with the church roof collection', replied the barman.

'At these prices I'm not surprised', said Oliver in a serious tone of voice.

'If you want to blame anyone for the prices, blame your two soggy pants friends', answered the barman raising his voice.

'What have they got to do with your greed?' asked Oliver.

'It was those two brats that organised the torching', replied the barman angrily, 'and now all my customers have found a better form of entertainment'.

'What entertainment?' asked Oliver, 'and what do you mean by torching?'

'Well', replied the barman, 'saying you're not going to buy a drink, you might as well join the rest of the blood thirsty bastards, I heard they are going to burn a nice lady by the name of Mary and if you hurry you might even catch the best bit'.

Oliver turned and made his way towards the door, he tried to run but some strange force similar to a wall of water caused him to move in slow motion. He turned left onto the road and there before his eyes was a gathering of people encircling what looked like a pole protruding from a bundle of twigs and straw. As he laboriously pushed his way through the circle he came face to face with John and Michael.

'What in hell's name is going on?' roared Oliver.

'It's all right kiddo', replied Michael, 'we got permission from the parish priest'.

'Got permission for what?' asked Oliver, his voice now echoing in confusion.

'Did you know the barman across the road told everyone that you are a wanker', said John.

'Yeah', said Michael, 'if you can't trust the barman then who can you trust'.

'What has that got to do with what's going on here?' asked Oliver once again raising his voice.

'Nothing', answered John, 'but it is a terrible thing to say'.

'He also told me that you are going to burn someone by the name of Mary', said Oliver, 'anyone I know?'

'No', answered Michael, 'just a Witch we caught with a poison apple'.

Suddenly Oliver heard the familiar voice of Mary screaming as a number of people carried her and tied her to the stake.

'Oliver, Oliver', cried Mary, 'Help me'.

'Forget her', said Michael in a sharp frost like voice, 'She's no good'.

'Fuck you', shouted Oliver as he pushed his way through the crowd towards Mary.

Oliver knew that somehow among all the madness, Mary was the only sane person left. He ignored the shouts of Michael and reached to untie Mary's hands from the pole. Suddenly he felt the heat of the flames engulfing him, as he looked for Mary's face through the smoke and flames, all he could find as he burned was a juicy red apple perched on top of the pole.

Oliver awoke four hours later with a cold drop of sweat flowing down the side of his cheek, and his right leg shaking frantically. Another twisted and merciless dream had entered his sleep to taunt him yet again with madness. Yet no matter how false or defiant his mind had chosen to express itself through sleep, at the very second he awoke, Oliver knew what was real and what was not. John and Michael were dead, never again to breathe mortal air or witness the new day with fond expectations. Their dreams were now frozen and shut away in some cavern hidden from time, locked away in a place where living eyes can never see. Oliver felt scared and alone, he sensed the cold hard steel of grief penetrate his pounding heart as fond memories sent shadows of loss across the walls of friendship. Oliver knew that somehow he would have to gather the broken pieces from the dust stained floor of life and face the coming days with strength and dignity. Throughout the months and years growing up with the troubles in Northern Ireland, he heard of death, he smelled it through the TV screen of the six o'clock news. Death was waiting around every sectarian corner, hiding behind every wall of hatred and snarling from the mouth of those who knew they could get away with it. It was easy to face death from a distance, to sympathise with others without ever touching the flames of their grief. Now Oliver was on the other side of the TV screen, and had joined the line of those who had been burnt before him.

Oliver made his way into the kitchen and like countless times before, took a chair beside the table. His mother who had by now stopped crying spoke to him in a soft almost quiet voice,

'Would you like a cup of tea son?'

Oliver replied in a tone that was unfamiliar even to himself,

'Please Mum'.

Oliver's Mother began the ritual of tea making and before long Oliver was tasting the sweet hot beverage that to him, no one else could rival. As he placed the cup temporary on the table, Oliver asked,

'Have you heard any more details on the killings?'

'A lot of conflicting reports', replied Oliver's Mother, 'I went out to the corner shop for a loaf of bread an hour ago and met Jane Bradley, she heard there may have been a gun battle. The shopkeeper himself said that they tried to knock down a policeman'.

'All a load of bullshit', replied Oliver as he stared into his cup, 'anything on the news?'

Oliver's Mother reached over and turned on the black transistor radio that was perched on top of a small shelf above the table. NATIONALIST AND SINN FEIN COUNCIL MEMBERS ARE CALLING FOR A PUBLIC ENQUIRY INTO THE SHOOTING DEAD BY POLICE OF TWO YOUNG MEN EARLY THIS MORNING. ACCORDING TO A POLICE SPOKESPERSON THE CAR THEY WERE DRIVING RAMMED A POLICE CHECKPOINT AND FEARING FOR THEIR LIVES, POLICE OPENED FIRE. THE YOUNG MEN WERE NAMED AS EIGHTEEN YEARS OLD MICHAEL RAMSEY FROM RIVER VIEW IN CASTLEDAWSON, AND SEVENTEEN YEARS OLD JOHN CONWAY FROM CURRAGH WAY IN MAGHERA. RIOTING HAS CONTINUED FOR A SECOND NIGHT RUNNING……….. Oliver reached over and turned the radio off,

'No sense in being reminded of the obvious', he said.

'I sat up the whole night worrying about you son', said Oliver's mother, 'and when I heard at first about reports coming in of a shooting outside Moneymore, I almost died'.

Oliver turned his head towards his mother, looking her

straight in the eyes and muttered,

'I lied about last night Mum, I'm sorry'.

'What do you mean you lied about last night?' asked Oliver's mother as alarms became evident in her voice.

'It's ok mum', answered Oliver quickly, in order to spare his mother any continuing grief. 'I had a date with a girl, we went to Portrush and after drinking too much I decided to stay the night. She got a friend to take her home and I got a room at the hotel'.

'My God son', said Oliver's mother, 'you shouldn't even be drinking at your age, never mind drinking too much'.

'I agree', replied Oliver, 'but I'm not really sure if it was too much drink, or tiredness'.

'What's the girl's name?' asked Oliver's mother.

'Mary', replied Oliver.

'Mary who?' asked Oliver's mother.

For one brief moment Oliver stopped from his thoughts and realised he didn't know Mary's surname, where she lived or her age.

'I forget her surname', answered Oliver, hiding the fact that he hadn't bothered to ask her.

'Well you better try and remember it for the next time you meet her, she won't be impressed if you have forgotten her name', said Oliver's mother, trying to bring some light into the conversation. Oliver began to think of Mary and wondered if he would ever meet her again. He had only known her for a short time, but he knew he loved her no matter who she was. Even through the terrible throbbing of pain and despair, the thought of Mary still kept a candle burning in his heart. Out of respect he would not call her again until he had mourned the death of his friends. The calling at the respective homes, the strong words of condolences and the prayers at the side of the coffins are rituals Oliver knew he couldn't perform. He cared to remember John and Michael as in life, not death, and remember the vibrant laughs and episodes they shared both legal and not so legal. He would attend each funeral separately as not to do so would be a crime against not only his conscience, but also their friendship. At this moment he could share some of, but by no means match the unbearable grief that two mothers were now enduring. Oliver knew that both John and Michael's mothers had shed their unfairly portion of tears, and the tears they would shed now, would be red and dripping from the heart. He began to digest the cruel way in which his friends died, and wondered if things had have turned out different, he too could be lying in a cold morgue alongside his two friends. If Mary had not instigated a date, his life could have ended and his mother would have to bear the torturous wraith of fate. Perhaps Mary was an angel who needed to earn her wings, he thought, and his life had been prolonged by someone who he may never see again. His thoughts were once again interrupted by his mother,

'I'll make you a bite to eat son, you must be starving'.

Oliver had been true not only to himself, but to John and Michael by staying away from the wakes. On the day of the funerals he dressed in the black suit he had bought before the heart rending death of his friends, and borrowed a white shirt and black tie from his father. Michael was to be buried after a service in the Church of Ireland in Castledawson at 11.00am, and John after Mass at the Roman Catholic Church in Maghera two hours later. As he made his way in his car on the short journey to Castledawson, Oliver could not rid himself from the heavy feeling that had attached itself to him since the deaths. A thousand questions were swirling around in his mind, and at this very moment he had no answers that would lighten the load. As he pulled up to attend Michael's funeral first, his heart sank even further as he witnessed Michael's mother being helped into the Church. He waited until most people had entered the church, then proceeded to follow an old well dressed couple and take a seat at the back. Before Oliver could gather his thoughts, the service began with the singing of a hymn, followed by some careful selected words from the Vicar.

'Michael was a fine young man', said the Vicar, 'cut down in the prime of his life. Those who knew him and loved him will give thanks to God for the happiness he give and the consideration he expressed. Michael was an honest caring individual who loved life, but unfortunately like so many others before and with no doubt after him, that life has come to an unexpected end. The Lord God as we the faithful know, is a merciful God, and through his mercy Michael will have eternal life'. Oliver like all the others listened to what the Vicar had to say, and smiled inwardly when he heard Michael being described as honest. Honest Michael he thought to himself, wouldn't think twice of robbing a bank. But the reality was as Oliver knew, Michael was as honest as most people alive. Oliver remembered when he found some lady's purse, and Michael insisted it was returned to the owner immediately. Michael was truly honest he thought, except to those who did not deserve honesty.

John's funeral in Maghera had been similar in almost every aspect, except the homily had been delivered in an air of condemnation.

'John along with his friend Michael', said the priest, 'had been cut down at the dawning of their youth, by armed men who claim to be upholders of law and order. Questions must be asked, and indeed answers must be given, as to why these young men, who were unarmed, should have died. Hanging over our province is a dark cloud of death and within that cloud there is secrecy and lies. I call on those who feel it is within their power to seek vengeance for these murders, to refrain because surely one murder cannot be justified by another. And I further call on those policemen who have one iota of conscience, to come forward and tell the truth about what really happened on that terrible night two days ago'.

Oliver's heart began to pound as he digested the priest's words. His mind returned to the night he was arrested and beaten, and he began to ask himself if perhaps John and Michael's death had been planned and executed deliberately. Maybe, he thought to himself, that he was going to meet a similar fate. Perhaps for some horrid reason he had pissed off a lunatic cop, and at this very moment he was planning to take out the third culprit.

Oliver arose from his seat in the church and made his way hurriedly to the exit. He didn't look right or left to see who had noticed him leaving, all he wanted was to escape the place of death and breathe the fresh air of life. On leaving the main building of the church, Oliver moved quickly down the narrow gravel path lined with grey and black headstones. On entering his car he started the engine and as dignified as possible, made his way in the direction of Magherafelt and home. He knew John and Michael were not in any church or chapel, and he would not watch the pine boxes being lowered into a hole in the ground. As far as Oliver was concerned, John and Michael were gone and no gravestone or sermon would convince him otherwise. As he turned onto the main Glenshane road, Oliver pushed the Meatloaf cassette into the cassette player and began listening to the song *heaven can wait*. Oliver felt the tears beginning to slowly flow down his face, and began wishing within the deepest caverns of his heart, that he could turn back time. He began to think of Mary and thought to himself that now would be an appropriate moment to hold her in his arms. As soon as the thought of Mary passed Oliver's moment of contemplation, the cassette player suddenly stopped and Oliver heard the almost distant voice of John taking its place with the words 'SHE'S NO GOOD'. Oliver felt a cold chill moving down his back, as he tried to stay focused on the road ahead. *Heaven can wait* continued from where it had been interrupted, and joined the rhythm of Oliver's shaking hands gripping the steering wheel as he pulled up outside his house.

As he turned the engine off, the music stopped also, and as he locked the car door, he very much welcomed the warm smile of his mother waving from the kitchen window. Oliver took a seat at the kitchen table and blamed the stress of the last two days for playing tricks on his mind. A large mug of steaming tea was welcome, and as she positioned a plate of sandwiches before him, Oliver's mother began to speak.

'How were the funerals?' She asked.

'Dead and dreary', replied Oliver before he began to bite hungrily into one of the egg sandwiches.

'There's an envelope for you', said Oliver's mother,

as she reached and handed Oliver a white envelope.

'Where did that come from?' asked Oliver as he looked at it in amazement.

'I don't know', she answered, 'I found it in the hall floor with your name on it'.

On opening the envelope Oliver could smell the familiar aroma of Mary's perfume, the note read MISS YOU, CALL ME ON THIS NUMBER....MARY. Oliver put the piece of paper back inside the envelope and slipped it into his hip pocket.

'Who's it from?' asked his mother.

'From the girl I stayed with the other night', replied Oliver.

Oliver did not want to worry his mother by concealing the contents of the note. He remembered how torn apart she had been the night of John and Michael's deaths, and he would never want to put her in that position again.

'I don't want you to be worrying about me Mum', said Oliver as he reached for a second sandwich, 'I have a girlfriend and if I'm not home at night it's because I am warm and safe in her house'.

'You might ring next door and let me know son, if you're staying overnight that is', said Oliver's mother.

'They don't have a phone in their house', answered Oliver, 'the nearest one is two miles away and nine times out of ten its vandalized. But if I'm not back by twelve any night, you go to bed in peace as you will know I'm staying the night'.

As soon as Oliver finished his tea and sandwiches he thanked his mother and made his way to his room to gather his thoughts. As he lay on the bed he began to wonder how Mary knew where he lived, for he could not remember ever telling her. He once again dismissed the freaky incident in the car and assured himself that a meeting with Mary would be just what he needed. As quickly as Oliver lay down on the bed, he arose again and made his way downstairs and out through the front door. He decided there would be no need for the car as it was only a short distance to the phone box, and besides, he thought to himself, he needed the time to consider what to say to her. He remembered little of the last time they met and he was ninety percent sure he had made a complete ass of himself. Mary would know nothing about John or Michael, except what she heard on the news, so he decided to leave them out of their conversation for the time being. As Oliver entered the red phone box, he took out Mary's note and was thankful for the soft smell of perfume to help him fight off the stench of urine and vomit. He carefully dialled the number and waited nervously for Mary's angelic voice to answer from the other side of the line.

'Hello', said a male voice from the other side.

'Hello', replied Oliver, 'could I speak to Mary please'.

'May I ask who's calling?', asked the male voice.

'Tell her it's Oliver', answered Oliver as he searched his pocket for more coins.

'Oliver! It's me', said the male voice.

'I beg your pardon', asked Oliver, 'but who are you?'

'It's me John', the voice replied, 'listen Kiddo, don't call this number again, I already told you SHE'S NO GOOD'.

Oliver froze with fear, he began to shake violently, and the tea and sandwiches that he had eaten earlier were now projecting from his stomach, and spraying the phone box floor.

What Oliver thought was the phone box floor,

turned out to be his bedroom carpet. He realized that the few minutes he had lain across the bed, in reality was almost an hour as he dozed off, and the sick soaking into the carpet assured him he had never been to the phone box yet. He reached for an old worn tee-shirt that lay on top of the small chest of drawers below his window, and proceeded to clean the undigested tea and egg sandwiches from his room floor. While doing so, Oliver discovered that in addition to his shaking hands, a cold sweat had gathered on his brow. He knew he needed to pull himself together and shake off the effect of his best friends deaths. It was not unusual to dream about a dead friend in his sleep, but to hear them speak while he was fully conscious was a dangerous revelation. Oliver decided that as it was getting dark, a trip to the phone box to phone Mary would be best left until the next morning, and until he got a good night's sleep.

CHAPTER 12

When Oliver opened the door of the red phone box, the stress of the day before had elapsed sufficiently for him to gain confidence. He lifted the receiver, dialled Mary's number and waited to hear her voice from the other side of the line.

'Hello', a female voice said.

'Hello', replied Oliver, 'Can I speak to Mary please'.

'You must have the wrong number', she said, 'there's noooo'. Before she could finish her sentence, another female voice mumbled something and took the phone saying

'Hello, is that Oliver?'

'Yes', replied Oliver.

'That's my sister messing around', said Mary apologetically, 'and how are you?'

'I'm ok', answered Oliver, 'I got your note so I thought I'd give you a call'.

'I'm glad to hear from you', said Mary, 'the last time we met was eventful to say the least, so I thought you might want to meet up again sometime'.

Oliver felt his heart starting to race at the thought of meeting Mary again. He was unsure of some of the events of their last meeting, but he had blamed himself and was certain he would never have the pleasure of her presence again. Gathering his composure and trying not to sound too enthusiastic, he replied,

'That would be great, just say where and when'.

'Oh let's see', said Mary, 'how about the park behind the swimming pool in an hour'.

Oliver was taken aback by Mary's sudden hurried eagerness to meet up, that he paused for a few seconds to try and gather his thoughts.

'Are you there?' asked Mary.

'Ahhh yes', replied Oliver, 'ok I will see you there in an hour'.

'Until then', said Mary, 'byeeee'.

Before Oliver had time to respond with his own goodbye, Mary put the phone down on the other side. Oliver departed from the phone box and began to hurry towards home. As he made his way through the door of his house, his first port of call was the bathroom and a hurried wash and shave the few bristles that were sprouting from his chin. He then proceeded to his room and to the contents of his wardrobe in the hope he would find something suitable for a meeting in the park. As he began changing into a clean pair of jeans and black tee-shirt, he thanked his mother inwardly yet again, for giving so much thought to his laundry. The room still had a slight odour of vomit from the day before, and he was a little happy that his mother had left the house earlier, for now was not a good time to listen to her complaints. Upon finishing dressing, Oliver afforded himself a quick glimpse in the mirror, fixed his denim jacket collar and set himself on his way to meet Mary.

When Oliver arrived at the park, there was no sign of Mary so he picked an empty seat and sat down to wait. The park itself was scarce of people, and as Oliver discovered like many times before, this was substituted by the generous amounts of dog shit scattered across the neatly cut green. As the waiting allowed him some time to think, Oliver began to run some questions through his mind. He began to wonder why Mary was in so much of a hurry to meet him now and why could she not have left it until tonight, at the very least. One question he was sure would be at the top of his list for Mary was, how did she know where he lived? The deaths of John and Michael were still very much in his mind, but all he could do was push them aside in the hope he could retain some of his sanity. He knew the full impact of what had happened had not found its way into his reality yet, and all he could hope for was a few days reprieve. His thoughts were interrupted by the warm rays of the sun on his face, and the tingling in his heart by Mary's arrival.

'Hello', said Mary, as she sat down on the park chair next to Oliver.

'Hello Mary', replied Oliver, 'not much life around this neck of the woods'.

'I like that', said Mary, 'I'm ok with throngs of people whenever it arises, but I do like peace and quiet most of the time'.

'I'm ok with peace and tranquility myself', answered Oliver, 'especially when I'm trying to sleep'. Mary laughed and reached over to throw a feint blow in Oliver's direction,

'Smart ass', she said humorously.

'How's life been treating you since we last met?' asked Oliver.

'Much the same', answered Mary, 'boring, boring and

boring'.

'And you?' asked Mary, 'did you get over the night in Portrush?'

'To tell you the truth', answered Oliver, 'I don't remember much about it, I was hoping you could fill in some of the blank spaces for me'.

Mary patted her hand gently on Oliver's knee and said,

'Not much to fill in really, you drank too much and passed out'.

'I don't remember drinking a lot', said Oliver, 'I do remember drinking one or two pints, but that's that'.

'Add another ten double whiskies and you might have got your sums right', replied Mary.

'And how did I end up in the bedroom?' asked Oliver.

'I had to get a couple of men to help me up the stairs with you, and when I got you to lie down on the bed you were raving like a mad man', answered Mary.

Oliver began to blush as he thought back to the night in question and how he must have looked like an idiot alcoholic. Oliver thought it would be wise to turn the subject away from the drunken night, so asked Mary,

'How did you know where I lived?'

'You told me in the bar in Portrush, do you not even remember that?' replied Mary.

'No I don't', answered Oliver, unhappy with the conversation turning back to the terrible night.

'You told me a lot of things', said Mary, at the same time reaching over to hold Oliver's hand. Oliver was happy Mary was now holding his hand, and took comfort from the fact that he must not have incriminated himself too much; otherwise Mary would not be sitting beside him now. He knew Mary was a decent girl, and any mention of what John, Michael and himself did would have either sent her running or allowed her to call the police. Nice and wonderful innocent Mary, he thought. Butter would probably stay hard in her mouth and he wanted it to stay that way. Suddenly Mary interrupted Oliver's thoughts by saying,

'When are we going to get it?'

'Get what?', replied Oliver while he still contently held Mary's innocent hand.

'Get the money from the bank job', answered Mary. Oliver's heart stopped beating, his brain suddenly froze and his arms and legs refused to take any more responsibility for his body. He tried to throw a glimmer of light into the situation, to revive himself from the terrible revelation that had just passed from the lips of Mary. He knew he must react quickly and reply to her allegation with a denial that even the very heavens would not question. Or he could decide to get up and run, leaving Mary to keep whatever else he told her to herself. But Oliver knew he couldn't run, he knew he had to take whatever punches were coming and gather the strength to reply back with his own.

'Why are you so quiet?' asked Mary.

'Well I'm in shock', replied Oliver, 'who wouldn't be when they just heard the person they were holding hands with, admitting to robbing a bank'.

'Come off it', replied Mary as she looked around to make sure no one was near enough to listen, 'You told me everything, and how you hid the money until the smoke cleared away'.

Oliver had now recovered and reviled himself inwardly for being so stupid. He knew Mary was telling the truth, because how else would she have known if he hadn't have blown it out through the breath of whiskey.

'So if I told you everything then', asked Oliver, 'why didn't you go to the cops?'

Mary quickly rose to her feet and angrily threw Oliver a barrage of words,

'Who do you take me for, we made promises and discussed our dreams together. Do you remember promising you would buy me a farm in America and we would breed horses, or are you pretending to forget that also? '

Oliver arose from the park seat and beckoned Mary to sit down again,

'I'm sorry Mary, but I was so blocked out of my mind that night, I can't remember a thing', he said.

'One thing I do remember', said Oliver, 'is you are here with me now, and for all my highwayman revelations, you still wanted to see me'.

Oliver reached out with both his arms and pulled Mary to him in an embrace, as she rested her head on his shoulder Oliver whispered in her ear,

'Ok sweetheart, you have me'.

When Oliver left the park with plans to meet Mary the next day, he sensed that a great weight had been lifted off his shoulders. Since John and Michael's deaths he felt that he had been left on his own to carry a heavy burden. Mary knew everything, and to his surprise, she was ready to become a willing accomplice. John had once warned him about drinking too much,

'One drink and your smiling at the cops, two and the cops are laughing', he would say.

Oliver vowed he would never allow the drink to loosen his tongue again. Never again would he be reckless with his own freedom or anyone else, and with his hand on his heart he swore discipline to both body and mind.

'Excuse me Sir', said a red haired man, catching Oliver by surprise.

'Yes', replied Oliver.

'Irish Republican Army', said the man, 'get into the back seat, someone wants to see you'.

Oliver noticed that the man had a revolver pointed in his direction, and with the sense not to argue, he climbed into the back seat of the yellow Ford Cortina. As Oliver tried to come to terms with the situation that he now found himself in, the red haired man pushed his way in beside him and closed the door. Oliver noticed that there was a man and a woman in the front seat, staring straight ahead, calmly watching the people and traffic going lazily by. At this moment he knew if a blood pressure test was to be taken, he would be rushed to hospital immediately. He could not gather even a shred of reason why he had been forced to be in the company of dangerous people, he had done nothing wrong to upset these people. Just as Oliver thought the silence would honour him with a massive heart attack, the man in the front seat with curly black hair turned around and spoke,

'How are you Oliver? I see you have lost your two mates'.

'You mean John and Michael?' asked Oliver.

'The very two', replied the curly haired man, 'shot down like dogs by the good old murdering bastard cops'.

'I don't know much about the details', said Oliver, trying to keep the fear from his voice.

'Well the details are', replied the curly haired man,

'the cops are on a shoot to kill policy, anyone they think is a republican or a supporter of republicans, is a legitimate target'.

'John and Michael were neither', said Oliver, 'they were just a couple of guys from another country who didn't understand nor wanted to understand politics'.

'That may be so', answered Curly, 'but the long and the short of it is they are dead, and they cops did it deliberately'.

'What do you mean deliberately?' asked Oliver.

'We have information that a certain inspector by the name of Norman Brown, ordered the shootings', replied Curly.

'But why?' asked Oliver, as the fear began to slowly turn to anger.

'We don't know why', replied Curly, 'but one thing we do know, if their friend had any balls in him, he would want revenge on Mr. Brown'.

Oliver's mind began racing, he knew he was sitting among The IRA and from what he had heard, their intelligence was very good. One thing that Oliver did know for sure, he wanted revenge for his friends' deaths, but whether he could shoot someone was another matter entirely.

'I would love to see that bastard six foot under, but what can I do?' asked Oliver.

'That's where we can help', answered Curly, 'we will follow him, find out his patterns and when we discover an opportunity, you can strike'.

'What do I strike him with?' asked Oliver.

'When the time is right, we will supply you with a booby-trap bomb fitted with a mercury tilt switch', replied Curly, 'all you have to do is attach it under his car and pop goes the weasel'.

Oliver tossed and turned in his mind the idea of shooting him, but now a more cowardly method had arrived to allow his testicles to crawl in a dignified manner out of their hiding place. The plan that Curly was proposing was frightening, but acquired no more courage than robbing a bank.

'Ok', said Oliver, 'I'll do it'.

'Excellent', replied Curly, who now began to reveal two neat rows of unwashed teeth, 'we'll let you know a day before the operation'.

'Do you need my address?' asked Oliver.

Oliver's question was greeted by the three occupants bursting out in laughter.

'It's ok', laughed Curly as he nodded to ginger to open the car door, 'we know everyone's address'.

Oliver was truly thankful that he was no longer in the car enduring the presence of Curly. His anger had got the best of him and he now began to regret the arrangement he had made with The IRA. He knew there was no other course of action but revenge, but a little longer to make up his mind would have been preferred. And as he made his way through the back gate of his house, he decided that a fishing rod and a few sandwiches might be a remedy to digest his hasty decision. It had been over a year since he went fishing, and the peaceful flow of the Curdian River had always ironed out any creases in his thoughts.

'Hello Mum', said Oliver, 'any chance of a few sandwiches, I think I'll go see If I can catch any of those brown trout everyone's raving about'.

'If it's the Curdian your going to, you won't catch anything there, Mrs Stone's husband was there all last week and the only thing he caught was a dose of ringworm climbing over that old iron gate'.

Oliver laughed at the thought of Mr. Stone's itchy rash and remembered when he used to swear blind that cat food was the only bate to use.

'I don't need to climb the gate', said Oliver, 'there's a gap only a few yards down from it'.

As his mother proceeded to prepare the sandwiches, Oliver gathered up whatever hooks and sinkers he had and threw them into the black cloth bag along with his reel. He thanked his mother for the sandwiches, said goodbye and made his way to the car.

The few miles that took Oliver to the Curdian River were free from any checkpoints, and slow moving tractors. Oliver pulled up on the grass beside the stone humpback bridge, and surveyed the scenery before him. Aside from the few ruined remnants of what once were houses, Oliver viewed the green fields peppered here and there with cows and the occasional goat. No human form could be seen as Oliver exited from the car with his black cloth bag, and made his way to the boot to retrieve the long waiting fishing rod. Oliver had put the fishing rod in the boot two weeks ago, but circumstances had barred its use until now. He made his way over the bridge, past the ringworm gate and through the gap between a hawthorn tree and a large black stone. As he settled down to arm the fishing rod with hook, line and sinker, it was not long before Oliver realised that in his hurry to get away, he had forgotten to dig a few worms up from the back garden. He smiled to himself when he began to think that even cat food would be better than nothing. Oliver decided that the missing bate would not deter him from relaxing, and he remembered how an old man taught him once to cast the line as far as possible, and reel it in. Some claim to have caught trout and eels this way, Oliver decided he would give it a try, but during the process he was not going to hold his breath. Oliver hungrily devoured his first sandwich before casting the line across the river, then slowly pulling the line back with the help of the reel. Another sandwich was quickly disposed off, while Oliver repeated the process of throwing the line out and pulling it in again. As Oliver pulled the line back for the third time he could feel a slight tug, and noticed as the hook got closer that something was dangling from the end. Oliver removed the object which was covered in green slime, and began to clean it with a well used handkerchief he had in his pocket. To Oliver's surprise, a gold ring began to slowly appear, and as he scrubbed further, a clear diamond revealed itself to Oliver's astonishment.

Oliver did not wait to see if the technique that had caught him a diamond ring, would work on the brown trout or eels. He quickly packed his gear, made his way back to the car and gunned the engine to take him home faster than he had arrived. His mind was racing as he thought about the ring and how it had got there in the first place. He knew who's ring it was and all that was needed to confirm his suspicions was his mother.

As Oliver pulled in beside his house, he locked the car door and hurried through the back door and into the kitchen. Oliver's mother looked up from reading a newspaper and said,

'Back so early son, I guess you're going to tell me about the one that got away'.

Oliver sat down on a chair opposite and replied,

'Nope, but I did catch a big one'.

Oliver's mother looked at him, her eyes searching the

table and his presence for any sigh of a fish,

'Then where is it?' she asked.

'Right here', replied Oliver as he placed the gold ring on the table before his mother.

Oliver's mother's eyes opened wide as she reached with her hand to examine closely the beautiful object. Oliver displayed a wide grin as he asked,

'Are you thinking what I'm thinking?'

His mother suddenly returned the ring to the table and said,

'You're too young to get engaged son'.

Oliver laughed and replied,

'No mother, it's not what you think. I was fishing in the Curdian River without worms and this is what the hook picked up'.

'Oh my God', answered Oliver's mother in disbelief.

'Is the story true?', asked Oliver.

'Yes son', replied Oliver's mother.

'Then what we have here is Robert and Winifred's engagement ring', said Oliver.

'What you have ', answered Oliver's mother, 'is a remnant of a terrible heartache'.

Oliver thought about what his mother had just said, and remembered the story she told him. He could not think why the ring had attached itself to his hook and not a thousand others. Perhaps it was just fate and his hook was the one, or maybe he had found it for a reason.

'Where is Winifred now?' asked Oliver.

'It's funny you mentioned that', answered Oliver's mother, 'I was talking to a lady outside the butcher's last week and she told me Winifred's back home and working in Magherafelt Hospital'.

'What's she doing in the hospital?' asked Oliver.

'Apparently', replied Oliver's mother, 'she trained to be a nurse in England'.

Oliver began to study the ring sitting on the kitchen table and wondered if he should call to the hospital and give it back. Whether she would accept it back, Oliver was unsure, but he knew it wasn't his and if he give it to Robert it would be pissed against the wall before the night was out.

'Ok mum', said Oliver as he stood up and placed the ring back in his pocket, 'I'm going up to the hospital to give this back to Winifred'.

'Do you know her surname?' asked Oliver's mother.

'No', replied Oliver as he made his way out through the door and the direction of his car.

'It's Bateson', shouted Oliver's mother as she watched her son nod and get into the car.

It took only a few minutes for Oliver to arrive at Magherafelt hospital, and a few minutes more to find a suitable parking space. On locking the car he made his way through the main entrance and straight across to the enquiry desk.

'Excuse me', said Oliver politely, 'could I speak to Winifred Bateson please?'

'Just wait a minute and I'll see if she's available', replied an ashen face man.

The man talked to someone on the phone and on putting the handset down he turned to Oliver and said,

'Take a chair in the Chaplin's room and she'll be down shortly'.

Oliver thanked the man and proceeded to walk the few yards down the long clean corridor that would lead him to the room of a million tears. As he entered the Chaplin's room and closed the door gently behind him he could feel an air of sadness throughout the room. He sat down on a chair beside the window and began to imagine the terrible news that families would have heard in this room. In this room, Oliver reminded himself, all hope of a patient's recovery was shattered by its very presence alone. Oliver's thoughts were quickly interrupted by a small blond haired nurse entering the room. She smiled at Oliver and sat down on the next chair beside him.

'Hello, someone told me you wanted to see me', said Winifred.

Oliver hurriedly surveyed the nurse beside him and came to a conclusion that years may have punished her, but a ray of beauty still remained.

'My name is Oliver, we have never met before but I just came to return something which I believe belongs to you', answered Oliver as he took the ring out of his denim jacket pocket and handed it to Winifred.

Winifred smiled at the object for a short time, but Oliver soon realised that tears were flowing down her cheeks. He remained silent, waiting for Winifred to ask questions, or turn the conversation in some way that he would know how to reply. Winifred stood up from her chair and walked slowly across the room. She stopped to stare at a poster which read, THERE IS ALWAYS LIGHT AT THE END OF THE TUNNEL, and without looking at Oliver she said,

'How did you find it?'

'I went fishing one day and forgot the worms, so I dragged the empty hook across the water in the hope that something would get snagged', he replied.

'I threw that ring into the river almost twenty years ago, didn't think I would ever see it again', said Winifred, as she made her way back to the chair and sat down next to Oliver again.

'Strange things happen', replied Oliver.

'My grandmother used to tell me strange things happen for a reason, although I can't think of any reason why this ring would turn up again', said Winifred.

'Have you seen him since you came back?' asked Oliver.

Winifred produced a handkerchief from the sleeve of her nurse's uniform and dried the remaining tears from her eyes.

'I thought I saw someone who looked like him lying on a park bench, but didn't stop to find out', replied Winifred.

Oliver knew that the person Winifred saw on the park bench was most likely Robert. He couldn't even consider telling Winifred of Robert's plight, as he knew this would most likely add to the heavy burden that her heart was now carrying. But something was pulling his own heart strings, and for reasons that he couldn't yet understand, he knew that he had a part to play in these two people's lives.

'Is it true what they say?' asked Oliver. 'You mean about Robert being cheated at cards?' answered Winifred.

'Yes', said Oliver.

'That part is true', replied Winifred, 'but what was untrue was Robert's commitment to us, because if he had been truthful, he would not have been gambling in the first place'.

'Do you still love him?' asked Oliver boldly.

'I will always love him', answered Winifred, 'there is not a single hour of any day that goes by, that I don't think of him'.

'Will you do me a favour?' asked Oliver, 'Will you

hold tight to that ring and agree to meet me again'.
Winifred looked at the ring, smiled and replied,

'Why? Are you going to invent some time machine
to go back and fix what was broken?'

'Just promise me you will keep the ring until at least
we meet again', pleaded Oliver.

'Ok', replied Winifred, 'you will get me here most
week days, just ask at the desk'.

When Oliver departed from his visit with Winifred,
he left with a firm commitment to himself, and
unbeknown to Winifred, her also. When he saw the
tears running down Winifred's face, he knew he had to
try in some way to seek justice for a terrible dirty deed.
The rain had now started to descend and before Oliver
reached his car, a thin streak of lightening flashed a
warning before a loud roar of thunder. As the car
pushed its way through the heavy rain and towards
home, Oliver did not notice how hard the wipers had
to work to open a path of sight. He did not notice the
cars and Lorries driving slowly with full headlights on,
or the middle-aged lady chasing her umbrella through
someone's garden. Oliver did not see the flashing
lights or hear the siren of the ambulance overtaking
him. The only thing that Oliver paid attention to on
that wet summer evening was the mirror above his
head, and John smiling at him from the back seat.

CHAPTER 13

The heavy rain that fell violently from the heavens the day before, had now dried sufficiently enough to afford some dry spots on the footpath. Oliver had arranged to meet Mary in Danny's Lounge at 2.00pm, and apart from the painful memories he had of the drinking times with John and Michael, he was looking forward to the meeting. Oliver was once again worried about his mental state, as the day before he saw, or what he thought he saw, was John smiling at him from the back seat of his car. Oliver knew that to think too deep about why he was experiencing the voices and hallucinations of John, would allow him few nights sleep. He knew it was best to brush them aside in the hope that they would subside in their own time. What he must focus on was the living and staying alive to enjoy the plans that he was putting together for himself and hopefully Mary.

As Oliver entered through the door of Danny's Lounge, he spied Mary, solitary in her beauty and sitting at a lonely table near the Jukebox. As he approached the table where Mary was lost in her own thoughts, he whispered in her ear,

'A penny for them?'

Mary looked up and smiled before she replied,

'My thoughts wouldn't be worth a penny'.

'If any of those thoughts are about me, then they sure as hell are not worth half a penny', replied Oliver as he sat next to Mary.

'Well', said Mary as she gently put her hand on Oliver's arm, 'if things work out for us, then those thoughts will be priceless'.

'I'll get you a drink', said Oliver as he rose from the chair, 'and no if's, things are going to fall neatly into place for us'.

Oliver moved away from the table and approached the bar, first ordering a glass of white wine for Mary, then a pint for himself. As there were few customers in the bar, the barman fulfilled the order quickly and Oliver returned to the table.

'I forgot to ask you what you wanted', said Oliver apologetically, 'so I took a guess for the fun of it'.

'What is it?' asked Mary.

'White wine', answered Oliver as he took a sip of his beer.

'Thank you', said Mary, 'you're a great mind reader'.

'Speaking of mind reading', asked Oliver, 'you had a worried expression on your face when I walked in, with all joke on the side, is anything bothering you?'

Mary put the glass of wine to her lips and returned it to the table without taking any and replied,

'Oliver, we are going to be together, and hopefully for the rest of our lives, so please don't make this more difficult than it is now'.

'Go ahead spit it out', replied Oliver, 'I promise whatever it is I won't scream at you'.

'Ok', answered Mary as she turned awkwardly towards Oliver, 'I need some money'.

'That's fine', replied Oliver as he took another deep drink of his beer.

'It's just a few hundred', said Mary acting embarrassed, 'I'm behind with the rent and its due tomorrow and its worrying me'.

'Don't worry love', answered Oliver, 'It's no problem, but I will have to go and fish it out'.

'Could you have it for tomorrow?' asked Mary in a tone of desperation.

'I can have it for you today', answered Oliver, 'just need to fetch the car and go for a little drive'.

'Can I go with you?' asked Mary, 'you said you would bring me when you go fetch it'.

Oliver emptied the remaining drops of beer into his mouth and placed the empty glass on the table.

'That's fine baby', replied Oliver as he rose from his seat, 'wait here and I'll go get the car, I'll blow the horn twice outside the door'.

Oliver made his way through the door and back out onto the street. Apart from the old couple walking on the other side, the street was empty. Oliver was taking by surprise by Mary's request for money, although he tried hard not to show it, for a brief moment he began to think that Mary might me using him for financial gains. That brief moment quickly passed when Oliver thought of their future together, and how everything he had would be given to her lovingly. As Oliver turned the corner at the bottom of the street, his thoughts were suddenly interrupted by the voice of Robert,

'Could you spare some change for a wee bite to eat son?'

Oliver looked at the person of Robert before him, and his heart sank at how a once proud man could so easily have been defeated by the shrapnel of life. His long black greasy hair fell neglected down the back of a grey thread-bare coat. His battered and dirt saturated jeans revealed the bare unwashed knees, and his black boots bore all the hallmarks of footwear who's walking days were well and truly over.

'How are you Robert?' asked Oliver politely.

'Not too well son', he replied, 'I haven't eaten a bite these last three days and I'm almost ready for the knackers yard'.

Oliver reached into his pocket and took a five pound note out,

'Here Robert, but before I give it to you I want you to promise that it will not be used for a bottle of cider', he said.

'Jee son you drive a hard bargain', replied Robert.

'I want you to go buy yourself a feed and meet me in Danny's Lounge at six this evening', said Oliver.

Robert threw Oliver a bewildered look and asked,

'Why, ah what's going on?'

'All I can say for now is, there is a barman in Draperstown who has ripped off a friend of mine, and I intend to get justice' replied Oliver.

Oliver could see the anger appear in Robert's eyes, as recognition of who he was talking about sprang to life.

'I know the bastard', said Robert.

Oliver handed the fiver to Robert and said,

'I'll see you at six, don't let me down'.

'I won't', answered Robert, 'you can bet your life on it'.

As Oliver pulled up outside Danny's Lounge, he pressed the horn twice and waited for Mary to exit the bar. A lot of thoughts were rushing through his mind, and he knew that the only way to deal with them was in sequence. His mother used to say to him,

'Never fill the kettle to high or it will boil over' and Oliver knew that in this particular moment in his life, an overflow was the last thing he needed.

'You made it', said Mary humorously as she climbed in beside Oliver in the car.

'I almost forgot about you', replied Oliver as he moved away from the kerb and down the main street towards the open country road.

'I'm really embarrassed about this', said Mary, turning her head to look out through the side window of the car.

Oliver reached over and playfully squeezed her knee,

'Don't be, if I needed a few quid, I wouldn't be embarrassed to ask you', he replied.

The truth is, thought Oliver, he would be embarrassed, and he knew it would have to be a life or death situation before he could acquire the nerve to do it. He never asked anyone for money in his life, accept from his mother, and even then he found it difficult to do so. As Oliver turned left onto a narrow road, he noticed Mary enjoying the view of the mountains before them, and took the opportunity to bring up the subject of America,

'When we go to the States, I'll take you to see the Ozarks', he said.

'What's the Ozarks?' asked Mary as she turned her face towards Oliver.

'It's mountains and forests full of little brown bears and giant rat-like creatures', replied Oliver, 'a friend used to live there, and he told me if you take away the poverty and unemployment, it would be the most beautiful place on earth'.

Mary turned away from Oliver again and proceeded to

stare at the countryside around her. Oliver was aware that she looked lost and in addition lacked any sparkle in her conversation. He put this down to her financial embarrassment, and was happy to wait until that part of their life together could be reconciled.

'We have arrived', said Oliver, as he turned into the wild overgrown yard of an old derelict farmhouse.
As he switched off the engine and exited from the car, Oliver looked around for any changes or signs of activity since he was last there. Apart from a few signs of cow claps, Oliver reassured himself that no one had been there. With Mary on tow, he pushed the green door inwards and entered the dark musty room of the farmhouse. As soon as Mary walked through the door behind him, Oliver turned on the torchlight he had in his pocket and closed the door. The contents of the room consisted of one battered, moth hole riddled armchair and a small table beside it. On the wall opposite the table, an old cast iron fireplace stood death-like, no longer needed to warm the body and soul of life on cold winter's nights. Oliver walked over to the fireplace and knelt down before it; he reached his hand up the chimney and pulled down a black plastic bag. Asking Mary to hold the torch, he put his hand into the bag and removed two bundles of twenty pound notes. Oliver handed one bundle to Mary, and stuffed the other into his coat pocket, and returned the bag to its soot stained hiding place in the chimney that would never smoke again.

'That's that', said Oliver as both Mary and himself made their way back to the car and proceeded on their way back in the direction of Magherafelt.

'I like your hiding place', said Mary interrupting the silence.

'Thank you', replied Oliver, 'it's the most obvious place to hide money'.

Mary laughed and could not resist the urge to reach over and kiss Oliver in the side of his cheek.

'What's that for', asked Oliver, showing a wide grin of semi neglected teeth.

'For being so naïve and innocent', replied Mary.

'Well it's like this', answered Oliver, 'If I was a policeman and I was looking for the proceeds of a bank robbery, I would say to myself, 'don't look up the chimney, only an idiot would do something so stupid, and the person who planned and executed this robbery is no fucking idiot'.

Mary laughed again, and Oliver was happy to see her in such high spirits. He knew she would come around to things and how they are, and now the situation of asking for money had turned from humility to amusement.

'Would you like to meet up later on?' asked Oliver, as he abided to the thirty mile speed limed approaching the town.

'I'm working tonight', replied Mary apologetically, 'but I would love to see you tomorrow, maybe go for a drive somewhere'.

'That would be great', answered Oliver, trying to keep the disappointment from his voice.

He was looking forward to spending more time with Mary, and had half expected to be with her into the wee small hours.

'Where would you like dropped off at?' asked Oliver.

'Here's fine', replied Mary, pointing to the phone box at the corner.

As Oliver pulled up at the side of the kerb, Mary reached across the gear stick and gently kissed him on the lips,

'Thanks for everything, will meet you here at one tomorrow', she said as she departed the car and closed the door behind her.

Oliver took off and blew the horn once, in recognition of Mary's hand waving as she made her way down the street. As he made his way up to the roundabout, he suddenly remembered his meeting with Robert at six. Oliver turned around the roundabout and back down the way he came, deciding it would be safer to leave the Capri at his house and walk up to Danny's Lounge. As he took a right turn, he noticed Mary's figure occupying the red phone box at the corner, and wondered what changed her mind when she was walking in the opposite direction. Oliver decided he would get a chance of another goodbye kiss by surprising her, so he quickly parked the car and headed off to surprise Mary on his way to rendezvous with Robert.

When Oliver reached the phone box there was no sign of Mary. He sighed at the thought of missing her, so carried on his way to Danny's Lounge.

On entering the bar he spied Robert at a table a short distance from the entrance, so he proceeded to the table and said

'Hello Robert, thanks for coming, would you like a drink?'

'Does a dog shit in the park', replied Robert.

'What are you having?' asked Oliver as he looked towards the bar.

'A pint of anything son', replied Robert.

Oliver arrived at the counter and within a few minutes arrived with two cold pints of beer. As he placed the two pints on the table and sat down, Oliver noticed that Robert had removed most of the contents of his glass before Oliver could get a sip. As soon as Robert surfaced from his beer plunge, Oliver spoke,

'I have asked you to meet me hear Robert because I think I can help you'.

'You mentioned a barman in Draperstown?', asked Robert.

'Yes', replied Oliver as he took another sip of his beer, 'can you tell me anything about him?'

'Well for one', answered Robert, 'he is a thieving bastard of the worst kind'.

'In what way?' asked Oliver.

Robert looked into Oliver's eyes and the expression on his face was one of loathing for the barman,

'He ruins lives, fills them with drink till its running out of their ears then he sucks the life's blood clean out of them', he said.

'Do you know anyone he hurt?' asked Oliver.

Robert reached for his half full glass and then pulled his hand back as if he had discovered that someone had just deposited a mouthful of spit into it,

'Me and someone I once knew', he answered with a shake of emotion in his voice.

Oliver took a drink of his beer and then said,

'When I said I can help you, I meant it, but I need your help too'.

'What do you have in mind?' asked Robert.

'The first thing is to devise a plan, I have a few things in mind but none definite', replied Oliver.

'Why don't we shoot the bastard?' said Robert, still not reaching for his pint.

'Because that would be too kind', answered Oliver, 'what we need is proof of something, everyone has a skeleton in the wardrobe'.

'I bet that scumbag has several wardrobes bursting with them', said Robert.

'No doubt', answered Oliver, 'but we need to see what's inside them'.

Robert made once more to reach for the beer and once more he pulled his hand away,

'You're a smart kid, how old are you?' he asked.

'Seventeen', replied Oliver.

'I was a smart kid at seventeen', said Robert, 'but now all the drink has killed my brain cells'.

'I don't think they are dead', replied Oliver, 'I believe they are only sleeping and it's time to wake them up'. When Oliver finished his sentence he arose from his chair and said,

'I think we both need a breath of fresh air, this place stinks of piss'.

Robert left his chair and followed Oliver through the door and out onto the street. An old Vauxhall car drove past minus an exhaust silencer as Oliver led Robert across the street and sat down on the summer seat outside the library. Reaching into his pocket Oliver produced a bundle of twenty pound notes and handed them to Robert,

'Here's some investigating funds, you'll need it to oil a few tongues', he said. Robert looked at Oliver and smiled,

'You're not surely going to trust me with that, how do you know that the only thing getting oiled is me?' asked Robert.

Oliver stood up and replied,

'I trust you because you left half a pint of beer sitting in the bar; will see you tomorrow night at the same time'.

Oliver patted Robert on the shoulder and proceeded

to make his way on the short familiar journey home.

When Oliver returned home he greeted his mother and decided he needed to have an early night. A lot had been going through his mind these last few days, including his meetings with both Robert and Winifred. Oliver knew he would never remain in Northern Ireland, but before he left he was determent to see justice done to the barman who destroyed a young couple's life. He was angry at all the people who looked and treated Robert like something out of the gutter, without first trying to understand how he arrived at his situation in the first place. As Oliver removed his clothes and boots and smothered himself between the cool clean sheets of his bed, he wondered what dirt Robert would find on the barman before their meeting tomorrow night. His thoughts were soon interrupted by his own breathing guiding him down the path of dreams.

'Can you see it?' asked John, as he pointed his finger in the direction of The Glen Shane Mountains.

'See what?' asked Oliver as he strained his eyes to see across the green fields before him.

'It's bloody obvious, you really need to get your eyes tested', said John in an irritated voice. Oliver strained his eyes even harder and all that came to view was a beautiful carpet of heather flowing down to lush green fields.

'If I knew what I was looking for it might be a hell of a lot easier', replied Oliver.
John stood up from the large grey stone he had been sitting on and turned to Oliver in anger,

'What to fuck is wrong with you kiddo, I'm trying to figure out if you are an idiot, blind as a fucking bat, or both', he roared.

'Stop shouting at me, can't you see I'm trying to sleep', answered Oliver.

'Trying to sleep my ass', said John, 'if I was lying dead in my grave, I could still see it'.

'The last I heard, you were lying in your grave', replied Oliver.

'There we go then', said John in a somewhat triumphant voice, 'point proven, I am dead in my grave and I can still see the fucking thing'.

Oliver tried again to spy what John was trying to show him but still to no avail.

'Maybe you can see it because you are dead', answered Oliver.

'Stop making excuses, dead people have poorer eyesight than the living', said John.

'Why don't you tell me what it is you want me to see', replied Oliver, 'then it might be easier'.

'How in the name of fuck am I supposed to tell you what it is when I'm dead', said John as he sat himself back down on the stone. Oliver looked straight ahead, up and down and side to side, and all he could see was the unspoiled green, yellow and brown of nature.

'I'll have to give in', answered Oliver, 'I throw my hands in the air because whatever it is you want me to see probably isn't there in the first place'.

'Trust me', said John, 'it's there before your fucking eyes'.

'You just admitted your dead and therefore if you no longer exist as a living human being, then what you want me to see doesn't exist either, replied Oliver.

John jumped up again from his stone seat and shouted,

'Are you calling me a fucking liar?'

'Not a liar in the mortal sense of the word', replied Oliver defensively, 'as we are both living in two different levels of consciousness, than what you see is different from what I see'.

'Well done kiddo', said John, 'you always have a fucking answer for everything'.

'I try my best', replied Oliver as he smiled in the direction of John.

John smiled back and said,

'Then all we need to do to solve our problem is that you come onto my side of the consciousness'.

'I wouldn't dare', replied Oliver.

'Why not?' asked John.

'Well in order for me to do that, I'd have to kill myself', replied Oliver, 'and I'm not about to do that, I'm too tired'.

'I suppose that is as good an excuse as any', said John, 'but think about it when you get rested'.

'Will do', answered Oliver as he stood up to take his leave from John, 'well you could at least give me a hint of what it was you wanted me to see?'

'Ok kiddo', said John, 'what's that red thing straight in front of you?'

Oliver looked across were john was pointing and saw a bright red phone box before his eyes.

'Now why in hell did I not see that', said Oliver as he stared dumbfounded.

'Maybe it's because you were scared of what you might find inside it', replied John.

Oliver turned to John in confusion and asked,

'What could I possibly find inside a phone box that would scare me?'

'Why don't you ask Mary, and while you're at it why don't you ask her why she fancies scruffy seventeen year old losers', replied John.

CHAPTER 14

When Oliver awoke the next day, the dream he had about John did not upset him as much as he thought it would. He had quickly learned that the dreams made no sense most of the time, therefore he could only attach it to his mixed up state of mind. He had decided that the voices he was hearing of John could best be described as worrying, and a trip to Matty might allow him some answers. Matty was an old woman who lived in a rural part of Mayogall and many people near and far had trusted in her ability to cure both illnesses of the mind and body. Oliver remembered when he was younger his mother brought him to see if she could banish the Old Hag from trying to suffocate him in his sleep. At nine years old Oliver was terrified of The Old Hag, and whenever she tried to smother him in his sleep, he prayed to St Michael the archangel to help him. Low and behold after several minutes of frantic praying, The Old Hag would disappear off into the night. It was only after reading a book during his last year at school that Oliver discovered that others called it sleep paralysis. However, whatever anyone wanted to call it, after having a chat with Matty he never had another episode.

When Oliver finished dressing he made his way downstairs only to find he was the only one left in the house. A note from his Mother read GONE TO COOKSTOWN MARKET. Oliver decided not to disturb the neatness of the kitchen, so put on his denim jacket and made his way to the car. On turning the key Oliver was surprised it started first time, as he had been having some trouble with it these past few days. He quickly made his way onto the main street and with no traffic coming in either direction; he turned right and proceeded on his way to Mayogall. After some minutes Oliver turned right again onto a narrow road and into a police checkpoint. In front of Oliver there was an old beaten tractor, and behind him a bread van. Oliver knew about the stories of the treatment at police checkpoints, especially to young Catholic men and he was glad that there were enough witnesses around. The policeman allowed the tractor to move on and then signalled with his hand for Oliver's Capri to move forward.

'Can I see your driving licence', asked the policeman as Oliver rolled his window down.

Oliver proceeded to search his pockets and around the interior of the car for his nonexistent driving licence.

'Sorry I haven't got it on me', said Oliver apologetically.

'You don't look old enough to have a driving licence, when did you pass your test?' asked the policeman.

'About fourteen months ago, and I'm nineteen', answered Oliver.

'Ok, what's the name and where are you going too?' asked the policeman.

'Oliver McKenna and I'm going to see my granny

who's sick', replied Oliver trying to keep his voice from faltering.

The policeman stared at Oliver, then looked behind at the line of traffic that had now gathered up and said,

'Ok you can go, but make sure you carry your licence with you in future'.

'Will do', answered Oliver as he rolled up the window and moved off towards his destination. Oliver was relieved he talked his way out of his predicament in relation to the police checkpoint. He was used to checkpoints being set around every bend, but most were army checkpoints and you could usually get away with showing any form of ID. Oliver soon put the incident aside in his mind and began enjoying the countryside around him, and the occasional smell of burning peat.

When Oliver pulled up outside Matty's house, he could smell the aroma of freshly baked bread coming from the half open door of her one bedroom thatched cottage. He leisurely exited from his car and walked across to the door and gently knocked three times.

'Come in Oliver', said a female voice from inside the cottage.

Oliver opened the bottom half of the door and accepted the invitation to sit down by the fire.

'How are you Oliver, how's everyone at home?' asked Matty.

'Everyone at home are fine', replied Oliver, 'how did you know my name?'

'I know everyone's name', replied Matty, 'and you were here before when you were nine years old'.

'You have a good memory', said Oliver.

'I wouldn't say memory', answered Matty, 'but my cat never forgets a face'.

Oliver looked over at the large white cat perched at the window and decided in the best interests of politeness, he would not question the cat's abilities.

'So Oliver', said Matty as she hurried to the kettle. 'While I'm making a cup of tea for us, you can tell me all about the voices you are hearing'.

Oliver stuttered as he tried to find a reply to Matty, and how she knew so much before he even opened his mouth.

'Don't worry son', said Matty, 'you don't have to question my knowing, just accept the fact that I do and that in itself will make things much easier for both of us'.

Oliver cleared his throat and said,

'Well it's like this, I keep hearing my dead friend John's voice and I'm beginning to think that I'm going mad'.

'Never fear madness', replied Matty as she went through the motions of chasing something unseen out the door, 'those damn fairies can never mind their own business, as I was saying about madness, madness is only a label attached to the truth'.

Matty handed Oliver an old crockery mug of tea and sat down opposite him by the fire.

'The truth?' asked Oliver, somewhat confused.

'Yes the truth', replied Matty as she took a sip of her tea and sat the mug on top of the small table before her, 'a majority of people are living a lie, for example when you got stopped by the police on your way here, you lied about having a driving licence'.

'Ahhh Ohh', replied Oliver as he tried to question her precise knowledge.

'No don't question my knowing, just listen', said Matty.

'Ok', replied Oliver, 'you were talking about a lie'.

'Yes, a lie is who most of us are, and the truth or madness is hidden and only allowed to emerge when we think no one will know', said Matty, 'whenever the truth slips out accidentally we condemn it to the asylum of our own hidden consciences, and therefore brand it unbelievable because it doesn't correspond to the lie'.

Oliver took another sip of his tea and tried in some way to digest what Matty had just told him. She had already proved beyond doubt that she had powers beyond anyone he had ever known, so he had no reason to question the truth in her words.

'Voices from those who have left this mortal world are common', said Matty, 'more common than we care to admit'.

'So what you are saying', replied Oliver, 'that it is normal to hear voices from the dead'.

'Most of us hear voices in our head and we shrug it off as echoes from our memories', said Matty, 'but some people have got what those in my profession would call the 'whishh', a gift to touch someone from the other place, for good reasons or ill'.

Oliver paused from taking another sip of his tea and asked,

'What do you mean good reasons or ill?'

'The whisper could be trying to tell you something, like how much the love and miss you, or warn you of some danger that you are unaware of', replied Matty.

Oliver sat his tea cup down on the small table beside him and began to once more turn his thoughts over in his head. He could not foresee any reason why John would want to speak to him, other than to warn him of some future bank robbery that could go wrong.

Oliver's thoughts were quickly interrupted by Matty's voice,

'Listen Oliver', she said, 'don't do it, I think you know what I mean'.

Oliver turned and looked at Matty, trying to keep the look of guilt from appearing on his face. He could tell from the way her eyes pierced his that she knew everything, so he decided it would be easier to say nothing, than try to deny his past venture and future intentions.

'We are living in black times', said Matty, 'and until some light appears you must be on your guard at all times'.

'I know Matty', replied Oliver, 'all there seems to be is death and tears'.

'Guns and alcohol', said Matty, 'are the instigators of death and pain, those who use either one to destroy happiness should be damned for all eternity'.

Oliver turned to stare at the old black and white wedding photo hanging above the light switch by the door. Robert and Winifred began to enter his thoughts, causing the dark shadows of sadness to touch his heart. If he done only one good thing in his life, he knew that it would be revenge against the hand of greed who took away their laughter. Oliver stood up from his chair and thanked Matty for the tea and good advice. As he departed out the door to venture on his journey back to Magherafelt, Matty spoke,

'I hope you don't mind me eavesdropping on your thoughts Oliver', she said, 'here's a little nursery rhyme to cheer you up'.

Oliver reached and took the folded piece of paper Matty handed him, he smiled as he opened the page to read what Matty had written.

187

INSIDE A BARN OF A FIELD JUST MOWED,
THE HAND OF GREED WILL PAY WHAT'S
OWED,
FIND THIS PLACE BELOW THE ROCK,
AND GIVE TO HIM THE HARDEST KNOCK.

There was no sign of the checkpoint that Oliver had encountered earlier, as he made his way back to Magherafelt. His visit to Matty had been interesting to say the least, but what was fascinating most of all was the note she had passed to him before he left. Oliver was fully aware throughout his life of what constitutes a hard knock, but somehow this knock was going to be different. With no thought of his meeting with Mary, Oliver parked the car outside his house, and proceeded to walk the short distance to Danny's Lounge. On entering he found Robert sitting at a table facing the door, and signalled his intention of getting two pints of beer. To Oliver's surprise, Robert pointed to a glass of orange juice and nodded his head. Oliver approached the bar and on receiving and paying for his pint, he made his way to Robert's table and sat down beside him.

'How's things?' asked Oliver, placing his pint of beer on the table before him.

'Ok', replied Robert, 'to say the least'.

'Did you go on that little venture we discussed?' asked Oliver.

'I sure did', answered Robert before taking a sip of his orange juice, 'and what I came up with is baffling'.

'In what way baffling?' asked Oliver.

'Well I did like you said and courted and then oiled the tongues of a few locals, and all I could find out is, he leaves the house every day between six and half past, but no one knows where he goes too', replied

Robert.

'Interesting', said Oliver, 'I wonder what he finds so important about those times of day'.

'Hell only knows', replied Robert, 'But I would give my right testicle to find out'.

Oliver took a swig of his beer and began to think about the note Matty had given him earlier. Suddenly he stood up from the chair and said,

'You might not have to sacrifice your testicle, let's go on a journey'.

Oliver and Robert made their way down the narrow and twisted country roads that would eventually lead them to Draperstown. Oliver had only one clue so far to go on, and that was to head for the mountains overlooking the market town. As he turned to steal a quick glance at Robert beside him, he could tell by the way he held his stare straight ahead, that he had no idea what was happening. As they entered Draperstown from the Desertmartin road Oliver could see plainly a huge piece of rock leaning over to look down on the valley below it, almost in a threatening manner. He steered the car in that very direction and as they continued on their way, Robert cleared his throat before asking,

'Would you mind telling me where we are going?'

'I'm not quite sure yet', replied Oliver, 'but I have a feeling we are going in the right direction'.

As Oliver continued towards the overhanging rock, watching it get larger and larger before his eyes, something caught his eye. There, perched neatly under the rock and within a neatly mowed field, stood a solitary barn, almost as if it was taken out of an oil painting. Oliver pulled the car up on the nearest waste ground and turned the engine off. Turning to Robert while pointing at the barn, Oliver said,

'Inside that shed you are going to get your vengeance'.

Robert looked at Oliver with both eyes wide in bewilderment and asked,

'Is that where he hides all the money he steals from everyone?'

'I don't know', answered Oliver, 'but one thing is for sure, he's up to something and we are going to find out here and now'.

Oliver beckoned Robert to follow him out of the car, and on locking it they made their way quietly towards the barn.

'Keep below the hedge line until we get as close as possible', whispered Oliver as they moved towards their destination.

Oliver did not know what awaited them at the barn, but he trusted Matty fully and could only imagine what lay before them. Robert could be right, he thought, there might be a large stash of stolen money, or perhaps he was brewing his own gut rot whiskey. As Oliver approached the dust stained window and stole a look inside, it was sometime before Oliver could be brought back to his senses by a violent nudge from Robert.

'What to fuck is it?' asked Robert.

'Listen Robert', said Oliver, still trying to find his voice, 'take these keys and go back to the car, there is a Polaroid camera in a bag behind the driver seat, bring it here'.

Robert took the keys from Oliver's shaking hand and as fast and quietly as he could, he proceeded to carry out the requested errand. While Robert was away Oliver allowed himself a few quick breaths, as he began to come to terms with what he had just saw. He had always thought himself wise to the world, except around girls, but he never in his wildest nightmares could have imagined what he had just viewed through the pane of weather beaten glass. Matty had mentioned in the note about giving him a hard knock, but Oliver was unsure as to who would have been thumped the hardest, the man inside the barn, or he himself. As Robert quickly arrived with the camera, Oliver first returned to the previous view through the window and took two photos. He then beckoned Robert to follow him to the side door of the barn, which they discovered was locked from the inside.

'Ok Robert', whispered Oliver, 'I need you to throw every ounce of your weight and strength at that door as soon as you hear the word three'.

Robert nodded in recognition of what Oliver had just said, and gathered himself for the task ahead.

'Ok', whispered Oliver, 'Get ready, one, two, three'. As soon as Oliver spoke the word three, Robert charged the door with every muscle in his body. As the door flung violently open, Oliver hurriedly dashed through the battered but now open door and began to click several times on the camera button. The sight that met Robert's eyes was as shocking to him as it had been to Oliver. He still remembered the face from those years ago that tormented him, but now it looked shocked and embarrassed. Below Oliver and Robert's feet spread out naked on a bed of straw was the barman who cheated Robert, and his adulterous companion, a white nanny goat with one lonely black patch on its head.

The silence that followed was broken only by the barman struggling to put on his clothes, as he let out the occasional grunt. Oliver and Robert were still shaken by the encounter, and choose to allow the barman a morsel of dignity by letting him cover his bare flesh. When the barman had eventually stood fully clothed, Oliver decided that the ice would need to be broken.

'You have three choices to make here and now', he said, 'Number one, you can find enough rope inside this barn to hang yourself, two, you can try to brave the storm of these photos printed on every newspaper on the planet, or three, you can give back what you have stolen from this man, plus fifty grand for fucking his life up'.

'I prefer the first option', said Robert.
The barman began to contemplate the serious situation he was now in, and knew that option three was the only course open to him.

'Ok, ok,' he muttered, 'tell me what I took off you and I will arrange to give it back'.

'Remember the farm a young couple wanted to buy off you, but you swindled the man out of the money?' Said Oliver.

'I, err, ahh don't recall', muttered the barman.

'You don't remember because you swindled so many people you perverted, sick thieving bastard', shouted Robert in anger.

'Aaa, honest', muttered the barman, 'I don't remember'.

'Well let me remind you sicko', roared Robert, 'The cottage and thirty five acres at Slieve Way, fuck face'.

'Ahh ye, yes, I remember, but my son's getting married next week and his new wife and him are settling down there'.

'Change of fucking plan then, get it signed over to

me before the end of the week, or your son's wife to be will run a mile after we are finished', replied Robert.

'Plus the fifty grand before the weekend', said Oliver, as he put the photos neatly in his pocket.

'Arrange all the legal shit and meet me at the diamond on Thursday to sign', said Robert, as he followed Oliver out onto the newly mowed field and back to the car.

On their way back to Magherafelt, Oliver and Robert remained within their individual reflections for some time. Oliver had firmly accepted the fact that the world around him was much darker than he first thought, and any argument to the contrary would be quickly diluted by a greater evil. How much he had taken in from the scene in the hay barn, and how much he choose to take in were indeed in bitter conflict. He knew Robert would get what was asked for, but he also knew that something else needed to be returned and the story had not yet ended. Oliver's thoughts were interrupted by Robert speaking,

'Will you drive me out to the place on Friday?' he asked.

'No problem', replied Oliver.

'It is going to be a painful visit', said Robert with sadness in his voice, 'I don't want to do it on my own'.

'Just let me know what time' said Oliver in a sympathetic tone, 'and I'll be there to collect you'. As Oliver pulled up near the kerb to allow Robert to disembark, Robert turned to him with a forced smile and said,

'See you on Friday around noon beside the bank'.

'Will do', answered Oliver as he watched Robert close the car door and proceed on whatever destination he choose to take.

As Oliver made his way towards the hospital, he knew the Robert and Winifred story needed to be written to the end. He only hoped that Winifred was still there, and they would get some time to contemplate the changing fortunes of Robert. As he pulled into the car park at the front of the hospital, with good fortune he noticed Winifred leaving the building and making her way home. As she was passing by Oliver's car, Oliver put the door window down and spoke,

'Hello Winifred, can you spare a few minutes for a chat?'

Winifred looked at Oliver in recognition and jokingly said,

'Aren't you a little young for trying to pick women up'.

'Better starting early and gain the experience', replied Oliver smiling.

Winifred walked to the passenger door, opened it and sat on the seat next to Oliver.

'Well young man', said Winifred, 'you stepped into my life like a ghost, finding my engagement ring, I suppose you're going to tell me you have found a time machine that will take me back'.

'Actually', replied Oliver, 'speaking of time machines, you might not be far off the mark'.

'Come again', said Winifred looking surprised.

'Well', said Oliver, 'remember the farm you and Robert wanted to buy and settle down in?'

'I could never forget it', replied Winifred, 'there is never a day that goes by when the thought of it sends a bolt of lightning through my heart'.

'I have a surprise for you', said Oliver, 'if you want to try again, the farm now belongs to both yourself

and Robert, along with the money to get it going'.
Winifred sat in silence for a few minutes and turned to
face Oliver with heavy eyes,

'Robert is a drunk, he is lost within that world', she
said.

'Trust me please', said Oliver, 'Robert was never a
drunk, after losing you and the farm he had nothing
else to turn too, the farm is back and all he needs is
you'.

'How did he manage to get it back?' asked Winifred.

'Let's say the pub landlord who robbed him had a
rattle of his conscience', replied Oliver.
Winifred put her hands on her head and rubbed them
across her forehead,

'Everything is coming at me too fast', she said, 'I'm
going to need time to think'.

'You know where the farm is', said Oliver, 'I'm
taking Robert out there on Friday, if you decide to
turn back time, we will be there around twelve thirty'.
Winifred reached for the door handle and exited from
Oliver's car, without another word she made her way
in the direction of where she lived alone, leaving
Oliver to drive off with the hope that she would
choose to return to her dreams of an unforgotten past.

CHAPTER 15

The day before had been a busy day for Oliver and the falling into bed had no sooner been accomplished when he had fallen fast asleep. As he awoke to a new day from the smog filled mind of sleep he began to realise that the previous day's proceedings had been no dream. What would come out of the horror inside the barn would be something beautiful, and he knew if all the pieces fell in place then that twisted vision was worth enduring. He began to think of how Robert and Winifred would have the chance to relive their dreams, and smiled inwardly as he pictured Mary and himself starting a family together in love and happiness. No sooner had Oliver brushed the word Mary across his mind, when the sudden realization that he had missed their date the evening before jumped up at him like a wounded wolf. Oliver suddenly sprang out of bed, quickly got dressed and ran downstairs and out the front door to reach the nearest phone box. As he dialed Mary's number, he waited for someone to answer before he pressed the coin into the slot.

'Hello', said a man's voice from the other side.

'Hello', replied Oliver trying to catch his breath, 'can I speak to Mary please?'

'Sorry', said the male voice from the other side, 'there is no Mary living here, you must have the wrong number'.

As he finished with the word number, Oliver could hear the receiver being put down on the other side. Oliver stood inside the red phone box and tried to catch his breath while recovering at the same time from the revelation he had just heard. When he gathered his composure he departed from the phone box and set out on his way back home. No sooner had Oliver left the phone box, when he heard it ringing. Oliver stopped for awhile and decided it would be best to go back and answer it as Mary might be trying to get one back on him. As he entered the phone box for the second time, he lifted the receiver and said,

'Hello'.

'I wasn't going to phone you back for standing me up yesterday', said Mary, 'but I took pity on you'.

'I'm soooo sorry', replied Oliver, 'the car broke down and I couldn't find a phone to let you know'.

'Hummm', replied Mary, 'I might let you off this one time, but you are going to have to make it up to me'.

'How about a nice lunch around one o'clock at the Parches Hotel?' asked Oliver.

'That might just do the trick', replied Mary.

'Maybe you would like to bring your male friend who answered the phone with us?' said Oliver, trying to keep the jealously from prodding his words.

'Maybe', answered Mary, but my sister would like to come too, after all its her boyfriend.

'Ok', said Oliver feeling relieved, 'I'll meet you at one there, just the two of us'.

'Until then', replied Mary, blowing him a kiss

through the phone before putting down the receiver. As Oliver made his way back home he was relieved that Mary had believed his story. He was happy that a date was forthcoming and he looked forward to seeing Mary's smile and to breathe the womanly aroma of her perfume. He also knew that in order to play his male duty, he would have to pay for the pleasure and another trip to the hiding place where he stashed the bank proceeds would have to be made. As he entered through the door, the vision of his mother standing in the hallway with a cup of tea in one hand and a plate of toast in the other, almost made him laugh out loud.

'Where in hell where you running too', she asked with a puzzled look on her face, 'I thought there was a bomb ready to go off by the speed you left'.

Oliver smiled and took the cup of tea out of his Mother's hand. As he walked into the kitchen he replied,

'I dropped my wallet in the phone box last night'.

'Did you find it?' asked Oliver's Mother.

'Yes', replied Oliver as he took a sip of his tea, 'good job no one needed to use the phone or I never would have seen it again'.

As he took a bite of toast Oliver's white lie to his Mother had not bothered his conscience. He was used to telling his Mother what she needed, not what she wanted to hear and the meeting with Mary was best kept from her ears, at least for the time being.

'What are your plans for today?' asked Oliver's Mother, 'I hope you don't forget that you live here'.

'I never forget that I live here', answered Oliver sarcastically, 'how can anyone forget that they live in such a beautiful house set among a lush landscape of terraced sectarian whispers and black shadows of empty futures'.

Oliver's Mother never replied, but grasped the moment to stare out the kitchen window and far away from Oliver's words. Oliver at once regretted what he said, knowing that it hurt his Mother deeply. When he was just a few months old, they had a chance to emigrate to New Zealand, but his Mother refused, quoting the words far off fields are green. Oliver could tell by her language as he grew up, that she would repent those words for the rest of her life. Oliver arose from the chair and addressed his Mother by saying,

'Only joking, there is nowhere in the world I would rather be'.

Oliver's Mother smiled at the humour directed from Oliver's words, and as Oliver opened the back door to face another day, she shouted

'Take care son'.

A fine mist of rain taunted the windscreen of Oliver's car as he made his way to stock up on his dwindling funds. He wondered to himself if he had been too generous when splashing out to others, but settled on the fact that their want had been greater than his. Oliver had never considered money to be a blindfold when others were in need, and he certainly would never allow his generosity to be smothered by greed. He had witnessed the humility of having little or nothing many times throughout his life, and as long as those scars remained, he would try whenever possible to spare others from those pains.

As Oliver pulled in beside the old derelict house, he cut the car's engine and swept the surrounding fields and hedgerows with his eyes, in order to satisfy himself that he was alone. As time was quickly catching up until his meeting with Mary, he departed from the car without locking the door and made his way into the darkness of the empty building. As Oliver had been in the old house several times before, he was fully aware where the money was hid. As he shone the torch light up the black soot stained chimney, his mind began to race with confusion. He knew he put it there, he was sure he put it there, but now it was not there. Oliver hurriedly shone the torch around the room, in the hope he might find the bag of bank robbery money lying in a corner or on top of the old woodworm table under the window. But all Oliver could find in that dark musty room was emptiness, and the realization that someone had been there.

Oliver quickly fired the car into life and started out on his way back to Magherafelt. As the car bumped and twisted its way along, Oliver's mood began to change from one of confusion to that of anger. There was only one person he showed where the money was and that was Mary. He also knew that the hills and the fields have eyes and it would be easy for someone to observe the movements of those coming and going from a building no one lived in. As he pulled up at the car park outside the Parches Hotel, he only hoped that those who stole from a thief were not tracking his movements.

As Oliver entered through the two large front doors of the Hotel, he noticed Mary sitting on a soft chair beside the dining room entrance. As he approached her he watched her expression for some minute flicker of guilt, something that would tell Oliver that she was responsible.

'How's it going?' said Oliver, as he took a chair beside her.

'Ok', replied Mary flashing Oliver a smile, 'I was thinking of standing you up, but took pity on you'.

'The money's gone', said Oliver in a low tone of voice.

Mary looked at Oliver surprised and asked,

'What money?'

'The fucking money from the bank job I told you about', whispered Oliver.

'Who else knew about it?' asked Mary.

'Just four people and two are dead', answered Oliver.

'That leaves you and who else?' asked Mary.

'You', replied Oliver, as he continued to search Mary's eyes for a sign of guilt.

Mary suddenly rose from the chair and began to walk in hurried footsteps towards the exit. Oliver getting caught off guard, took a few seconds longer to pursue her in the same direction. As both Mary and Oliver left the hotel and out onto the cool air, Oliver grabbed Mary by the arm and said

'What to hell is wrong with you?' he asked as he tried to hold her back.

'Fuck you', answered Mary in anger.

'Hold on', said Oliver as he pushed Mary against a shop wall.

'You think it was me', said Mary.

'What got that idea in your head?' asked Oliver.

'When you said I was the only other person who knew, you pointed the finger straight at me', replied Mary with anger in her voice.

'I'm sorry if that is how it came across', said Oliver apologetically, 'but I never meant to accuse you'.

'Why would I want to steal a couple of thousand pounds, and ruin all our plans?' asked Mary.

'Listen', said Oliver, let's go sit in the car, its warmer'.

Oliver pointed to his car parked across the road and Mary eventually followed him. As they closed the car doors, Oliver turned to Mary and said,

'We can't go for a bite to eat like we planned, I'm skint'.

'Mary managed a weak smile and replied, 'It's ok, I'm skint too'.

'We will have plenty of time for wining and dining when the money comes rolling in', said Oliver, as he tried to console his financial grief.

'What did you say?' asked Mary as she looked strangely at Oliver.

'I said we will have plenty of time for wining and dining when we get rich', replied Oliver.

'Ahh', said Mary, 'I could have swore you said something else'.

'Like what?' asked Oliver, surprised at Mary's sudden change of facial expression.

'You're no good', replied Mary.

'No', said Oliver, 'just the getting rich thing, would never say a thing like that'.

'I must be starting to crack up', replied Mary as she managed a smile.

'My mum told me of someone she used to know years ago' said Oliver, 'who went to bed one night feeling dizzy and woke up the next morning speaking fluent French'.

'Bollocks', replied Mary as she slapped Oliver's knee playfully, 'you're winding me up'.

'No', replied Oliver, 'she had to learn to speak English all over again'.

'And what about her husband and family?' asked Mary, 'did she know them?'

'Yes', replied Oliver, 'she knew them all, in fact

nothing had changed except her language and she couldn't understand a word they were saying'.

'So what you are saying', said Mary, 'is that she woke up unable to understand anyone, that must have been very frightening for her'.

'It was', answered Oliver, 'but as her husband couldn't understand French, he didn't have to understand her constant nagging'.

'Ahh, very funny', said Mary, 'I might wake up tomorrow speaking German'.

'Or even worse', replied Oliver, 'You might wake up speaking English'.

Oliver's mild laughter was interrupted by a sudden slap, as if someone had just been smacked across the face. As he turned sideways to look at Mary, he could see a look of shock written across her face.

'What's wrong?' asked Oliver.

'You fucking sick bastard', answered Mary as she opened the car door and quickly exited from the car,

'You won't get the chance to hit me again'.

As she slammed the door, Oliver watched in shock as Mary walked away, holding her hand to her face as she muttered some words to herself. Oliver wanted to leave the car and run after her, to beg her to explain what was wrong. He wanted to shout her name across the road, to yell at the top of his voice for answers. But he couldn't, he didn't want to try, because at this very moment the rear view mirror revealed to him all that he needed to know.

Oliver's fear was accelerated for a few seconds by the sound of three taps on the driver's window of the car. Relieved to see someone who was still very much in the land of the living, he turned down the window and greeted Robert.

'Shit man you scared the crap out of me'.
Robert smiled and replied,

'You don't look the type that scares easy'.

'Never judge a book by its cover', replied Oliver trying to hide the shake from his hand.

'It's all on for tomorrow', said Robert.

'Ok', answered Oliver, 'I'll pick you up at the phone box after you get it all signed, sealed and delivered'.

'Thanks kid', said Robert, 'come to think of it the whole thing is scaring the crap out of me'.

'Well get to the toilet quick and I'll see you tomorrow', replied Oliver as he turned the key and give life to the engine.

'Ok kid', said Robert, 'take care'.

Oliver turned out of the small almost empty car park and made his way towards home. His mind was jumping back and forth again, and the thought of John appearing again left him puzzled. What Oliver couldn't come to terms with was why Mary behaved the way she did, and stopped short on believing that it was John who told Mary she was no good before slapping her. He convinced himself that dead people are dead and therefore have no physical presence. It would have taken a physical hand to slap Mary, and unless he was going nuts and did it without knowing, nothing could turn from the fact that Mary had faked it for some reason known only to herself. As he pulled up beside his house, Oliver began to think of the missing money and suspicion began to creep in to point the finger at Mary. He had quickly allowed Mary into his darkest secrets, without first allowing himself enough time to get to know her. Perhaps she needed the money for some life or death situation, and was too embarrassed to ask him for more. But the more

Oliver tried to paint Mary with the brush of guilt, the greater his heart beat to the hurried rhythm of her innocence. Oliver knew Mary loved him, and he loved her more than his own life. He knew the path of destiny was laid out before them as one, and that would eventually lead to peace and happiness. They might have their downs and ups, but Oliver was wholly convinced that they would grow old together. As Oliver locked the car and walked towards the back door of his house, he had convinced himself beyond any reasonable doubt, that the beautiful, angelic Mary was innocent.

'Did you hear the news son?' asked Oliver's Mother, as Oliver sat down on a chair at the kitchen table.

'No', replied Oliver, 'What's happened again in our good wee Northern Ireland?'

'They shot two young lads dead in Bellaghy', she replied.

'Who shot them dead?' asked Oliver, 'the police? the IRA? UDA?'

'The police', answered Oliver's mother as she sat a plate of stew on the table, 'they held up a post office and as they were coming out the police were waiting on them'.

'Did they not call out a warning or anything?' asked Oliver.

'Last news I heard, an eye witness said that both had their hands in the air', replied Oliver's mother.

'Put the radio on', said Oliver as he began to eat his stew, 'the news will be on in the half hour'. Oliver's mother reached over to the old black transistor radio and flicked the switch.

A NATIONALIST COUNCILLOR IN BELLAGHY HAS CALLED FOR AN INDEPENDENT

INVESTIGATION INTO THE SHOOTING DEAD OF TWO POST OFFICE ROBBERS IN THE TOWN EARLY THIS MORNING. AS MORE AND MORE PEOPLE ARE COMING FORWARD CLAIMING BOTH MEN HAD THEIR ARMS RAISED, THE COUNCILLOR IS ADAMANT THAT THE POLICE ARE OPERATING A SHOOT TO KILL POLICY. *'I HAVE SPOKE TO A NUMBER OF MY CONSTITUENTS WHO WITNESSED THE KILLING OF THESE YOUNG MEN AND ALL HAVE VERIFIED THAT THEY MEN INDEED HAD THEIR ARMS RAISED IN THE AIR.* ***HAS ANYONE YOU HAVE SPOKEN TO INDICATED THAT THE POLICE WERE IN DANGER OF BEING FIRED UPON?*** *TO THE CONTRARY, EVERYONE HAS STATED CATAGORICALLY THAT AT NO TIME WERE THE POLICE IN ANY DANGER. THERE ARE UNCONFIRMED REPORTS CIRCULATING AROUND THE COMMUNITY THAT THE MEN WERE NOT CARRYING REAL FIREARMS BUT REPLICAS.*

Oliver's mother reached over and turned the radio off,

'I can't listen to anymore of that', she said, 'it's making me depressed'.

Oliver continued to consume the warm plate of stew before him, giving the impression that the incident he had just heard was about someone else and it didn't concern him. But Oliver knew in his own mind, that it could just as easy have been them when the robbed the bank on Main Street. The painful part of it all was he needed to do it again, and the following news report had just added another notch to his over tight stomach. Every time he listened to the news, there was nothing but death and destruction. Bombs ripping buildings and people apart all in the name of freedom and equality. The mothers and fathers, sons and daughters tore apart with grief and consciences devoured in the jaws of a necessary evil. Oliver wanted so much to leave the mayhem, to take Mary and go to another place, another land where a red sky at night meant something warm would greet the new day, not something black, charred and ugly. He knew that one more Bank job would be his last, and his dreams would heavily outweigh the risk. The couple of thousand he lost in the derelict building would never have been enough, so the next job was inevitable.

'Do you want anymore?' asked Oliver's mother as she reached for Oliver's empty plate. 'do you hear me?' she said, 'wake up'.

'Na…no', answered Oliver in a broken voice. The rattle of his plate going into the sink, and the roar of a car with no silencer passing by outside his door were just two of the many things Oliver didn't hear. All he could hear were the words two thousand vibrating inside his head, keeping in time to the beats of his heart. Two thousand pounds is what he lost, two thousand was not enough to get him away, and two thousand was the exact sum that Mary quoted when he told her of the money's disappearance.

Oliver lay on top of a clean bed within his clean room and turned the words around in his head two thousand times. There was no way of Mary knowing the exact sum left in the bag, and he could not remember ever telling her. Mary's guilt began to pound the walls of his affection, as Oliver tried to defend them with every ounce of his love. What would not go away was the plain and bare fact that too many coincidences were being flung at him at once, and he couldn't tell which ones were true or false. He didn't want to believe that Mary would betray him, and above all he couldn't face the sharp knife edged reality of breaking up. He knew that in order to free him once and for all from the torture of suspicion, he would have to confront her with the two thousand pounds question.

'What in hell's fuck are you doing', asked John.

'My feet are killing me', replied Oliver.

'But that's fucking ridiculous, if anyone sees you they'll lock you up in a nut house', said John.

'Why?' replied Oliver, 'I'm only relaxing my feet in this warm stream, what's so nutty about that?'

'What's so nutty?' mimicked John, 'why don't you take a look at yourself in the mirror?'

'I took a look at myself in the mirror this morning', replied Oliver, 'still as handsome as ever'.

'Stop assing around', said John, 'get your feet out of there now, that water is too fucking warm'.

'It's you who will be taking a trip to the nut house', replied Oliver, 'what's wrong with warm water flowing smoothly over my feet?'

'I don't believe I'm hearing this', said John as he stamped his feet in frustration, 'what sort of a dumb idiot are you?'

'Why don't you pull your shoes and socks off and join me', replied Oliver.

'Listen Oliver', said John in a desperate tone of voice, 'you have got to stop what you're doing'.

'Ok Johnny old son', answered Oliver, 'give me one

clear and present reason for depriving myself of this luxury'.

'Because the water is too fucking warm', replied John, 'you cannot use warm water on your feet in your situation'.

'What situation?' asked Oliver.

John turned around to Michael who was sitting high on a horse dressed as a Cowboy and said,

'Can you believe this dumb fuck, for shit's sake tell him'.

'Your situation requires your feet to be cold', said Michael.

'And who in their right mind wants their feet to be cold?' replied Oliver.

'A right minded person in your situation needs to take cold feet', answered Michael.

'Two thousand cold feet', said John in a sharp frosty tone of voice.

CHAPTER 16

When Oliver awoke from his dream he could feel the warm water from the bathroom sink pouring over his feet. Sitting on the window sill with his feet dangling into the basin, be came to the quick conclusion that he was losing his mind. As he made his way back to bed he began to analyse the paradox of the dream's contents, and surrendered himself to the truth that his mind was moving faster than he could think. The incident with Mary and the suspicion in relation to the money, had allowed him no peace and he vowed before the day was out he would have the truth whether he liked it or not. As Oliver climbed back into bed and smothered himself under the blankets, he could see a faint glint of daylight stealing its way between the curtains. He looked at the clock on the bedside cabinet and closed his eyes after first reminding himself that 6.23am was not his time for getting up.

The note sitting on top of the kitchen table was not alone in bearing witness to his mother's absence. Oliver could smell no aroma of eggs or toast, no familiar whiff of brewing tea leaves or rattle of cup on saucer. He looked at the clock to familiarise himself with the time and despite the hands reading 10.14am, Oliver had no cause for concern. Today would bring something wonderful back in from the dark, and witness justice in the form of Robert walking through the door of his long lost farm house. Oliver knew also that sometime today he would have to face Mary with a few serious truths and however hard those truths turn out to be, he knew his state of mind depended on an outcome. Sleep walking was something he had never attempted before and on being introduced to it for the first time, he decided against its friendship.

As he struggled with the teapot and cups, Oliver surrendered himself to the fact that tea, bread and butter would be the only fuel that would start him through the new day. He had never been one to pry into the skills of the kitchen, so as a consequence, his breakfast would reflect that failure to harness the simplest form of survival. Oliver had grown entirely dependent on his mother for even the smallest of things, and he shuddered to think how he would cope on his own in a foreign country. Not only was he unsure whether Mary could cook, but if she would even be coming with him at all. What he lacked most of all in his life was certainty, and Oliver was getting impatient with all the tangled threads of destiny. The coming days were vital, for Oliver had decided that sooner if not later, he was leaving behind the land of a thousand bleeding hearts. Even if one more fountain of tears was added by his mother on account of his absence, Oliver knew that the pain of staying would be far greater.

Oliver opened the car door and climbed in behind the steering wheel, at the same time reaching over to wipe the moisture from the interior of the windscreen.

For a few seconds the white envelope, wrapped in clear plastic and positioned behind the wiper did not catch his attention. When Oliver eventually caught sight of it, he reached his hand out through the side of the half open door and retrieved it. On quickly opening it the note read MEET ME AT THE DIAMOND AROUND FIVE, WE NEED TO TALK……MARY. Oliver was happy that Mary had instigated the meeting, as he was unsure how he was going to bring it about himself. He was glad she realised also that they needed to talk, as Oliver could not bear the icy blade of goodbye. As Oliver gunned the car into life and set out to pick up Robert, he knew that the cogs of change were beginning to gather momentum, and soon a change would be floating above the clouds and beyond.

' Good afternoon', said Oliver, as Robert climbed into the passenger seat next to him.

'Is it really', answered Robert.

'Why not?' asked Oliver as he steered the car down Main Street and out into the countryside.

'I must have spent the whole night thinking', replied Robert, 'and I might sell the place and go off abroad somewhere'.

'What brought that into your head?' asked Oliver with an air of surprise in his voice.

Robert turned and stared out the window at the countryside passing him by,

'The whole excitement of getting the farm back made me oblivious to one very important missing piece', he said.

'And what is that?' asked Oliver.

'Her', answered Robert.

'Her?' asked Oliver in feint surprise.

'Winifred', answered Robert, 'I haven't got anything back, a few acres of land and a house does not make a home, and unless you have a split personality, the place is going to feel damn lonely'.

'Once you have a few animals and a dog running around, the whole place will feel a whole lot different', said Oliver.

'Don't like the thought of all that shit', replied Robert, 'there are only certain circumstances when a whole pile of shit becomes logical'.

'Since when does shit ever become logical?' asked Oliver.

'When no matter how nasal whacking and stomach wrenching it really is, you couldn't live without the smell', replied Robert.

'Whenever the time comes that I cannot live without the smell of shit', said Oliver, 'I'll just find myself the nearest and deepest well and throw myself down it'.

As Oliver and Robert pulled up outside the small farmhouse, another car had arrived before them and now stood parked near the gable wall.

'Someone doesn't want to let the place go after all', said Robert as he eyed the car with suspicion.

'There is someone inside I think you should meet', said Oliver.

'Meet?' asked Robert in surprise.

'Just go ahead, trust me', answered Oliver.

Robert opened the passenger door and on closing it, made his way slowly towards the back door of the farmhouse. Oliver watched him go and noticed he walked as if he was moving through an open minefield. The years of a broken heart soaked in alcohol had taken its toil and unless some new shot of life was injected into Robert's vein of hope, an early grave would be the only outcome. Oliver surveyed the scene before him, the whitewashed stone walls, the old run down out buildings and the weeds dominating the yard due to years of neglect. He had wondered how a person could be so greedy, that they needed to take away not only the life's blood of the old farm, but also of a young couple who worked hard and dreamt the same dreams. Oliver knew that those years could never be got back, and he also knew that the old place's future depended on what walked out the back door of the house that bore similar scars to those who were now inside it. The moment alone allowed Oliver time to think about the note Mary left, and once again struggle with the fact that she left a note outside his house, yet didn't call in while she was so close. He still was not able to read Mary, but Oliver could not deviate away from the pangs of love or the dreams they had planned together. Unlike Robert, Oliver would fight for his dreams and try with every breath of his body to make them come true. Robert had followed millions of others and shrouded the bitterness and pain under an admission of defeat. Oliver knew that Robert's love for Winifred should have been stronger and braver than life itself and because of that, evil should not have been allowed to ferment for all those years.

Oliver opened the car door and on closing it, he made his way towards the figure of Robert beckoning him to come inside. As he followed him in he could see Winifred sitting on an old well worn chair beside a fireside that had stopped breathing many years before. The musty smell of emptiness had left its footprint on every floor and wall, and as Oliver sat down on a chair next to the table he knew that something else was about to greet the inside air.

'Hello Oliver', said Winifred in a level tone of voice.

'Hello', replied Oliver, 'how do you like the place?'

'Nothing that a gallon of petrol and a match wouldn't cure', answered Winifred.

'What about a gallon of paint and a paintbrush', replied Oliver.

'Wouldn't make a bit of difference', answered Winifred.

'We have decided to sell the place', said Robert butting into the conversation. 'too many unpleasant memories surround it'.

Winifred and Robert eyed Oliver for a response, both bearing serious straight faces. Oliver had no response to give them, he knew it was their decision together and years have a strange way of changing how people think. He looked around once again and tried to draw some flicker of life from the remnants of what once was a home.

'I'm sorry you both think that way', said Oliver as he searched for words to give some hope to Winifred and Oliver, 'but you are both adults and its logical to believe you are doing the right thing'.

'Oh very much the right thing', replied Winifred, 'we were once young and foolish and our souls were etched with simple expectations. Now we are old and seek greater things in life, and long to reject the narrow minded cultural attitudes'.

'Winifred and Myself have decided that it is best this way', said Robert as he shuffled his feet through the old newspapers and books lying on the floor.

'I guess that is it', said Oliver, 'do you want a lift back into town Robert?'

'No its fine, I'll get a lift back with Winnie', he

replied.

'Stop it you brute', said Winifred as she threw a mock punch at Robert, 'you know I hate it when you call me that'.

As he made his way back outside, Oliver could tell by that one short incident that things were not as he had come to believe. The way in which both Winifred and Robert had answered his questions, had been subdued, almost as if they had found a pot of gold and didn't want him to know. As he opened the car door he could hear both Winifred and Robert approaching behind him, but it was only as Oliver sat down on the driver's seat and looked out the window, that everything became clear. Oliver filled with happiness as he watched Winifred and Oliver stand before him holding hands and smiling from ear to ear. He could see by their expressions, the way they locked their hands together, that no one would ever part them again.

'I was right after all', said Oliver, 'a gallon of paint and a brush'.

'No', answered Winifred, 'the petrol and match are still the option but we might as well sell it and use the money to start anew'.

'Any idea where?' asked Oliver.

'Not yet, but we'll let you know at the wedding', answered Winifred.

'And all this was decided in fifteen minutes?' asked Oliver in amazement.

'No', replied Winifred, 'it took me fifteen years to plan it if things ever turned out as they did'.

'I'm really happy for both of you', said Oliver, 'sometimes something or someone appear in our lives for better or worse, leaving us to wonder if destiny has already been written for us'.

'It's strange you say that', said Winifred, 'I remember caring for an old lady a few years ago in hospital and she told me the strangest thing. She said that a boy who had a mind much older than his years would guide me back home'.

'Do you remember her name?' asked Oliver as he started the car to drive off.

'I can't remember', replied Winifred, 'it might have been called Hattie'.

'I will see you two later', said Oliver as he slowly moved away from the farmhouse and the couple who had found each other again after fifteen years. Suddenly Oliver heard Winifred calling his name and on turning down the window, he heard her shout,

'Matty, her name was Matty'.

On the road back to Magherafelt, Oliver took little notice of the trees and fields that blotted the landscape on each side of the road. He didn't care if the stray cow would run across the road in front of him, or the soldiers standing at the side of the road would try to stop him. He could not get his mind off the name that Winifred shouted at him as he left. The name vibrated through his head and his confused state of mind had no answers as to why the name was Matty. The chances of the Matty he knew and the one Winifred described being different people were very slim. If he was born to help fulfill other people's destinies, not his own, Oliver knew he would be very disappointed. He had his own dreams, his own expectations and owned nine tenths of his mind. The other tenth he knew was rattling around somewhere upstairs but he had yet to find it. Strange things were happening all around him and that knowledge he could only keep to himself for fear of other people's scrutiny. The incident with Mary in the car laid open those wounds to someone else, but Oliver hoped Mary would soon be discarded as someone else. After seeing Winifred and Robert reunited, Oliver vowed he would do what was necessary to keep Mary and himself together.

When Oliver pulled up beside his house, he didn't bother locking the car but quickly made his way inside to get ready for his meeting with Mary at five. His mother had still not returned, so Oliver decided to run himself a bath and remove the dirt and smell that could come between a beautiful girl like Mary and his good self. He knew he must look his best, even if that included washing inside the ears that Oliver had not washed in a long time. On completing the arduous task of getting clean, Oliver dried himself off and made his way to the bedroom to done his best outfit. On entering his bedroom Oliver noticed how disorganized it was, owing to the absence of his mother. On opening the wardrobe he was happy to see his clothes ironed and hung on hangers. Although happy, Oliver was not surprised as his mother had always been two steps ahead of his needs and that he was truly grateful. On getting dressed in his black jeans, blue denim jacket and new white tee-shirt, Oliver decided a quick view in the mirror before he left was a good idea. On looking in the mirror Oliver expected to see a clean cut self dressed in his best and a smile of approval. To his horror all he could see was a battered and broken self, with blood gushing out from a small round hole in the head. Oliver froze with fear, the hair that once sat neatly on the back of his neck, now stood upright. For a few seconds Oliver believed he was dead, and only on taking a second look did he realize that his imagination was running wildly away with itself. On looking again Oliver could now see the clean cut figure he wanted to see in the first place, and as quickly as his legs could carry him, Oliver made his way out of the room and on to his meeting with Mary.

When Oliver drove up to the Diamond, at first he could see no sign of Mary, so he parked the car in the town's only designated car park and waited. A few minutes later the front passenger door opened allowing enough room for Mary to get inside. On closing the door behind her Mary spoke in an almost out of breath fashion,

'What to fuck is going on Oliver?'

'What do you mean?' asked Oliver staring at her confused.

'The last time we met', replied Mary, 'when I was so violently assaulted'.

'Listen', protested Oliver, 'I never put one hand on you'.

'I know', replied Mary, 'when I got home that night I realised you had both hands on the steering wheel when it happened'.

'Thank you so much', said Oliver in mock relief, 'but that doesn't remove the fact that I might be sitting beside an escapee from the county nut house'.
Mary turned to Oliver with an angry expression written across her face,

'I'm not impressed by your jokes, I haven't slept since it happened', she stressed.

'Ok', said Oliver, 'let's go back to when it happened and piece it together bit by bit, so that we might be able to find a rational reason of how it happened'.

'I was sit..never fucking mind a rational reason',

replied Mary raising her voice, 'how can you find a rational reason for getting your hair grabbed from behind, and then being slapped across the face?'

'Well', answered Oliver, 'I have heard about people who are subject to what some people call spinal shocks, that is when a jerk from some part of the spine simulates a movement, or in your case a violent simulation of being assaulted'.

'Are you pulling my leg?' asked Mary.

'No, cross my heart', answered Oliver, 'I remember reading a story of a man who claimed that every so often a number of demons would kick the living shit out of him. Every time he made the claim, he had a few bruises to back it up. So some do it yourself demon hunters decided to lock him in a padded room to make sure he wasn't inflicting the injuries on himself. Low and behold, they looked into the room one evening and there he was kicking around on the floor as the unseen demons give him a damn good thrashing.

'You're not going to tell me that I'm possessed?' asked Mary.

'Well in your case I'm not quite sure yet', joked Oliver.

'Well what happened?' asked Mary.

'What happened what?' answered Oliver.

'The story, the man kicking around on the floor', answered Mary impatiently.

'Oh that', teased Oliver, 'well of course when they witnessed it for themselves they decided that an exorcism would be required to free the man from his torture.

'Hold on a minute', said Mary, 'did you really read about this or are you just making it up as you go along?'

'I told you', replied Oliver, 'it's the truth, cross my heart a thousand and one times'.

'Ok, get on with it', said Mary.

'I am trying to get on with it, but someone keeps interrupting me', replied Oliver in protest.

'Go on', said Mary anxiously.

'Ok', replied Oliver, 'so the demon bashers decided to hold an exorcism and called in a few of their heavies to carry it out. On the night of the battle of good v evil, they laid the man down on a specially made bed and strapped him down good and tight. In case the demons were stronger than the straps, the posted four big strong men at the bedside and proceeded with the exorcism.

'What happened?' asked Mary unable to wait for the ending.

'He died', answered Oliver.

'What do you mean he died?' asked Mary in a tone of disappointment.

'I mean the man died, ceased to exist', replied Oliver.

'How did he die?' asked Mary, 'did he die of exhaustion? Did the demons kill him? What to fuck happened?'

'Apparently the man was epileptic', answered Oliver, 'and no one decided to investigate this as a reason for his behaviour, so when he took a severe fit while he was strapped down on the bed, the demon bashers were more concerned with the unnatural than the natural, and low and behold the poor man choked on his tongue'.

Mary remained silent for a few minutes before she decided to speak,

'You don't think I'm epileptic do you?' she asked.

'Certainly not', answered Oliver humorously, 'I think you are the real thing'.

Mary forced a smile towards Oliver and then turned to stare out the window at a passing police land rover. A short time later she turned and asked Oliver,

'When's the next bank? I want to get away from his dump'.

'There is a something we need to get sorted first', said Oliver.

'I know what you mean', replied Mary, 'but I'm not sleeping with you until we get out of this hole and far away'.

Oliver was taken aback by Mary's statement and reached deep within himself for an answer. He knew he was guilty of sexual thoughts of Mary and himself, but he never contemplated anything happening until they were married. Oliver was fully aware of how shy he was in relation to women and only remembered kissing one girl when he was eight years old. At that moment Oliver came to the stark realisation that sitting beside him was a fully grown woman, and he was just a child. He knew he could match most adults in many things, talking and fighting to name but two, but when it came to the real thing, he was just like any other child looking to hide behind their mother's apron. All Oliver could manage to say in reply to Mary's statement was

'When a you if ter aa'.

Mary laughed and said

'What was that load of shit you just came out with?'

Oliver could feel both cheeks on his face beginning to kindle and knew in order to take the situation back into his control he needed to do something fast.

'Did you take the money Mary?' he asked.

Mary remained silent for a moment as she stared straight into Oliver's eyes and suddenly said

'What is it with you; I told you I didn't take it'.

'You and I were the only ones who knew it was there', replied Oliver, still holding Mary's stare.

'When are you going to start trusting me?' asked Mary in anger.

Mary proceeded to empty her purse out onto her lap and shouted

'For fuck's sake take a look, do I look like a person who just stole two grand'.

Oliver watched as the contents of Mary's purse poured onto her lap, and counted no more than a few pence.

'How did you know there was two grand in the bag?' asked Oliver.

'I guessed, I used to work in a bank and I learned the amount inside any bag just by looking at it', replied Mary.

Mary's reply was met with silence as Oliver digested what Mary had just told him. The excuse she handed him was not impossible, he had heard of people who could count how many pennies were in a bag, just by looking at it. Oliver's thoughts were suddenly interrupted by Mary saying,

'I know there is a bank in Cookstown where they have two hundred grand dropped off every month'.

'I was already thinking about that one', replied Oliver.

'No you were not', said Mary, 'this one is down George Street and it's the last place in the world where you would expect so much money'.

'How do you know all this?' asked Oliver.

'I was in the dentist's waiting room one morning looking out the window, and low and behold the van pulls up across the street', replied Mary, 'I checked the date which was the first day of the month and called the following month and bingo'.

'And you are sure of the amount?' asked Oliver.

'One hundred thousand in each bag, trust me', replied Mary smiling.

'Put your stuff back into the purse', said Oliver, 'you're making me feel embarrassed'.

Mary returned the few coins and stamps back to her purse, while Oliver once again returned to his thoughts. He knew Mary was telling the truth and now he wanted to kick himself for doubting her sincerity. The bank job would be the answer to both their dreams and if it could be pulled off soon, his life would change for the better, quicker than he thought.

'Do you want to go and see it tomorrow?' asked Mary, interrupting Oliver's thoughts once again.

'Yes', answered Oliver, 'Let's get the wheel turning'. Mary reached over and kissed Oliver gently on the lips, sending tingles to Oliver's already awakening hormones.

'Meet me here at ten tomorrow morning', said Mary as she departed from the car leaving Oliver yearning for another kiss.

CHAPTER 17

The new day was much the same as the day before, and the day before that. It consisted of Oliver rising to the smell of his mother making breakfast, or the emptiness of her absence. Some mornings the sun would sneak a view from between the curtains, other times it couldn't care less. Oliver sat on top of the bed trying to shake the last few remnants of sleep from his head, and wondered if things would ever really change. He liked the comforts of his home and loved how his mother fussed around him, but as he grew older his heart throbbed for something different. His imagination was beginning to wander far beyond the parameters of his own shadow, and Oliver feared that he would lose them both.

As Oliver sat at the kitchen table he could hear his mother humming a tune lowly to herself and remembered the time when she wasn't afraid to sing it out loud. Traditional Irish tunes sung to the ear shot of listeners other than Catholic could have a detrimental effect on the songster's health and well being Oliver was aware of the mental and physical consequences of stones or petrol bombs being flung through someone's window, as the television and radio news reports held little back.

'Anything nice happen last night?' asked Oliver as his mother sat his breakfast down before him.

'Just the usual bombings and shootings', replied his mother, 'nothing unusual'.

Oliver thought about those two words 'nothing unusual', and realised that in all its rawness, they meant exactly what they said. Outside the ruined buildings and demolished lives, nothing unusual would mean someone getting up to go to work, or attending Sunday services. In Oliver's world a hand grenade lands on someone's doorstep, and in the world facing it, that grenade is replaced by a newspaper. His world reminded Oliver of an electric fence he saw stretching across a field to preserve the grass on one half. On one side the ground was trampled and muddy; on the other side it was clean and green. Oliver felt like one of the cows staring across at all the juicy ripe grass, but unable to touch due to the pain of electricity passing through their bodies. Oliver's electricity was poverty, and the only way to escape was to gather courage and charge through the pain.

At 10.00am Oliver pulled up at the Diamond and had no sooner done so, when the passenger door opened and a not so smiley Mary climbed in beside him.

'Good morning', said Oliver, 'You look a picture of morning health and vitality'.

'Don't talk', replied Mary in a tired voice, 'I had the worst night's sleep in my entire life'.

'Did the excitement of bags of delicious money keep you awake?' asked Oliver humorously.

'I wish', answered Mary, 'but the bloody alarm clock kept going off all night'.

226

'Why didn't you switch it off?' asked Oliver as he put the car in gear and moved off in the direction of Cookstown.

'I did switch it off', answered Mary, 'but the fucking thing kept switching on again'.

'I had a dream like that once', said Oliver, 'I kept getting up the whole night in my sleep and closing the room door'.

'This was no dream', replied Mary, 'I even took the battery out of the damn thing and still it woke me up again and again with its bloody bleep'.

'Why didn't you take it and throw it in the bin?' asked Oliver.

'I would have if the night had went on any longer', replied Mary.

'What really happened', said Oliver, 'was you dreamt you took the battery out and all the things you done to the clock to stop it from functioning were imaginary, not physical'.

'Imaginary my ass', replied Mary, 'I banged my toe twice on the side of the bed and have the bruises to prove it'.

Oliver turned the sharp corner at Moneymore road and continued on his way to Cookstown. As he passed a mental hospital on the left hand side he nudged Mary on the elbow and pointed,

'Do you want me to call in and see if there are any nice comfy beds?' he asked sarcastically.

'Don't start', answered Mary, 'I'm really beginning to think that I am, starting to lose my mind'.

'Don't worry', joked Oliver, 'at least you will be free from all the worries of the world'.

'I'll keep the worries of the world if you don't mind thank you', replied Mary.

Oliver stopped at the stop sign as they entered Cookstown, and then turned left and continued to drive up the main street. He studied closely how tired Mary looked, and thought about all the strange things that had been happening to her. Oliver believed that behind Mary's thick shell, there was other problems trying to eat their way outwards. Oliver remembered Mary looked a troubled soul when he first met her, but now the black bags of sleeplessness were beginning to reveal themselves even to the casual glance. He wanted to ask Mary about her troubles, to ask her to let go of whatever it was that was turning her mind. But Oliver was afraid of taking a step too far, so decided to defer the matter until they knew each other better.

'This is it', said Mary, 'Just pull up here outside the bakery'.

Oliver pulled up beside the bakery and switched the engine off. He stared at the bank across the road on his right, and wondered how someone could put so much money into such a crumbled run down building.

'I know what you're thinking', said Mary, 'but don't let appearances deceive you, the money is there'.

'Are you sure those bags were not full of letters or rubbish for that matter?' asked Oliver.

'You have got to trust me', answered Mary, 'I know what I'm talking about'.

'So when is the next drop off?' asked Oliver.

'Tuesday, that's four days from now', answered Mary.

'Shit that doesn't allow much breathing space', replied Oliver, trying to keep the alarm from his voice.

'I believe it is better to act as soon as possible', replied Mary, 'there is a rumour the place might be closing down, perhaps condemned or something'.

'Surely they can't close something down in a matter of five weeks', said Oliver, 'leaving it to next month would allow us more time to plan it'.

'It only took two days to close the Post Office at the end of the street', replied Mary, 'and besides, what is there to plan?'

'A lot of things', answered Oliver.

'All it takes', said Mary, 'is allow ten minutes for those who drop off the money to disappear, then go in fast and grab the bags before they have time to unpack them'.

'Just as simple as that', said Oliver sarcastically.

'Well if you're not up for it I'll do it myself', replied Mary.

'I do believe you would', said Oliver as he turned to smile at Mary.

'So is it on or not?' asked Mary.

'It's on', replied Oliver.

Mary turned to look across at the bank and said,

'That is our ticket to freedom'.

As Oliver turned the key to start the car and move off, he replied,

'Let's hope it's not our ticket to hell'.

As Oliver and Mary left Cookstown to return to Magherafelt, Oliver's mind began to toss and turn on the idea of committing himself to a robbery with little time to plan. He was both excited and scared, excited that his world was about to change for the better and scared that it might change for the worse. He was now putting his complete trust and judgement into Mary's hands, and all he could do was pray that she knew what she was doing. The women he had known in his life had proven much stronger in courage and organisation than any men. The last time he had carried out such a daring and dangerous act, John and Michael had been by his side. Now it would only be Mary. Oliver knew he had to distil both their fears and produce some kind of bravery that would see them through until the end.

'Ok', said Oliver trying to keep any remnants of fear from his voice, 'the night before the robbery we stay in a hotel room in Cookstown'.

'Do we really need to?' asked Mary.

'Yes', replied Oliver, 'we need to be as close to the operation as possible, in case of any mishaps or checkpoints on the way there'.

'I don't agree', protested Mary, 'we could leave an hour or two earlier'.

'No', replied Oliver, as he raised his voice enough to let Mary know that he was taking control of the situation, 'we are staying close to the target the night before or it's not going to happen'.

Mary shrugged her shoulders in surrender and turned to stare out the window as the car made its way into Magherafelt.

As Oliver took his leave from Mary, the thought of not seeing her for three days was outweighed by the heavy responsibility that had been placed before him like a bolt of lightning. Two hundred thousand was a lot of money, but common sense allowed him the knowledge that no matter how easy it looks, anything could go wrong. As he pulled up beside his house, Oliver turned the ignition off and decided he would sit a while in the car to gather his thoughts, before going inside. He began to act out the robbery in his head, searching for loose ends and trying to be positive. The answer to what he would do with the money could only be left until the all clear. But Oliver knew that the country and town he had spent so many happy and sad days were going to be left behind, quickly disappearing in the rear view mirror of Mary and himself speeding off to fulfill their destiny together. His heart began to beat faster as he grasped the realization that his being was starting to grow. The branches of his tree of life were stretching beyond the enclosure that had imprisoned him since birth, and the spring of his contentment would blossom forever. Oliver's thoughts were suddenly interrupted by someone tapping the side window of the car. Oliver reached for the handle and opened the window of the car.

'Hello Ollie old son'.

Oliver looked into the face of a man he had never seen before and replied

'Hello'.

'The boss wants to see you at eleven tomorrow morning at the diamond', said the stranger.

'What do you mean the boss?' asked Oliver.

'You and him had a chat a while ago in the back of a Ford Cortina, be there', replied the stranger as he walked away.

Oliver turned the window back up and leaned back on the head rest. He knew he would have a meeting with the IRA some time, but he wasn't expecting it this soon. The thought of his two friends being gunned down in cold blood had never left his mind, yet he wasn't sure if he was capable of meeting fire with fire. He knew in his heart of hearts that this killer policeman needed to be stopped before he murdered someone else.

Oliver left the car and made his way into the house. As he walked through the back door and into the kitchen, he began to notice the small things that lent themselves to the character of a home. The grey and black transistor radio that perched on the kitchen table, which through more years than Oliver cared to remember, spat out more bad news than good. The old dark wood clock that hung on the wall stared at him through time, as if to say every hour holds its own secrets. Oliver stared at the gas cooker and noticed how clean it still looked despite its years of faithful service. Everything around him bore the mark of strangeness, yet they had always been there. Even his mother who like some machine presented him with a cup of steaming tea, sounded unearthly as she spoke.

'Why don't you catch your fucking self on, and stay away from that evil bitch'.

'What did you say?' asked Oliver as he tried to confront the shock of his mother's language.

'I said the stew will me another half hour', she replied as she took a chair beside Oliver at the table. Oliver shook his head wildly in order to remove the loose fragments of insanity from his thoughts, and reached for his cup of tea. As he returned the mug to the table, he noticed that behind the greying hair and wrinkling lines on his mother's face, a beautiful lady could still be evident. Oliver knew he had a lot to thank her for, as she alone had been his shelter through life, while his father kept an extremely low profile.

'Mum', said Oliver as he leaned back on the chair beside the table, 'do you regret anything about your life?'

Oliver's mother looked into his eyes and forced a smile,

'I regret a lot of things like most people, but learn to

live with them', she replied.

'Do you regret giving birth to me?' asked Oliver.

'I don't regret giving birth to you son', she replied as the tone in her voice lowered, 'I regret what I brought you into, and the situation that you are in now'.

'There are others born into a worse situation', said Oliver.

'I know', replied his Mother, 'but I have no doubt their parents regret leading them into a world where hope is only available to those who can afford it'.

'I believe in destiny', responded Oliver, 'I believe that every road we walk upon whether it be smooth or bumpy, leads to somewhere that we have been before'.

'There are some religions who believe in reincarnation', said Oliver's Mother, 'if that's the case then I would like to come back as a worm'.

'Why a worm?' asked Oliver in surprise.

'Because I would crawl under the ground, and stay away from the filth and lies of so-called humanity'.

'A bit like burying your head in the sand', said Oliver, 'I think the best idea is to stand up tall and grab anything you can as it passes by'.

'Son', said Oliver's Mother, 'things are going to change here for the better, it may not be in my lifetime but it certainly will be in yours'.

'I will not hold my breath', replied Oliver as he reached to take another sip of tea.

'Nevertheless', said Oliver's Mother, 'if I was your age I would be planning to get out of this hell hole of a country'.

'Don't worry Mum', said Oliver as he rose from the table to go to his bedroom, 'the plan is in motion'.

Oliver removed the floor board in his bedroom and removed the black plastic bag containing the Webley

.455. He sat down on the bed and as he removed the revolver from the bag, a sudden pain shot through his heart. The last time he had the weapon in his hand; John and Michael were beside him in this very same room. Now as he opened the chamber to check that the bullets were ok, he wished with all his heart and soul that they were still alive. This time he was frightened even more, because he knew he would be on his own. With Mary by his side, Oliver knew he would have extra baggage. He would have preferred Mary to take a back seat and leave the bank job to him, but unfortunately Oliver knew that Mary's insistence would overcome any barriers that he chose to lay before her. Tonight he would clean the gun with the tin of three in one oil that sat at the back of the wardrobe. He would wash and shave the few hairs that had been appearing on his chin recently, and afterwards he would settle between the crisp clean sheets of his bed and try to get a good night's sleep. Oliver knew that sleep would be difficult, and was clearly aware that sometime in the very near future, he could be given the chance to sleep for eternity. Sometime between dropping Mary off and now, he had thought to himself how easy it would be to just walk away from everything. From Mary, the bank job and the IRA's assistance in seeking revenge. He could pack his few belongings and drive off into the sunset, closing the door behind on all that caused his nerves to be tested. But Oliver knew that for the rest of his life, the two words 'what if?' would haunt him day and night. Mary's beautiful presence and a chance of a good and prosperous life together outweighed any excuse Oliver could produce, so come rain or sunrise on that day of days, Oliver would once again stand among the shadows of men.

'I wandered lonely as a cloud', said Oliver as he tried to remember William Wordsworth's poem about daffodils.

'It's not lonely as a cloud', protested John, 'it's lonely as a shroud'.

'Don't be stupid', replied Oliver, 'it was cloud, I can remember that cruel bastard of a schoolmaster beating it into me at school'.

'What the cruel schoolmaster taught you then and what is reality now are two different words', argued John. 'And the word then might have been cloud, but now, today, this very moment in time, the word is shroud'.

'You can't change the word on a poem just because it's a different moment in time', stressed Oliver.

'Ok', replied John, 'when you referred to the cruel bastard of a schoolmaster, let's say that he was both a schoolmaster and he was cruel. But the question of authenticity lies within the word bastard, and in what context the word bastard is used'.

'The schoolmaster was a bastard because it adds spice to the foul recipe of his description', replied Oliver.

'Ok', continued John, 'let's say both the schoolmaster's parents were without question, and we use the word bastard to insult him deservingly, do you agree it's ok to call him a bastard?'

'Of course I agree', answered Oliver.

'Then it's ok to replace cloud with shroud', said John.

'No its not', protested Oliver angrily, 'William Wordsworth wrote the poem and used the word cloud to compare his solitary stroll, and when he says cloud, no one other than him has the right to change it'.

'But Willie has already said it's ok to change it', replied John.

'You are bullshitting me', said Oliver, 'you never met the man'.

'If you don't believe me ask Michael' replied John.

'John's telling the truth', said Michael, 'Willie said that it's ok to use shroud if there are no clouds in the sky'.

'I don't believe a word either of you are saying', said Oliver, 'you are trying to screw with my head'.

'No one's trying to screw with your head', replied John, 'we have full confidence in you screwing your own head up, why do we need to bother?'

'Then why do you keep sticking your nose in where it doesn't belong?' asked Oliver.

'My nose always belongs where I stick it', replied John.

'Yes Oliver', added Michael, 'John's nose is always in the right place'.

'So what both of you are saying', said Oliver, 'is, it's ok to interfere with the living and causing havoc when you have no bodily right to do so'.

'You are going to love this', said John excitingly,

'Here Michael, tell old Ollie here how we did it'.

'Well', replied Michael, 'old Pete who guards the gate loves to hear the story of how we robbed the bank in Magherafelt, he can't understand why we were allowed in after committing such a sin. So while I keep him busy, John slips out the side of the gate'.

'What happens if he catches you?' asked Oliver.

'Stop trying to change the subject', answered John, 'we did mention the word shroud'.

'Ok for the sake of argument', said Oliver, 'let's say its shroud, since when have you seen a shroud wandering alone?'

'You are alone since we left', answered John.

'And your wearing a shroud', said Michael.

Oliver looked at the long white robe-like item of clothing covering his body and tried to scream. He tried to call out for someone to save him, to hold and reassure him that everything before his eyes was not happening.

Oliver threw the bedclothes from his face and gasped for air as he quickly realised that another dream had paid host to his attempt at sleeping. As he laid his head on the pillow he was only too aware of the magnitude of the dream he just had, and for the first time in years he began to pray. Oliver could still feel his heart beating wildly inside his chest, as he surveyed the small fragments of lights from a distant vehicle creeping under the bedroom curtains. He did not look to see what time it was, nor did Oliver guess, all that he had in his mind at that very moment was the words of a prayer his mother taught him, and the deep, thriving longing for peace.

CHAPTER 18

The Ford Cortina was parked exactly where the stranger had told him, and as Oliver approached the back door, a man jumped out and beckoned him in, before closing the door behind him.

'Hello Oliver old son', said Curly as he turned around to face Oliver from the front passenger seat of the car, 'hope the world is treating you ok'.

'As well as can be expected', replied Oliver, trying to hide the slight quiver from the tone of his voice.

'As long as your well as can be expected, then there's not much to complain about', said Curly as he subjected Oliver to another satisfied smile.
'I hope you haven't forgotten our last little talk, I hate people who forget little talks'.

'I haven't forgot anything', replied Oliver.

'Good man', said Curley, 'I don't forget anything either, here's a little gift on behalf of the boys and myself'.
Curley handed Oliver a brown cloth lunch bag and said
'Be careful with it, its fragile'.
Oliver took the brown bag and set it gently on his knee; he knew only too well its terrible contents and

began to wish this meeting had never happened.

'On Monday night from 10.00pm onwards a grey Volvo will be parked behind Dawson's hotel in Cookstown', said Curley. 'The registration number is DJI 222, don't write it down it must be kept in your head only. There is a magnet attached to the device, so place it under the driver's side floor of the car, pull the yellow clip out of the side and get as far away from the scene as possible. I guarantee you Oliver old son, that cop who murdered your two friends will be going straight to hell'.

'Are you sure it's not going to go off prematurely?' asked Oliver with concern leaking from his voice.

'Ye of little faith', replied Curley, 'everything is as sound as a pound, at least until you pull the yellow clip'.

Before Oliver had time to ask any more questions, the man beside him opened the door, got out and signalled Oliver to do the same. As Oliver slowly stepped onto the pavement, the man got back into the car and all three occupants took off down the street leaving Oliver with nothing more than a package of death and a pounding heart.

Before Oliver departed on his journey to visit Robert, he made sure the bag was hidden well in his bedroom. At first he wanted to keep it in the boot of his car for safety reasons, but thought better of the idea in case it was discovered at a police or army checkpoint. The road to Robert's farm graced Oliver with not only the pictures of mother nature's green and spotted land, but visions of fear and doubt. He could not escape the remnants of opposing views on, for or against, and as a result he began to worry inwardly if his metal would carry him through. The image of Robert raising his hand to greet him as he pulled into the farmyard distracted Oliver away from the grinding of his thoughts.

'Hello Oliver old son', said Robert as Oliver turned the driver's window down.

'Hello', replied Oliver, 'how's life been treating you since we last met?'

'A lot better to say the least, would you like a cup of tea?'

'Would love one', answered Oliver as he made his way from the car and followed Robert into the house. As Oliver sat down on the table next to the window overlooking the front yard, he noticed the female touch of Winifred. The odour from the flowers placed in the yellow vase in the centre of the table coupled with the wake of Winifred's perfume embraced the old run down kitchen with the scent of life. Robert whistled lowly to himself as he poured the tea, and within that short moment, Oliver allowed himself some joy in the fact that he had been party to that very happiness.

'Have you thought of what you might do yet?' asked Oliver as Robert set a cup of very strong tea before him.

'We don't yet know what's best', replied Robert as he sat on the chair opposite Oliver. 'Winifred thinks America would be the best idea to start again, but I don't know'.

'I know the feeling', replied Oliver, 'I sometimes get so confused I put my underpants over my head'. Robert laughed wholeheartedly as he said,

'Now that's what I call screwed up'.

'I know an old lady called Matty, I believe Winifred has heard about her, she might be able to throw a bit of advice your way', said Oliver.

'I heard someone mentioning her name once or twice, but I had no reason to call on her at the time', replied Robert.

'Well why don't you call in and see her, and tell her I sent you', said Oliver.

'Winifred will be back around five so I'll put it to her, replied Robert. 'I know for one thing, neither of us can make up our minds one way or the other, so no harm in giving it a try'.

'Having the power to look into the future would save a hell of a lot of headaches', said Oliver as he poured the remaining contents of his tea into his mouth.

'Knowing who was going to win The Grand National long before the race starts would make a nice winning in the bookies', joked Robert.

'Or the football pools would be even better, fancy half a million quid', replied Oliver.

'Have you any plans yourself?' asked Robert.

'A few curdled thoughts here and there, but America does spring up a few times, have you ever heard of a place called Stockton in Missouri?' asked Oliver.

'Only places I heard off are the big cities like New York, Chicago or Boston' answered Robert.

'I used to know someone from Stockton, we were very good friends and I promised myself I would go there and see what's left of his family', said Oliver.

'Sometimes promises are hard to keep, sometimes bloody impossible', replied Robert.

'Well I will try my best', said Oliver, 'there is one thing I do believe in and that is providence'.

'I hope you're right', said Robert, 'and if we can ever make our minds up to go to the states, you are welcome to join us'.

'I thank you for the invitation', said Oliver as he arose from the table to leave, 'time will tell us soon enough, what direction we should take'.

The direction that Oliver now choose to take was to the graveyards were both John and Michael were buried. It was a calling he tried to avoid at all costs, even on the day of the funerals, but now he convinced himself that some courage could be drawn from the stark reality of the death of his two friends. As he slowly walked down the narrow stone path of the graveyard, Oliver viewed the hundreds of graves, and the headstones with etched memories of those who once had dreams and hopes. At the end of the path he stopped before a gravestone which read MICHAEL RAMSEY DIED 14TH JUNE 1982. As Oliver stared at the gravestone he could almost feel Michael standing before it and making jokes about his new place of residence. Oliver wanted to feel anger and hate from the scene before him, but all he could feel were the tears slowly tumbling down his face. He had no words to say, no outward prayers to bestow upon the dearly departed. All Oliver could feel was emptiness and strong emotional echoes of a young breath erased from the annals of life. Whatever Oliver wanted to say to Michael was kept silent to the ears but heard loudly by the soul, and as he made his way back to the car, he only hoped his legs would be strong enough to carry him there.

As Oliver made his way to the graveyard in Maghera he suddenly came upon an army checkpoint stationed just over the brow of a hill. Oliver had to quickly apply the brakes in order avoid colliding with a land rover dangerously positioned with flashing lights.

'Have you any identification?' asked the soldier in a local accent.

Oliver began to rummage through his pockets, and then replied

'Sorry, I have nothing on me'.

'What's your name, where are you coming from and where are you going?' asked the soldier.

'My name is Oliver McKenna, and I have just come from Castledawson', answered Oliver, 'I'm on my way to the chapel graveyard in Maghera'.

As soon as Oliver finished with the information requested, the soldier looked over at the other soldier standing beside an old stone wall and nodded his head.

'Ok get out of the car', said the soldier in a threatening voice.

Oliver stepped out of the car and was quickly searched and ordered to lie spread-eagle on the road. As Oliver lay on the road he began to remember the local regiment his Mother warned him about. Some people in this regiment hated Catholics and would sooner put a bullet into them at any excuse. Oliver remembered his mother's words, 'these are not real soldiers so don't give them any excuse, be polite and only answer when spoken too'. After what seemed like eternity, the soldier told Oliver he could go, and moving himself from the road Oliver made off in the direction of Maghera.

It only took Oliver twenty minutes to pull up outside the Catholic graveyard and turn off the ignition of the car. Oliver breathed a sigh of relief and was content that the incident at the checkpoint passed off without any violence. As he commenced his walk to find John's grave, he noticed that despite the different religions, both ended up as one with bereavement.

The headstones all resembled each other and each was similar in the fact that they all were loved and missed by someone. When Oliver reached John's grave, the headstone read JOHN CONWAY MURDERED ON THE 14TH JUNE 1982 RIP. Oliver noticed, like the graveyard in Castledawson, an air of peace flowed over each grave like an eternal feathered bed. Graveyards were the last places he wanted to be reminded of, before his dangerous mission ahead, but he owed it to both John and Michael. He knew this would be the last time he would see their names written in stone, from this day forward their memories would remain forever etched in his heart. As Oliver turned to walk down the narrow gravel path that would lead him through the grey painted gates and back to his car, his eye suddenly caught something strange staring at him from one of the headstones. Oliver stopped and rubbed his eyes in bewilderment as he thought he saw his own name on one of the gravestones. The moment was suddenly interrupted by the sound of two gun shots in quick succession, and the dull thud of the bullets hitting the pillars of the gate where he should have been standing. Oliver flung himself hard onto the freshly cut grass and took cover behind one of the gravestones. The firing of shots at both Catholic and Protestant Churches had been commonplace and Oliver knew no reason why they should be interrupted on his behalf. As he waited for more shots to be fired, Oliver could hear the loud roar of a motorcycle accelerating off and into the distance, and hopefully taking with it any further threat to his life. As Oliver remained safely behind the stone epitaph, he could hear the cars and people carrying on oblivious to what had happened.

'Perhaps'. Oliver thought, 'they mistook it for a car backfiring as cars often did, or someone taking a shot at a crow trying to help itself in the barley field just across the road'.

As he gathered himself up from the grass, Oliver scanned the path he intended to take and moved slowly and cautiously towards the gate. Looking up and down the road as he exited through the gate, Oliver hurriedly opened the car door and without loitering, took off in the direction of the last person he wished to visit.

Oliver was surprised to see Matty's door wide open, yet no physical sign of her appearing to greet the person or persons entering her yard. He switched off the engine of his car and waited a few minutes to allow Matty to finish any chore she may be doing, before she came out to greet him. As there was no sign of the old lady, Oliver left the car and walked through the open door of the cottage, after first knocking and calling out her name. Oliver wondered why Matty would have left her door wide open, and could only assume she was not far away. As he sat down on the old worn brown leather chair next to the fire, the hiss from the kettle hanging from the iron crook above the smouldering clods of turf, invited him to avail of a much wanted mug of tea. As Oliver poured the steaming hot water into the teapot and added the tealeaves, he knew Matty wouldn't begrudge him the opportunity to help himself. He had a long and stressful day and the chair by Matty's fire, and hopefully her company, would offer to Oliver a soothing hand. He knew that Matty would know everything that was about to happen, and Oliver was hoping that perhaps she could offer him some advice or warning. As he took a sip of his tea from the old crockery cup that Matty had offered him before, he wondered if he would heed any advice she would give him. Other forces much stronger had now entered Oliver's world, and a powerful magnetic force was pulling his common sense away from his heart. Oliver knew it was time to say goodbye to his life as he knew it, and the checkpoint and the shots fired at the chapel gate had reminded him only too well of how much he wanted to escape. He cast his eyes around the inside of Matty's two room cottage and noticed how simple her life was, and how content she remained within the cobwebs, and the black and smoke stained walls and ceiling.

'Perhaps within these walls', Oliver thought, 'unseen creatures or beings were watching him now, and recording his thoughts to play back to him when he is dead'.

The brisk movement of a hungry mouse, or a daddy-long-leg dancing within the spotlight of a brown stained bulb, were both remnants of a larger being. Oliver knew that he too was one of those remnants of something bigger, and like the creatures, he also hungered and longed for a brighter light. As he took another sip of the strong tea, Oliver could feel the tealeaves gather between the spaces in his teeth, and wondered how he would look in the mirror when he smiled. To Oliver's surprise, he could not find a mirror of any shape or form on Matty's walls, and strained his neck to try and make out even a faint glimpse of his reflection on the dusty window. The place at the window was reserved for Matty's cat, and Oliver began to wish that both the cat and Matty would hurry back. He did not want to stay long in

Matty's house without her presence, and as he waited patiently, the only noise he could hear was a gentle wind blowing fragments of dead grass through the door and onto Matty's grey stone floor. Before Oliver decided to go, he looked around for something he could leave a note to thank Matty for the tea, and how disappointed he was that he missed her. On top of the table was an old used white envelope and a pencil, so Oliver wrote, SORRY I MISSED YOU AND THANK YOU VERY MUCH FOR THE TEA….OLIVER. As Oliver made his way out the door he noticed he still had Matty's pencil in his hand, so he turned around and walked back to place the pencil back on the table. As Oliver placed the pencil on the table beside the envelope, he stared at the writing that had now replaced what he had written. I'M SORRY I MISSED YOU TOO AND YOU ARE WELCOME TO HELP YOURSELF TO A CUP OF TEA ANYTIME…..MATTY. Oliver walked out the front door and climbed into his car without giving what he had seen a second thought. As he started the engine and made his way back to Magherafelt, he knew he had no reason to be amazed by anything he saw or heard within the walls of Matty's little whitewashed cottage, because inside Matty's home, reason had no place.

When Oliver returned from making his rounds, he walked through the back door like he had done many times before, and greeted his mother as she listened to the radio perched on the kitchen table.

'Hello Mum', said Oliver, 'anything strange happening?'

'Depends on what you call strange', replied his mother, 'a baby was born in Belfast with six fingers today'.

'Are you sure it had six fingers', said Oliver, 'it might have been five fingers and a thumb, or four fingers and two thumbs'.

'What difference does it make if it's one thumb or two', answered Oliver's mother, 'whatever it is, it's one more than normal and the bible's thumpers are climbing on board the nutty wagon'.

'What are they crying about then?' asked Oliver.

'They are saying that a sixth child born on the sixth of the month with six fingers is a sign that the devil is coming', answered Oliver's mother.

'Well God bless us and save us', replied Oliver, 'and there's me thinking that the devil was already here'.

'I think it's about getting more money into the collection boxes than anything else', said Oliver's mother, 'they can't even leave a pure innocent child alone'.

'No', answered Oliver, 'they kick them before the midwife has time to wrap them up, what a lovely world we live in'.

'If you believe in reincarnation', said Oliver's mother with some amusement escaping from her voice, 'maybe the child was a spider in their last life'.
Oliver laughed and answered,

'No spiders are lucky, so no way would it have been born in this damn place, and besides spiders have eight legs'.

'Stupid me', said Oliver's mother, 'would you like some stew son?'

'I would kill for a bowl of stew', answered Oliver.
Oliver's mother arose from her chair and went about her business of filling a bowl of Irish stew and setting it before the hungry Oliver. Oliver thanked her and

began to eat it quickly. A lot of things were now flowing through his head, and he knew he would need a checklist prepared for his departure the next day. As he finished the last of his stew, Oliver thanked his mother and said,

'I'm staying overnight at a friend's house tomorrow night, so don't be worrying'.

'Who's your friend?' asked Oliver's mother.

'Just a friend', answered Oliver, 'someone's birthday party and we have decided to stay up late playing cards'.

'Will you be home in the morning then?' asked Oliver's mother in a concerned tone of voice.

'Tomorrow afternoon', replied Oliver.

'You know I worry when you are out all night', said Oliver's mother.

'You don't have to worry, I told you', replied Oliver, 'I will be safe behind closed doors'.

'I don't care what you say', said Oliver's mother, 'I will be worried sick until you are back inside these walls'.

'You are beginning to sound like a prison warden, when you mention the words inside these walls', replied Oliver humorously.

'When you grow up and have children of your own, you will know what I am talking about', said Oliver's mother.

'No matter', said Oliver as he rose from the table, 'I'm telling you now that I will be as safe as the Bank of England'.

As Oliver sat on top of his bed he began to create a list of everything he must do in his head. He pulled a black sports bag from the bottom of the wardrobe and proceeded to pack a few clothing items. He then recovered the revolver from its hiding place and placed it inside the bag between a pair of jeans and a clean tee-shirt. Oliver then retrieved the lunch bag that The IRA had given him and made his way down the stairs and out to his car. Oliver opened the back of the car and placed the two bags on the floor beside his tool box. He made sure the car was locked securely, and returned to his bedroom, and once again to his thoughts. As the most important things were now in the car, Oliver began to go through the list in his head to make sure nothing was forgotten. He remembered gloves, but on discovering he had none, decided to either purchase them before tomorrow night, or wear socks on his hands. There was one more item on the list, but Oliver concluded there would be nothing gained by rattling around the wardrobe again, so would be best left until the morning. Oliver began to think of Mary and wondered how she was coping as the time was drawing them closer to their destiny. He was frightened, yet at the same time there was a growing feeling of excitement. The journey to John and Michael's graves left him with a stronger reason for both revenge and escape. If knowing what they might have known now, Oliver had no doubt that both of them would have encouraged him to make the break. There was nothing left for him in this country only tears, tears and more tears. Soon he would do what generations had done before him, cross the great wide Atlantic Ocean to seek a better place. Forty eight hours from now both Mary and himself would be together forever, inseparable both physically and spiritually. He would send a letter to his mother, leaving out the rawest detail and explaining that Mary and him are in love and have moved to fulfil their dreams together. After recovering from the initial shock, he knew his mother would agree that theirs was the wisest decision. Oliver would also explain to his mother that as soon as they get settled, she would have the opportunity to come and visit him in America. Oliver hoped that he would be able to get some undisturbed sleep tonight, for he knew tomorrow night would be almost impossible. The night before would leave his head buzzing with a thousand possible things that could go wrong, and less a thousand that could go right. He would ask John and Michael to stay away from his dreams tonight, in the hope that they would understand what lies ahead. He would pray for a peaceful sleep and an enormous pot of undiluted courage.

CHAPTER 19

The day before had arrived and John and Michael had either heard his plea, or had no intention of calling on him in the first place. Someone coughing as they passed by his back gate outside had heralded Oliver back from the relative peace and safety of his sleep, to the world of conflict and fear. He did not have to stretch his arms or yawn to fully wake up, Oliver was fully conscious as soon as his eyes opened. The long thin laser rays of morning sun, revealing particles of unseen dust had no bearing on his entry into reality; Oliver had arrived on his own free will, helped along slightly by the quickening of the blood through his veins. Oliver paused to consider sympathetically all those both past and present, who waited to look danger straight in the eyes. He knew how they felt as the minutes trickled slowly by like sweat flowing down the brow of a labourer on a hot summer's day. He thought of his grandfather and stood beside him as he awaited the loud shrill of the whistle of death, calling them to feed the spitting hunger of the German machine guns at The Battle of the Somme. But unlike his grandfather, Oliver knew that if he survived the clutches of death, his life would change for the better.

252

His grandfather did survive that terrible day, but Oliver remembered the stories his mother told him of the piece of shrapnel that was so close to his heart it could never be removed safely. For thirty years he rode his bike to deliver the post through fair weather and foul, and for thirty years they waited for him never to return alive. On the first of July 1946, thirty years to the day he went over the top, Oliver's grandfather died by the roadside with a scattered bundle of eagerly awaited letters paying host to the wild buttercups and grass at the side of a lonely mountain road. His mother told him once that the young of that generation were so naïve that everything they read in the newspapers was believed as gospel. She said that they were so brainwashed that when the whistle blew to climb out of the trenches to feed the German machine guns, even the dead stepped out of their graves to obey.

After Oliver got dressed he made his way down the stairs and into the kitchen. A note on the table from his mother authenticated the absence of anyone else in the house, so Oliver continued to make the final preparations for his departure. His stomach had strictly forbid any nourishment from taking up residence for various reasons, so Oliver ignored what his mother wrote in the note, and left the porridge untouched. Before Oliver opened the car to climb in, he remembered the bag in the wardrobe and returned to fetch it. He placed the bag in the back of the car, fired up the engine and proceeded on his way to the diamond to collect Mary.

Not much was going on as Oliver made his way up the main street and surveyed the movement of a small number of people and cars. Oliver noticed that each person looked subdued, almost robotic as if they were programmed to go nowhere. Most of the shops and businesses were painted grey, and those that were not, sported a darker colour. Oliver wondered if the colours on each side of the street truly reflected the mood of the people who lived there, and hoped that someday those colours would get brighter.

Mary was waiting patiently as Oliver pulled up at the diamond to collect her. Oliver noticed she only carried a small sports bag and commented as she climbed in beside him in the car.

'You're the first woman I ever saw who didn't carry a shit load of suitcases when they went to stay overnight'.

'I travel light', replied Mary as she closed the door of the car, 'it's easier to run'.

Oliver moved off and as he turned the corner onto the Cookstown road he said,

'Mentioning the word run is not a promising start to our expedition'.

'It may not', answered Mary, 'but now that we are closer to it happening, I'm shitting myself'.

'Don't worry', said Oliver jokingly, 'I brought enough toilet roll for both of us'.

Mary's face showed no reaction to Oliver's attempt at humour, and Oliver could tell that Mary was starting to crumble. He knew that he and he alone would have to be the pillar to hold the plan together and he also became quickly aware, that if he didn't, it would fall apart faster than it had been put together. As they passed through Moneymore and on to Cookstown, Oliver noticed that Mary's face looked far away and lost, even as they passed places that they both had joked about before.

'There's the mental hospital', said Oliver trying to catch Mary's attention.

'I'm beginning to think it's a good place to be at this very moment', replied Mary.

'We could always put it back for another time', said Oliver.

'No', answered Mary as she tried to put some strength into her reply,

'Let's get it over with'.

As they pulled into the car park at the back of the Cooks Hotel in Cookstown, only a small number of assorted cars dressed the narrow parking strips with dull colours. Oliver switched the engine off and viewed the four story building before him, with its signs of aging already evident by the missing patches of plaster, laying bare the edges of stonework from a distant era. He had often heard old stories that the building was haunted by the ghost of a world war two pilot who left his pregnant girlfriend behind in one of the rooms, promising to return after the battle of Britain. The young girl was eventually caught up with by her parents who took her away and hid the disgrace in a convent. The young pilot was killed in a dog fight over Dover and some say he made good his promise to return and can be seen walking from room to room after midnight, searching for his sweetheart.

Oliver and Mary entered through the two heavy wooden doors of the hotel and made their way to the desk before them. A middle aged lady wearing over sized black rimmed glasses greeted the couple with a husky voice escaping between two rows of false teeth.

'Good afternoon', she said, 'can I help you'.

'We would like a double room with two single beds', replied Mary.

The woman opened a large book before her and answered,

'We have one at the back, would that suit you?'

'That will do fine', replied Mary.

'How long will you be staying for?' asked the lady.

'For one night', answered Mary.

The lady reached above her head to a long line of keys and on finding the right one she said,

'The room number is 18 and that will be forty pounds'.

Oliver put four ten pound notes on the counter before them, and followed Mary as she took the key and made her way to room 18. The hotel smelled of dampness and cigarette smoke as they walked along the narrow corridor and up a flight of dark wood stairs. On entering their musty room, Oliver made his way to the window and looked out across the car park. Oliver knew that in that car park, that very night, someone was going to receive a nasty shock. He had been surprised at Mary for asking for a room with separate beds, and was unsure how to approach a question that he himself had little knowledge of. He was only too aware that sleeping with Mary had crossed his mind quite often, but knew that the night before they were about to commit robbery, it would be the last thing on both their minds.

'I'm not sleeping in the same bed with you', said Mary as if she had just read Oliver's mind, 'it's best to leave things of a more intimate nature until the smoke clears'.

'I hope you don't snore', said Oliver jokingly, as he sat down on the edge of one of the single beds.

'I snore like a horse', replied Mary, 'so I hope you brought your earplugs'.

'Don't need earplugs', answered Oliver as he bounced up and down on the mattress as if to test the springs, 'a damned good slap with a well aimed pillow always does the trick'.

'Don't miss', said Mary forcing a smile as she made her way into the small bathroom adjacent to the room, 'I always reply with something harder'.

While Mary decided to soak herself in a hot bath, Oliver made his way out the back of the hotel to view his surroundings and map out the best way of escape. He noticed there was two ways into the car park behind the hotel, the one that they came in and the other that led onto the street where the bank was situated. Oliver decided it would be best to leave the car where it was and cross the car park on foot to the bank. On their return they would leave the way they arrived, and quickly make their way back to Magherafelt via a back road. The cold breeze blowing up from a passing alleyway did not halt the mix of fear and excitement that was still flowing through Oliver's veins. As he stood opposite the bank and surveyed the old run down building, he fostered a sense of pride for Mary and her sharp eye and wit that uncovered a true jewel in the crown. Never in his wildest dreams would he ever expect so much money to be stored in such a ramshackle of a building. On his return to the hotel, Oliver took note of every alleyway and side street that led from the bank to the car park, and wished that the waiting would be over. As he returned back up the stairs and into room 18, he prayed from within his soul, that a favourable destiny would greet him with open arms, and carry him through the next twenty four hours.

On entering the room, Oliver found Mary lying on

top of the bed with the bed cover lazily flung over the top of her. He climbed on top of the bed next to her, neatly placing the pillow under his head and spoke,

'Do you fancy something to eat?'

'No', answered Mary, 'food is the last thing running through my head at the moment'.

'Ok', replied Oliver, 'but I'll take a run out later and pick up a couple of fish suppers, best not to show ourselves too much around town'.

'I'm not really worried either way', said Mary, 'I just want to get this bloody thing over with'.

'Did you sleep much last night?' asked Oliver.

'No', replied Mary, 'again, I will not sleep until this is over'.

'Things will work out ok', said Oliver trying to console Mary, 'I have a good feeling about things. I took a walk down to the bank and it's almost like it's just lying there asking to be robbed'.

'Let's hope someone else doesn't decide to rob it at the same time, it might be appealing to others', said Mary.

'I heard of that happening before', replied Oliver.

'Your joking', said Mary.

'No joking', answered Oliver, 'and it was not only two gangs hitting the same bank, but three.

'Now you really are taking the piss', said Mary as she raised her eyebrows.

'I swear', replied Oliver, 'the three gangs hit the bank at the same time and an argument brewed between them who should get robbing the bank. After about half an hour they agreed to share the loot, and while they were sharing it out in the middle of the bank floor, the police had ample time to surround the building and catch them'.

'What a bloody mess of foolishness', said Mary.

'I guess so', answered Oliver, 'I think they call it Murphy's Law, anything that can go wrong, will'.

'So what you are saying', said Mary, 'is that if there is a chance of getting caught tomorrow, we will'.

'Yes and no', replied Oliver, 'yes if we allow ourselves to be a victim of chance, and no if we don't'.

'Did anyone ever tell you that you were clever for a seventeen year old?' said Mary.

'Many times', replied Oliver sarcastically, 'although my brains must be in my bottom, because the all told me I was a smart ass'.

'Good one', answered Mary as it brought another smile to her face.

As dark began to close the day, Oliver made his way out of the hotel and walked to the chip shop about four hundred yards away from where they were staying. As he returned with the fish and chips, he found that Mary had fallen asleep so decided that sleep would have more benefit to her than a handful of greasy food. As he sat on the small narrow armchair overlooking the car park, Oliver picked a few morsels from his fish and chips, then decided to banish the remainder to the bin. He was not as hungry as he thought, and as the time slowly ticked its way closer to the day of days, he knew he would follow in the footsteps of Mary and food would be the last thing on his mind. The dark night before him had arrived quickly and Oliver stared at the lights of different lives taking their place among the black shadows of existence. He knew some would be content within their own creation, whether it be business or home. He could also understand why some would be unhappy and only whiled the days away nursing their regrets and lack of vision. As Oliver returned to lie down on the bed, he knew within himself that action would equal movement and without movement, the world was going nowhere.

When Oliver opened his eyes nothing had changed within the room. Mary was still fast asleep and the smell of vinegar from the dormant fish suppers had decided to stay. Oliver looked at the round white wall clock on the wall above Mary's bed, and the time read 11.45pm. Oliver jumped to his feet almost stumbling onto Mary's bed; he cursed himself for falling asleep so early. He wanted to deal with the grey Volvo before 11.00pm as he would not have looked suspicious hanging around the car park. But Oliver knew it still had to be done, so picking the car keys from the small table beside the window, he made his way once again out onto the car park.

When he arrived at his Ford Capri, Oliver opened the door as quiet as possible and reached into the back seat, and retrieved the lunch bag carrying the surprise. He softly closed the door and made his way across the car park in search of the grey Volvo. As some of the lights covering the car park were faulty, Oliver was thankful for the obscurity of darkness. He was also aware that he could not distinguish the colour of the Volvo so he would have to look out for the number plate. Oliver noticed the stillness of the night air and the uncanny silence of the market town. Although it was a Monday night, Oliver expected more movement of people, or the occasional bark of a cautious dog. The number plate CJI 222 greeted Oliver like a long lost shoe or a displaced tool. It stood out before him like a portrait of doom calling Oliver to fulfill his calling. Oliver knelt down behind and read the number plate once again to make sure that some poor innocent driver would not receive what he did not deserve. He removed the object from the bag and crawling on his hands and knees, Oliver made his way to the driver's side of the vehicle. The car was high enough off the ground for Oliver to push his head and arms under to place the device beneath what he could make out as the driver's seat. The device stuck solid to the underside with the assistance of the magnet, and Oliver pulled the yellow clip out to prime it as Curly had instructed. Oliver quickly removed himself from the vicinity of the vehicle and made his way back in the direction of the hotel. The lunch bag which was now empty of its contents was disposed of in the black bin beside the back entrance, and Oliver made his way back to his hotel room and the security of closed doors.

'Where have you been?' asked Mary as Oliver entered the room.

'Out visiting a dear old friend', answered Oliver with a half smile.

'I didn't know you knew anyone from around here?' said Mary, 'I thought we were supposed to keep a low profile'.

'Nothing to worry your good self about', answered Oliver as he made his way to the bathroom, 'just a favour for an old friend'.

As Oliver sprinkled the cold water over his face, he was amazed at how untouched mentally he had been by the event. The process took no more than twenty minutes, and Oliver compared it to being no more stressful than a walk to the corner shop. He knew that Mary was a little taken aback by his dear old friend excuse, but what she didn't know at this very moment in time would not hurt her. As he made his way back into the room, Oliver removed his coat and shoes, and lay down on the bed.

'Who's your dear old friend?' asked Mary.

'I'll tell you tomorrow after the job, no point in getting carried away with things that are not relevant to what we are really here for', answered Oliver.

'I hope you are not planning something behind my back', said Mary as she sat in a dressing gown on the side of the bed.

'Don't be getting paranoid', answered Oliver, 'we are in this together just you and me; no one else knows what's going on'.

'We allow ten minutes after they drop off the money and then go in fast and grab it', said Mary, 'that's the plan'.

'Whatever you say boss', answered Oliver with a smile.

'Another thing', said Mary, 'I don't think you should load that gun, I'm frightened of us shooting someone'.

'What happens if they decide to be awkward and refuse to hand over the dosh?' asked Oliver.

'Threaten them with the gun', replied Mary, 'you don't have to shoot them'.

'I firmly believe that there is nothing like a couple of fire crackers above someone's head to persuade them to your way of thinking', said Oliver.

'I don't like it', replied Mary with a worried expression on her face.

'Just leave the firearm rules to me', said Oliver calmly, 'I'm not going to shoot anyone'.

As Mary seemed to accept Oliver's judgement in the use of live ammo, Oliver began to contemplate the reality of having someone refusing his criminal demands. More than anything in his heart, Oliver knew he could not shoot someone dead, but the prospect of injuring that person or persons to accommodate his escape, was an option reserved for that very moment. Tomorrow would be one of the biggest robberies he will ever have carried out, and without any reservations, his last. Mary and him had plans for the future together, and Oliver was looking forward to the beginning of something wonderful. He valued Mary's decision to sleep in separate beds, and took comfort from the realisation that Mary was decent and respected her body. Oliver knew that if Mary could be true to herself, then there is no reason why she could not be true to the right person in her life. And as Oliver closed his eyes to beckon sleep to help him while away the hours, he was truly convinced that he was the right person.

'Do you Oliver take Mary for your nagging wedded wife, to be pissed on and shit on, to receive boot prints on your face?'

'Hold on here', protested Oliver as he interrupted the ceremony, 'these are not wedding vows, who in their right mind would agree to this'.

'I would', answered Curly as he shuffled up beside Oliver and Mary at the altar.

'You have got to be joking', said Oliver, 'how would anyone who bombs and shoots people, be in their right mind?'

'Bombing and shooting is just a hobby, I also like gardening', replied Curly.

Mary suddenly steps forward and holds Curly by the hand,

'Before we go any further with this ceremony both

Curly and I have a confession to make'.

'Confess my dear children', said the priest with two gold shining front teeth.

'Both Curly and myself', answered Mary as she got closer to Curly, 'love gardening'.

As the congregation let out gasps of astonishment and shock, Oliver grabbed Mary's other hand and said,

'Let's get on with the bloody ceremony; I'm sick of this silly nonsense'.

'There will be no ceremony', stated the priest, 'both Mary and Curly are hereby excommunicated from this church, so fuck off both of you'.

As both Mary and Curly commenced to exit the church holding hands, Oliver angrily shouted at the priest

'Since when does gardening become a bloody crime?'

'The purple and orange striped book on cannon law states quite clearly in Chinese that gardening between two consenting adults is a holy disgrace', answered the priest.

'Who in hell, or this damn congregation can read Chinese?' asked Oliver.

'Well you don't need to be a coalman to realise that those in hell cannot read one word of Chinese, otherwise they wouldn't be there in the first place', answered the priest, 'as for the congregation, they all can read Chinese'.

'Excuse me', interrupted a small skinny middle aged man, 'I don't know Chinese'.

'Then get your scrawny ass out of here you little bastard', roared the priest.

'I suppose it's time I left too', said Oliver, 'I don't know one word of Chinese either'.

'It's ok', replied the priest, 'blind people are exempt

from the law'.

'What are you talking about?' protested Oliver, 'I can see perfectly well'.

'Well your wife that did not be, and soon to be cast down into hell with all the other filthy gardeners, registered you on the application as blind as a fucking bat', answered the priest.

'Why would she do that?' asked Oliver in bewilderment.

'Perhaps she didn't want you to see the marriage vows that she had written herself', answered the priest.

'Even if I was blind, which I am not, I could still hear every word', said Oliver.

'Yes indeed', replied the priest, 'but sometimes what we hear is not always what we see'.

CHAPTER 20

As the sunlight shone through the window and into Oliver's eyes, he could hear Mary's voice bringing him back from another dream that made no sense. A number of various vehicles could be heard in the distance coming or going to their destinations, and a few muffled footsteps could be heard from the room upstairs. As Oliver rubbed his eyes and yawned into another day, he could hear Mary say,

'Oliver, Oliver, what time is it?'

Oliver looked at the wall clock for a few seconds and replied,

'A quarter to nine'.

Eight forty five or a quarter to nine, it did not make any difference to Oliver what way he presented it. He arose from the bed, put on his shoes and jacket and made his way down to the car. On the back seat he removed two bags and returned to the room. Mary had already dressed and was making her way into the bathroom to answer the call of nature and freshen up. Oliver removed his jacket and first reached into the heaviest bag and removed the revolver. He opened the chamber and checked that all cylinders were loaded with brightly polished brass bullets. He then removed his tee shirt and replaced it with the vest he carried in the bag. He placed the heavy revolver into the waistband of his jeans and finished by putting his coat back on to hide the weapon. Almost at the same time as he had finished, Mary made her way out of the bathroom and proceeded to pack her things. Oliver entered the bathroom, and after urinating in the toilet bowl, he washed his hands and face with soap and cold water. Both Oliver and Mary finished gathering up their belongings, and on leaving the key in the door, they headed towards the car park and to Oliver's Ford Capri.

When they reached the car, they put what they had taken from the hotel and placed it in the back of the car. Oliver locked the door before handing the keys to Mary and almost in a robotic fashion; they both made their way towards the bank.

As they reached the front door of the bank, Oliver was surprised by how calm and relaxed he was. He did not experience any fear, only a small trickle of excitement could be felt running down from his head to the pit of his stomach. The van that delivered the money had left ten minutes ago, and now they were climbing the three small steps and through the door. Oliver pulled the gun from the waistband of his trousers and shouted

'Robbery, everyone put your hands above your head'.

As the small number of employees followed Oliver's orders, Mary stepped forward and grabbed two heavy cloth bags that had been sitting on the counter. Oliver knew the plan, Mary was to leave the building first and calmly carry the money to the car. Oliver would allow three minutes in order for her to get a head start, and then he would quickly follow. As Mary departed out through the doors with the bags, Oliver knew that this was the first day of his life. As he waited the three minutes he caught sight of Michael at his left side, and turning to his right, there was John smiling that confident grin he was renowned for. He was happy to see his friends again, standing by his side in his hour of need. One more face stared at Oliver from across the floor, a face that Oliver knew so well, yet never physically met. He was happy to see his grandfather for the first time, standing in his First World War uniform and saluting Oliver for his act of courage. His time had come to depart the building and on reminding the staff to keep their hands up for five minutes after he left the building, he noticed a middle aged lady with tears falling from two bright blue eyes. He was sorry he had frightened her and without thinking apologised to the staff for any fear that he may have caused them. The door that would lead him onto the street drew closer, as he made his way to freedom. Oliver could hear a scream, a cry that reached somewhere in his heart that he may have recognised, he turned around once more and saw the lady being held back by staff as she tried to escape their grasp. He could still see the fear in her eyes, her head shaking from side to side and the words 'NO' being flung at him like winter hail battering a cold corrugated tin roof. Oliver turned away and stepped out onto the brightness of an early sun, and a gentle soothing breeze.

The first bullet caught Oliver in the left shoulder, flinging him against the grey brick wall and causing more shock than pain. The second, third and forth peppered his chest causing him to fall forward smashing his jaw on the second step leading from the building. The rest of the machine gun bullets finding their way to Oliver's body left their bitter marks without pain. Oliver no longer felt the angry fingers of death, for he now lay motionless and bleeding from seeking the fortunes of love.

After putting two cloth bags of money into the boot of the car, Mary climbed into the front passenger seat and passionately began kissing the male driver.

'I'm so fucking glad it's over', said Mary as she applied a stick of lipstick to her lips with the help of the car mirror.

'I thought you were enjoying yourself', joked the male driver before drawing on a cigarette.

'Enjoying myself my ass', replied Mary, 'the little bastard almost made me vomit, did they finish him off?'

'Over a hundred rounds fired, I guess they finished him off good', answered the male driver grinning.

'Let's get out of here', said Mary as she buckled up her seat belt.

The Male driver started the car and began to move off at the same time as an ambulance could be heard approaching the outskirts of the town.

'I wonder who his dear old friend was?' said Mary as the car proceeded up the hill.

The explosion ripped through the car killing both Mary and Inspector Norman Brown instantly. Within those small microseconds of remaining life, Mary consciously found her answer.

The Ambulance driver and one of the policemen at the scene carried the stretcher with Oliver's blood stained body and placed it into the back of the ambulance. A nurse climbed into the back beside the body and the policeman commented,

'Nothing you can do for him in there love, he's had it'.

The nurse reached over and closed the back doors of the ambulance, locking out the stare of the policeman on the other side as the ambulance moved off.

Two women on each side of a young lady are comforting her after the ordeal of first the robbery and then the shooting. The young girl is shaking with emotion, and the outer edges of her blue eyes are red from crying. A policeman approaches with a notebook and pen and asks her

'Are you able to give a statement love?'

The lady turned to the policeman and replied in a soft American accent

'Take this down; I witnessed a cold blooded, calculated and premeditated murder'.

'What about the bank robbery?' asked the policeman.

'What about the murder?' replied the lady before breaking down again and crying.

As the policeman moved away, one of the ladies comforting her said

'Now there love, you'll get over it in a few days'.

The lady stopped crying for a few seconds and turned to the lady saying, 'I think he is my husband'.

Robert lifted his cup of tea from the table and as he stared out the window he downed the last dregs. He could hear a rooster crow from across the yard, and as he set the empty cup back on the table, Winifred gently closed the bedroom door behind her and sat down at the other side of the table facing Robert.

'What's the verdict?' asked Robert with concern ebbing from his voice.

'I give him another shot of Morphine and a sleeping pill, he needs to rest'.

'Poor bloody kid', said Robert.

'I don't give a fuck what you say or what anyone else says', roared the policed inspector. 'I have half the people in Northern Ireland driving or catching buses to Cookstown, trying to catch fivers and tenners floating in the air with their hands or nets or whatever else they can get their hands on. I have two dead plain clothes detectives being swept off the fucking car park behind Cooks hotel, and now you're telling me another corpse has vanished into thin air'.

'Yes sir', muttered the police sergeant, 'he was confirmed dead at the scene of the crime and took away by the ambulance'.

'Did a doctor confirm him dead at the scene, or did someone just suppose he was dead?' roared the inspector.

'There was a lot of shots fired', replied the sergeant nervously.

'And what of the ambulance?' shouted the inspector as he applied a dry handkerchief to his head.

'The hospital confirms that no ambulance was called for', answered the sergeant.

'Ahhh fuck', moaned the inspector, 'this is getting worse'.

'Witnesses are also confirming that one of the robbers was a woman fitting the description of detective constable Mary Anderson'.

'Something stinks here', said the inspector, 'call a meeting for five this evening'. 'what else is it?' asked the inspector as the sergeant remained standing.

'There is an American lady crying at the desk, insisting that she sees you', answered the sergeant.

'What does she want? whatever it is tell her I'm busy', said the inspector.

'She said that the police murdered her husband', replied the sergeant.

Stockton Missouri three months later.

'How are you feeling?' asked Winifred.

'Still stiff and a little sore, but thankful I'm living', answered Oliver as he lay in the hammock, enjoying the view of a clear night sky.

'I'm glad we came here', said Winifred, 'it's so peaceful'.

'What I can't understand' asked Oliver, 'is, how did you know what was going to happen?'

'I got a call to the hospital from Matty and she told me what was about to happen', answered Winifred.

'Don't ask me how she knew, but she said you were in mortal danger'.

'I knew an old drinking friend who has a small garage and who regularly services the ambulances', said Robert as he took a sip of his coffee, 'so I slipped him fifty quid and I knew then he wouldn't be returning to the garage that day'.

'Robert collected me outside the hospital and we rushed to Cookstown as fast as we could', said Winifred, 'but when I saw you lying in a pool of blood I nearly died myself, I really thought you were dead and I only discovered the bullet proof vest when we were driving away'.

'Where did you get that vest?' asked Robert.

'I swapped it for a bag of turf', answered Oliver as he smiled to himself.

Oliver closed his eyes and breathed in the warm fresh Missouri air, as he thanked God for the love of the people around him. He surrounded himself with contentment, looked forward to a life free from the pains and humiliation of religious persecution. He had written to his mother and she was pleased that he had finally made the journey that she had longed to take herself. Oliver remembered the letter that had arrived today from his mother, so he opened his eyes and reaching over to the table beside him, lifted the letter and opened it.

Dear Son

I hope this letter finds you well and you find peace not only within yourself, but all around you. I have something important to tell you, so I hope you are sitting down. A week after you left, a policeman arrived at the door and asked me some questions. He asked for you first and when I told him you were living in America, he then asked if you were married. I laughed and told him you had only just turned eighteen, and as far as I knew, had only one casual girlfriend in your life. He then informed me that they had a lady in the mental hospital who claims to be your wife. The policeman told me that the doctors said that she had been traumatised by some event in her life. When the policeman left, something inside me began to take pity on the poor woman, so the next day I took the bus to Antrim and called into see her. For God's sake son you need to come back as quickly as possible, something is terribly wrong.

Mother.